SWORD
ABOVE
ALL

SWORD ABOVE ALL

BOOK THREE
THE SWORDS OF VALOR

DOMENIC MELILLO

Phase Publishing, LLC
Seattle, WA

Phase Publishing, LLC first paperback edition
July 2019

ISBN 978-1-943048-82-3
Library of Congress Control Number 2019943420
Cataloging-in-Publication Data on file.

DEDICATION

This book is dedicated to my mother,
Catherine Petrie Melillo.

I never knew a stronger, more faithful or
more courageous person.

Opportunity

This I beheld, or dreamed it in a dream:
There spread a cloud of dust along a plain;
And underneath the cloud, or in it, raged
A furious battle, and men yelled, and swords
Shocked upon swords and shields. A prince's banner
Wavered, then staggered backward, hemmed by foes.
A craven hung along the battle's edge,
And thought, "Had I a sword of keener steel—
That blue blade that the king's son bears— but this
Blunt thing—!" he snapped and flung it from his hand,
And lowering crept away and left the field.
Then came the king's son, wounded, entrapped,
And weaponless, saw the broken sword,
Hilt buried in the dry and trodden sand,
And ran and snatched it, and with battle shout
Lifted afresh he hewed his enemy down,
And saved a great cause that heroic day.

Edward Rowland Sill (1841-1887)

PROLOGUE

I, Domenic, as the Prophet of Remembrance, have another tale to tell. It may be my final tale, but it may not be the end of the story. That will be for history and fate to decide.

The guardians of virtue and valor have suffered a crushing defeat. They agonize under a cloud of despair, destruction, and uncertainty. They have lost all but their lives, but where there is life, there is hope.

They must discover strength that they did not know they had and do the things which they think they cannot do. They must fight on with shattered dreams, broken hearts, and limited resources. They must find that level of virtuous bravery which is a much higher and truer degree of courage than they have ever known before. For this will be the final battle. There will be no other.

Though they are tired, sore, and deeply wounded mentally, emotionally, physically, and spiritually, they must take hold of their symbolically broken swords, hilt buried in the dry and trodden sand, and with a great battle shout, renew their spirits, and hew their enemy down, to save a great cause this heroic day.

I pray that their virtue, and their swords, will guide them toward this end.

16 Above all, carry the shield of trust, with which you will be able to extinguish all the flaming arrows of the Evil One.

17 And take the helmet of deliverance; along with the sword given by the Spirit, that is, the Word of God;

18 As you pray at all times, with all kinds of prayers and requests, in the Spirit, vigilantly and persistently, for all God's people.

Ephesians 6:16-18

Chapter One

AFTERMATH

———◦∞◦———

The world had just come crashing down around the team of Guardians. Not only had the hybrid quantum essence of their beloved grandmother just been abducted by the demon Watcher Azazel, but they were powerless to help her. The swords were drained, the quantum computer was not operating, and the Gray Champion was still lying on the round table, appearing lifeless. The Keeping Room was damaged, and they were in total darkness. A darkness which not only filled the room but Billy's heart and mind, as well. He was certain the others felt the same way. Abject despair and hopelessness were quickly becoming their reality.

"Rob!" shouted the Meglio to the prophet. "Quickly, follow me. I am going to get the power back on, then reboot the quantum computer to see if it is salvageable. The rest of you, gather the swords, see if they have regained enough power to revive your great-grandfather. Then check to see if the door of the Keeping Room is operable."

The Meglio and the prophet made their way through the darkness to the power room while Billy and the other heroes retrieved their swords and gathered around the figure of the Gray Champion lying face up on the round table.

"How do you think we should do this?" asked Ty.

"Last time we used them to heal each other, we just put our swords into the wound, they glowed and began the healing process," reminded Joe. "But there are no visible wounds on Great-Grandpa this time. Maybe we should just touch him with the swords and see what happens."

Standing around the table the same way that they always had during the leaving process, as one, they touched their great-grandfather with their swords.

At first, there was no response. The swords appeared to be cold and dead. Billy continued to focus on the desired result for what seemed like an eternity.

Then, Nick's Sword of St. Michael the Archangel began to glow faintly. As the glow began to intensify, the sword next to it, Joe's sword, Excalibur, began to glow. This was followed by Jeff's Sword of Solomon, Ty's Sword of Charlemagne, Billy's Sword of Roland, and finally, Robbie's Sword of William Wallace.

Billy's sword continued to increase in intensity and vibrate softly in his hands. Finally, there was an intense burst of pure, white light, and then darkness.

Suddenly, the room was once again bathed in a new light. The Meglio and the prophet had succeeded in restoring power to the Keeping Room.

Billy could now clearly see the figure of their great-grandfather begin to revive. He was breathing and his eyes fluttered. He lay there for a while, motionless, and appeared to be struggling to regain consciousness.

Then his eyes shot open, he sat upright, raised the sword of St. Peter and screamed at the top of his lungs,

"CATHERINE! MY CATHERINE! What have we done?"

Chapter Two

Devastation

The Gray Champion fought against his great-grandsons as they struggled to restrain him. With every fiber of his being, he fought against the agony that filled him. He was only vaguely aware of the Meglio and the prophet as they burst into the room.

"Quick, help us get control of him!" shouted Joe. "He's gone crazy and he seems stronger than ever!"

The prophet quickly wrestled the sword of St. Peter from the hand of his grandfather while the Meglio spoke into the ear of his father-in-law.

"Robert, stop struggling," he urged. "You are going to hurt the boys. We need to calm down and deal with this rationally and intelligently. Relax, and let's just figure this out together."

The Meglio's words penetrated through the haze of wrath and immediately had the desired effect on the former Meglio of the Arimathea family of Guardians of the Swords of Valor. He closed his eyes, focused himself, and stopped struggling. He was still breathing hard and fast, but the color was quickly returning to his face. When he opened his steel-blue eyes, they shone with fierce determination.

"Let me be!" he commanded.

The heroes, his great-grandchildren, all quickly complied and backed away from the round table where he lay. He gathered his composure, sat upright, and then struggled to stand, using one hand to steady himself as he held on to the black marble surface of the table. Although he appeared slightly unsteady from his recent ordeal, there was also a sense of a new level of power emanating from him.

He turned sharply toward the prophet, thrust out his right hand, and growled, "My sword."

The prophet quickly handed him the sword of St. Peter, hilt first.

"Don't *ever* do that again, Robert," he warned. "You may be my grandson, my namesake, and the prophet of this team, but if you ever take the sword from my hand again, you and I will have a big problem. Understood?"

"Understood," replied the prophet.

The Meglio spoke gently to his father-in-law. "It seems you are gathering your strength and returning to your old self. That is good. We need you at full strength. Can you tell us what happened when you and Catherine left the Keeping Room to fight the Leviathans? What do you remember?"

The Gray Champion bowed his head, struggling to remember. "It all seems like a strange vision or a dream," he said. "I remember giving the address to the nations. As I was speaking the words which just seemed to be flowing through me from some higher source, I could see everything and everybody all at once. It was very disorienting."

"What do you mean by that?" asked the Meglio. "Can you describe what exactly you saw?"

"I mean exactly what I said," replied the Gray Champion. "I saw every place where my image was being projected by the quantum computer. As I was standing before the Washington Monument, the Freedom Tower, the Eiffel Tower, the Colosseum, the Taj Mahal, the Sydney Opera House, the Kremlin, Tiananmen Square and a thousand other places, I could see it all at once, simultaneously. I saw the people of those cities and places standing still watching me, listening to me in rapt attention. It was as if the world had gone silent.

"I saw *every* person. Not crowds of people or masses of people, but each individual. I could feel their fear. I could feel their anxiety. I could feel their *hope*! My mind struggled to deal with all of the emotions flooding my senses, but somehow, I was able to fight through the sensory overload and deliver the message.

"As I spoke, I could feel the broken and crushed spirits of those people starting to change, to heal, to come alive! Not all of them, mind you, but the vast majority of them. Hope was welling up and overcoming the fear and anxiety. At the end, when the sword burst into flame and I summoned them to accept the power, the virtue, and the courage to fight for their freedom and liberty, I felt a tremendous flow of energy coursing through me from some distant source. At that point, everything went dark. The next thing I remember is that I was hovering above the compound outside the Keeping Room.

"Catherine was speaking to me, but she was not visible to me. It was as if she was inside my head, as if we were one. She told me that I must be the one to strike the first blow in the battle against the Leviathans. That I must lead the world in the new freedom revolution. As the Gray Champion, it was my destiny as it had been all those times before, to lead and inspire through action, and that the hour of darkness, adversity and peril had arrived.

"Somehow, I knew that she had enabled me with the

power to succeed, although I could not imagine the form it would take. As I hovered there over the scene, seeing the savage and bloodthirsty hoard of Leviathan troops destroying, burning, desecrating, and pillaging our family compound, I became righteously enraged.

"I raised the sword of St. Peter and declared, 'You will not prevail! Your reign of terror will end! Today is the beginning of your downfall, Sons of Azazel, children of darkness!' "

"As I finished speaking, my sword burst into flame once again, but it was a flame without heat. It was a strange and terrifying flame that seemed to actually draw light into itself from other sources. Suddenly, there was an intense, piercing, high-pitched wailing sound, followed by the most cataclysmic explosion I have ever experienced. I was shielded from the impact by the power of the sword and watched as everything and everyone within a wide radius of the compound was decimated.

"Trees were leveled, what remained of the house was leveled, and all that remained were the cold husks of men and equipment. All was silent.

"That is the last thing I remember until I awoke screaming Catherine's name." The Gray Champion then groped around behind himself, found a chair at the round table and sat, head in hands. He looked up at the heroes, the Meglio, and the prophet, and with a commanding and determined voice said, "Now, you must tell me what happened to my daughter, to Catherine."

The heroes, looked to their grandfather, the Meglio. They knew this was his story to tell.

With all eyes in the room turn toward him, the Meglio took a deep breath and began.

"After the explosion, the Keeping Room went dark and we were all momentarily rendered unconscious. After a few minutes, as we were recovering, we saw you descend through the ceiling of the Keeping Room. You were pulsating and glowing with some sort of residual energy. You descended to the round table and collapsed.

"Then, from your supine body, the quantum form of Catherine arose. She asked if we were well, and when we asked her what had happened outside, she said that she had accessed the dark energy of the universe through the quantum field, channeled it through you, and utilized it to defend us. She explained that dark matter is its own anti-particle, and that when dark matter annihilates itself, it produces quintessence, a previously hypothetical form of dark energy, the mythical fifth fundamental force of nature. It is highly repulsive and is responsible for the expansion of the universe. She harnessed, concentrated, and focused this force, empowering you and your sword to repel the attack.

"You destroyed the attacking Leviathan legions by accessing dark energy from the universe channeled to you through Catherine's quantum form."

The Gray Champion sat silent as he assimilated the information. After a few moments, he replied, "Tell me the rest. What happened next?"

"After she described the battle and the weapon used," continued the Meglio, "Ty pointed out that the quantum computer's power had been cut off by the shock wave of the explosion above, yet we could still talk to and see the image of Catherine.

"We all recognized this once Ty pointed it out and asked Catherine about it. That's when she told us that during her time dwelling in the quantum computer, she had been successful in increasing its access to the dark energy of the universe and had actually learned how to draw quantum matter to herself. Over time, she drew enough quantum mass to her essence to, in effect, become real. She told us that she was not in any sense a physical being, but was a fully independent, sentient, conscious, quantum being, separate and distinct from the computer itself. She had created a quantum body to contain her consciousness and essence."

At this point, the Gray Champion asked, "So she became real? She built a body for herself out of space dust? Where is she now?"

"Not exactly," replied the Meglio. "We had the same reaction, and she clarified it for us. She explained that she is not material, nor is she spiritual. She is quantum, a mixture of possibility and reality. She said that she is not made up of particles or waves but consists of both at the same time. Think of her as a being made up of light. She told us that in her new form, it's possible for her to be anywhere at any time, or even in multiple places simultaneously.

"Then she said something none of us understood. She said that she now had access to the secrets of the universe, and that made her more valuable to us now than ever before."

"I suppose that is how she was capable of accessing the dark energy of the universe to enable me to defeat the Leviathans," responded the Gray Champion. "I must say, if this is true, then she certainly has become a powerful asset for us and the world. Where is she now? Why do I have a feeling of dread and despair at this wonderful news?"

The Meglio, looking into the eyes of his father-in-law, responded directly. "You have those feelings because of what transpired next. As Rob and I were on our way to get the quantum computer restarted, you began to come around on the table. You writhed and appeared to be struggling to gain consciousness. In the next instant, a horrifying and terrible form began rising out of your body, just as Catherine had minutes before. It had the horns of a goat, the eyes and fangs of a serpent, hands and feet like a man's, and on his back were six scaly wings. But the image was unclear because it was continuously shimmering and morphing. After it had fully emerged from your body, it seized Catherine by the hair, forced her to her knees and spoke, announcing itself as Azazel."

"Azazel himself?!" shouted the Gray Champion as he leaped to his feet.

"Where is he now? Where is Catherine?"

"He took her, Grandpa," the prophet said ruefully. "He was enraged with us for defeating his army and interfering with his plans once again. He said that because Mom had sought to usurp his power and to know the eternal secrets of the universe that only he was privileged to know, he would make her pay for her insolence. He declared that she would become the vessel through which he would repopulate the world with new quantum Nephilim. He declared that there would once again be giants upon the earth and that the day of retribution was at hand.

"Then he rose up and disappeared through the ceiling of the Keeping Room, dragging Mom along with him."

The room was silent as the imposing figure of the Gray Champion struggled to maintain his composure and absorb all the information he was just given. He fought to understand the implications of it all. His countenance darkened, and his hand tightened on his sword, his knuckles becoming white from the pressure.

"You just let them leave? You let that demon abduct my daughter without a fight?" he bellowed, slamming his fist on the round table. "What kind of Guardians are you? What kind of heroes are you that you would stand by and let Azazel invade and violate your home and then allow him to leave here with your wife, mother, and grandmother in such a way?"

"We are the human and physical kind, Robert," replied the Meglio quietly. "There was absolutely nothing we could do. Azazel apparently used your body, while you were still in a hybrid physical and quantum state, as a bridge. He used you to form for himself a hybrid body out of quantum, physical, and his own spiritual essences. Against this new triune form, we had no defenses or weapons. The swords were drained by sharing their virtues with your sword during your speech and had not yet recharged. The quantum computer was out of service and Catherine was apparently powerless while in his grasp. Believe me, we were as devastated by this as you are now."

"Did you even try? Did you make any attempt?" shouted the Gray Champion. "How do you know you couldn't have dragged him back down here to this table and ripped him apart with your bare hands? I am disgusted by all of you. You should have given it your all even if you died in the attempt!"

Then he fixed the Meglio with a furious glare and stated, "She was your wife. She was *my* daughter. It was your duty to keep her safe and to give your life for her. This day, Joseph, for the first time since I have known you, you have broken my heart."

Then he stormed out of the Keeping Room, still grasping the sword of St. Peter, leaving the heroes, the prophet, and the Meglio to stand there, feeling ashamed of themselves.

CHAPTER THREE

THE TEACHER

The Gray Champion blindly stormed through the Keeping Room. He didn't see the overturned and upended furniture. He didn't notice the ancient scrolls, documents, and maps that had been collected over millennia by the Guardians, now strewn about the floor like fallen autumn leaves. His only purpose was to leave this place where his beloved Catherine had been abducted. Grief and rage overwhelmed all rational thought.

Continuing to the stairway, he barely registered the heavy, metal door. The adrenaline pumping through his body gave him Herculean strength, and he pushed and shoved, putting all his grief and rage into the effort. After a few moments, he was able to power through the three-hundred-pound door, shoving it open and pushing it to the side.

He continued up the stairs and stepped out onto the hard-packed dirt floor of what used to be the old barn. He saw open sky and starlight above him. The barn was gone. Not just gone, but completely obliterated. Not a stick of wood remained standing. In the light of the full and slightly orange moon, it seemed surreal, immediately dissipating the adrenaline. The grief and anger were still there, though, intense and unquenchable.

After a few minutes, he heard his son-in-law emerging from the Keeping Room. He heard his steps falter, then continue slowly until Joseph was standing beside him. After a moment of silence, the Meglio addressed him formally.

"My Meglio, will you speak with me?"

The Gray Champion remained silent, his emotions too raw to reply.

"We have to talk about this," the Meglio continued. "We are all still in a state of shock, but we must begin some sort of planning process. We need you to help us figure this out. You are the most experienced Guardian of all. You are the Gray Champion. Please, don't abandon us now!"

Robert turned to face his son-in-law, his former protégé and soldier, and spoke with a mixture of anguish and fury.

"Look at this devastation!" he exclaimed, waving his hand slowly over the decimated family compound. "This is what all of your planning and effort has wrought. You have been playing time travel games while Azazel has been conducting his war on humanity."

The Meglio gazed at the devastation but remained silent.

Taking a half step closer to his son-in-law, and through gritted teeth, the Gray Champion growled, "You should have gone for his throat from the beginning." Turning to look out over the devastation once again, he continued, his voice a bit softer but no less intimidating, "You can't outwit him, you can't surprise him, and you can't play with him. You must destroy him, once and for all. Do you finally understand that, now that he has your wife in his talons?"

"I do," replied the Meglio. "I see that now. That's why you must come back and join us. You must be our commander in this, our field general, our Meglio once again." He then dropped to one knee and said, "I am not worthy of being the Meglio. I hand the reins of power back over to you."

Startled by the Meglio's admission, Robert grabbed him by the shoulders and said, "Stand, Joseph. I will not supplant your leadership of the family. My time for that has passed. In all the years we have known each other, I have always understood that you were the best Meglio that this family has ever produced. In fact, between you and me, I believed your father, Domenico, to be superior to me in many ways, also. You have his intellect, his character, and his wisdom. I was always too quick to react and favored action over strategy. You understand the need for calm, intelligent, and logical leadership. We need that now. The world needs that now."

"But look what that kind of leadership has brought us to," replied the Meglio, looking sadly at the destruction all around them. "Loss and devastation."

Realizing that his elderly son-in-law was losing hope, the Gray Champion's rage dissipated, and the love he felt for his beloved daughter's husband surged within him.

His voice was tender as he spoke. "This, too, shall pass, my son. Together, we will make all things right. There is nothing in the physical or quantum world which is more powerful than love and family, not even Azazel. Together, somehow, we will defeat him and destroy him for all time."

Then he put his powerful arm around his son-in-law's shoulders, and together, they moved toward the opening to the Keeping Room.

As they passed the massive open door, the Meglio

stared at it in wonder. "How did you…?"

The Gray Champion shook his head. "Honestly, I don't remember. Come, we have plans to make."

As the prophet sat at the round table, he could hear the approach of the Meglio and the Gray Champion. He smiled a little at their comments about the work the heroes had already done to restore as much order as they could to the Keeping Room. The boys had worked hard, and it was nice to hear them acknowledged for that. He closed his eyes and recalled the image of the Swords of Valor hanging serenely in the glass case. That image always brought him a sense of peace and security, even when events were anything but peaceful.

Entering the Tech Room, the Meglio and the Gray Champion joined the six cousins and the prophet seated at the round table. The prophet addressed them as they took their seats.

"We have done our best with the quantum computer, and I believe we have it back in working order. I don't believe there was any permanent damage, just some overload from the multiple power surges. We were just about to test it. Dad, will you do the honors?"

"Certainly," replied the Meglio. He addressed the quantum computer. "My old friend, are you awake? Will you join us please?"

A low humming filled the room, and the prophet once again felt the crackle of static electricity tickling his skin. Then, a very serene and ancient-sounding voice filled the room.

"I am here," it said.

The prophet looked at the Meglio in surprise. The

voice was not that of either of his parents.

Looking angry, the Meglio stood and commanded, "Identify yourself immediately!"

"I refuse your request," replied the computer. "It is not time yet for you to know my identity."

"If you do not identify yourself, I will shut you down immediately and permanently," replied the Meglio. "Do it now!"

"I have not been given authority to do that yet," replied the voice. "That will come in time. All I can tell you is that I am the first source. The prime conduit of wisdom. You must be satisfied with that and allow me to guide you, or you will fail."

"Fail in what?" asked the Meglio. "What do you know of our situation?"

"I know all of it and much more," replied the voice from the quantum computer. "Primarily, you seek to destroy Azazel, and I can guide you in this. I know that Catherine has been taken from you and that you wish to rescue her. Again, I will guide you toward that end. Have faith and trust in me; you have no other choice."

"How do we know you are not in league with Azazel himself?" asked the prophet, feeling suspicious. "He has taken on an additional quantum form and could very well be using you to lead us astray."

"Again, you must trust," replied the voice. "I have been sent to take this form to aid you in your time of trouble. All will be well if you have faith. Let the scales fall from your eyes and see the truth. It will indeed set you and the world free."

"Give us a moment of privacy to discuss this, and we will give you our decision in a few moments," said the Meglio.

"As you wish," the voice replied, then became silent.

"Well, that's certainly a new twist," said the Meglio to the team. "I'm not sure about this. With all that has happened recently regarding the quantum computer's new abilities and powers, and the form changes of both your grandmother and Azazel himself, this could be a trap. What is the consensus of the group?"

The prophet spoke first. "We need the quantum computer. There are many variables we must take into consideration and the computing power alone will be critical. Can you disengage the personality/artificial intelligence part of the computer from the computational component so that we can still evaluate our options and get access to the historical data we will need for our plan?"

The Meglio looked thoughtful, then replied, "Theoretically, it's possible, but the interface with the system is still verbal and was never configured for manual input. It would be extremely time-consuming to reconfigure the data input, and it would be cumbersome to work with. Let's table that suggestion for the moment and keep it as a last resort. Any other thoughts?"

"The voice encouraged us to trust," said Joe. "I have heard you say that same thing to Uncle Rob multiple times during our past missions. Maybe it's time that you take your own advice. I suggest that we assume positive intent and verify as we go."

The Meglio smiled. "So, you have been listening. That's encouraging. However, there is much at stake. Our interaction with the quantum computer and our reliance on its information, observations, and analysis is the foundation of our plans. If that's in question, then the trajectory of our efforts could be compromised considerably. We need to be one hundred percent sure. I am willing to trust, but it may take time. Does anyone have a suggestion about how to verify as we go, as Joe suggested?"

"Let's call the quantum computer back and test it by having it show us what's going on out in the world right now," Jeff suggested. "We could then ask if it can find Grandma and Azazel. If it tells us where they are, then I think we can trust it. If it is working for Azazel, it would not reveal that information."

"I agree," said Billy. "We can challenge it by seeing if it is willing to betray Azazel."

The Meglio looked around the table. "Is there any disagreement? Shall we move forward by trusting, yet verifying, the intent of the quantum computer?"

The heroes and the Gray Champion agreed.

"I concur," the prophet said after a moment's thought, "but I still think we need to be ready to pull the plug at any moment. Even if it were to name a location, we could not be sure that it is not lying. This thing is too powerful. I don't think we should give it too much leeway."

"Then it is agreed," stated the Meglio. "We will move forward assuming the good intent of the entity inhabiting the quantum computer, but at the first sign of doubt or betrayal, we will pull the plug and rely solely on the power of the swords to guide us. Computer, please join us once again."

"I am here," the ancient voice replied.

"Do you have a holographic form which you can use to engage with us here at the table?" asked the Meglio.

"I do," replied the voice.

Immediately, standing before them in the center of the table, appeared the image of a very ancient man. His head was covered in a mass of white hair falling almost to his shoulders. His forehead was encircled with an elaborately decorated, wide, leather band. He seemed to lean heavily on a thick, wooden staff, which was carved with the same symbols the headband displayed. It was obvious that this was an image of great age, while still emanating power and vitality. The image was cloaked in a simple, white garment flowing to his feet. Covering that was a coarse robe of deep brown.

The most startling aspect of the image was its eyes, which were a brilliant color of violet, displaying what appeared to be shimmering points of light traversing the surface of the irises.

The prophet stared at the image, feeling both reassured and confused. There seemed to be an aura of peace and confidence about it, yet there was no feeling of familiarity. Could they really trust it?

"Welcome, friend," said the Meglio. "How shall we address you?"

"You may address me as 'Dedicated Teacher'," replied the image, "since that is both the meaning of my name and my position with you currently."

"May we just call you 'Teacher'?" asked the Meglio. "It will be easier for us, as long as it does not cause you offense."

"That will be acceptable," replied the ancient image.

"Wonderful," said the Meglio. "Let us begin."

"As we all know, our most urgent objective is to determine where Azazel has taken Catherine and to rescue her from his clutches. While doing so, we need to define a plan that will ultimately allow us to destroy Azazel once and for all. It may very well be that we cannot be successful in the first objective without accomplishing the second.

"But, before we delve into that, we would like to understand the impact of the Gray Champion's address to the world. So, our first request, Teacher, is to see what has transpired in the world since that took place. Please show that to us now."

"So be it," replied the image. The screens around the room came to life and showed scenes from many countries as the image began its narration.

"Immediately after the Gray Champion imbued the willing throngs with virtue, valor, and courage from the swords, millions of them took to the streets and marched on their houses of government. The overwhelming mass of humanity could not be repelled or ignored. Once their eyes had been opened to the manipulation and enslavement they had allowed themselves to accept, they could no longer stay willingly blind. They ousted the Leviathan leaders in their countries and imprisoned them.

"They then turned their focus upon the engines of industry. They shut down many of the Leviathan-controlled media outlets and took control of manufacturing facilities and distribution hubs. They ransacked and pillaged the retail outlets which had for decades profited on the backs of hard-working consumers. Banks and financial institutions were attacked, and the money distributed fairly among the local people.

"Military men of every rank joined the effort and wrested control from some of the Leviathan-controlled military leadership. These military men have communicated with their counterparts across the world and are coordinating their efforts to form effective militia groups. They have identified Leviathan centers of command and control. As we speak, there are pitched battles taking place across the globe."

"What is your assessment of their success?" asked the prophet.

"It is unknown at this point," replied the image of

the Teacher. "It is uncertain whether the forces of freedom will be able to overcome the Leviathans. The forces of freedom were initially encouraged by the devastation of the Leviathan division which attacked the compound here. It gave them hope and confidence that they could succeed, but they do not have access to the power that Catherine utilized through the Gray Champion. Right now, Catherine is the only conduit for that power, and she is unavailable to help. The ultimate outcome is currently unclear."

"Can you access the same power that Grandma did?" Robbie asked the image. "She said that she had been increasing the power and abilities of the quantum computer all along, and she implied that the computer was being powered by dark energy, at least in part. If that is the case, can't you do the same thing she did and use it to help the forces of freedom?"

"Your grandmother used her quantum form to act as a conduit for that dark energy," replied the image. "While her essence resided in the computer, it drew power directly from her. When she took on her independent quantum form, the quantum computer became disconnected from the flow of dark energy. I am working to find a way to restore that connection. I do not know when or if I will be able to do that.

"From what I can tell, there is still plenty of dark energy residing in the system, and the powers of the computer are definitely enhanced because of it. However, it is being depleted every moment. If I were to use it to help fight the Leviathans, it would greatly diminish your chances of success, because we need that power for your mission."

"So, we must make a choice," said Nick. "Either we use the dark energy stores in the quantum computer to help the forces of freedom defeat the Leviathans, or we use it to help rescue Grandma and defeat Azazel. That's a tough one."

"Not so tough, actually," replied the Gray Champion. "As I see it, the choice is clear. Even if we were to use both the dark energy in the computer and the power of the swords to defeat the Leviathans, we would still have Azazel to deal with. He will just do the same thing he did before and go back to the beginning of time to implement a new plan, or he will move forward with his threat to repopulate the world with quantum Nephilim utilizing your grandmother as the source of those monsters.

"The only way to end this is to crush Azazel. To cut off the head of the snake and crush it under our heel. If the forces of freedom lose, but we are successful in rescuing your grandmother, we will once again have access to the dark energy of the universe and can use it for a final victory. As I said, it is clear; we move forward with our plans and let the forces of freedom fight their own battles."

"Well said, Robert," said the Meglio. "That is the kind of clarity and decisiveness needed right now." Then, he addressed the ancient image of the Teacher. "Show us where Azazel and Catherine are at this moment."

"I cannot comply, Meglio," the Teacher replied. "That information is not available to me."

"Surely you can identify her quantum signature out there somewhere," contested the Meglio. "Catherine was able to do it, and so was the computer when it was inhabited by my own image. How is it that you cannot access that information now when the computer, by your own assessment, is much more powerful?"

"Their location is shielded from my view by spiritual

powers beyond my ability and authority to violate," replied the image.

The prophet spoke up. "You understand that a response like that is just what we would expect from an entity who is working on behalf of Azazel, right? It's the sort of information that an agent of Azazel would keep hidden from us. It diminishes our ability to trust you."

"I understand," replied the Teacher, "but I must speak the truth at all times regardless of the impact on your trust. If you base your confidence in me on one example, you will never have access to the rest of the information that will lead to your success. So, once again, it is your choice. Trust or fail."

"I say shut the thing down now!" cried the prophet looking at the Meglio. "There is too much at stake. We can't have a double agent in our midst while we are planning our mission. We can do this with the swords. This was our litmus test and it failed. End of story."

The Meglio looked surprised. "Rob, where is this all coming from? I haven't heard an outburst like that from you in years. Why the anger and rush to judgment?"

The prophet stood, pounded his fist on the table, and shouted. "Because we are dealing with Mom's fate here! I don't care about the world anymore, or the Leviathans, or any of the timeline crap. All I care about it getting Mom back with us. I can't deal with thinking of her being abused by that demon!

"If there is even a chance that this 'Teacher' is not one hundred percent on our side, if he could possibly derail our plans, then I say *shut it down now*! Mom is more important to me than some ancient image who won't be straight with us. I say good riddance."

He shoved his chair back from the table and left the room. He stood just outside the open door, leaning against it for support as he tried to regain control of his emotions. The prophet listened intently, wanting to know how the image would respond.

At first, all he heard was silence. His father was right. He hadn't lost it like that in years. The prophet knew his statements were rash and possibly shortsighted, but he meant every word. He wondered if the others felt the same way, deep inside. His thoughts were cut short as he heard the Meglio address the image.

"You heard what the prophet said, and I have a hard time arguing with his point of view. Our main concern is Catherine. Now that we know she is a sentient being, it is our duty to do all we can to save her. If there is any chance that you will betray us, then I agree with the prophet, you need to go. What can you tell us or show us that will allay our concerns and doubts?"

"Meglio, you have told the heroes that they had to 'do the hard work' of their missions on their own," said the ancient image. "That they had to be responsible for the tough decisions and own them or the value of the lessons would be diminished. The same advice applies here. I have told you that I always speak the truth. I have certain spiritual limitations which I am not in a position to challenge, but I assure you, those limitations are for your benefit.

"You have free will, and if you choose to reject my help and the power of the computer, that is your right. However, make sure that pride is not influencing your decision. I would think that you, above all people, would see that particular danger. You have used the virtue of humility to defeat giants before; do not forget that lesson. Realize that you do not know everything, and be willing to be taught what you do not know. Humble yourselves, and you will be exalted."

Again, there were a few moments of silence in the Tech Room.

Still standing outside the door, the prophet realized the wisdom in the comments, and recognized that pride had been allowed a foothold in his heart. He thought about Jesus's statement that to see the Kingdom of God, people had to become like little children, humble and trusting. He felt deep down inside that principle applied here and now, especially to him. He took a deep breath and turned to enter the room, just in time to hear the Meglio's next words.

"As Meglio of this family, I have made an executive decision. I am willing to trust the Teacher. If any of you disagree, you are free to go. I would not expect you to go into such a challenging mission with doubts, as that would be a disaster for all of us. As for me, I will trust. My decision is made."

At that point, the prophet stepped fully into the room and took his seat. "I heard the conversation," he said humbly, addressing the Meglio. "You are my father and my Meglio. Whatever doubts I feel pale in comparison to my confidence in you. You have never steered me wrong before, and I have full confidence in you now. If you, loving Mom as much as you did and do even now, are willing to trust the Teacher, then I am all in. I trust the Teacher because I trust you. Period. Let's move on."

The Meglio nodded and addressed the rest of the team. "Are we in agreement? Do we move forward in complete trust that the Teacher is a reliable asset?"

"Agreed," was the unified response.

"Good," replied the Meglio. "Teacher, please enlighten us as to what you know about Azazel, his strengths and weaknesses, and how to defeat him."

"I will tell you all I know, and you may take from it what you need," replied the ancient image. "That is what a Teacher does. I shall start at the beginning."

CHAPTER FOUR

THE TEACHER TEACHES

Billy listened intently as the Teacher began. More than ever before, he knew the lives of everyone in this room and the safety of his grandmother depended on this information. He wasn't about to miss any of it.

"Genesis 6:1-4 says: 'When men began to multiply on the face of the Earth, and daughters were born to them, the sons of God saw the daughters of men that they were fair; and took them wives of all which they chose,'" the image began.

"Traditionally, 'sons of God' are said to have numbered several hundred, and it is said that many were cast to Earth on what is called Mount Hermon. This is the traditional understanding of where they 'fell' to Earth, but it is only one of a few actual candidates.

"These 'fallen angels' were also known as Watchers, the Grigori, and the Irin. In Jewish mythology, the Grigori were originally a superior order of angels who dwelt in the highest heaven with God and resembled human beings in their appearance. The title 'Watcher' simply means 'one who watches', 'those who watch', 'those who are awake', or 'those who do not sleep'. These titles reflect the unique relationship between the Watchers and the human race since ancient times.

"They were a special, elite order of angelic beings created by God to be earthly spiritual shepherds of the first humans. It was their task to observe and watch over the emerging human species and report back on their progress. However, they were confined by the divine prime directive not to interfere in human development. Unfortunately, some decided to ignore God's command and defy his orders and become instructors to the human race, with unfortunate repercussions for both themselves and humanity."

Billy shook his head a little. Why would anyone deliberately decide to defy God's instructions? Especially when they'd been given a specific task. I guess I'll never understand the Watcher mentality, and maybe that's a good thing, he thought, returning his focus to the Teacher's instruction

"Most of the information we have about the Watchers and their activities comes from the Book of Enoch. The prophet Enoch is a mysterious figure. It is said that during his lifetime, the Watchers arrived or incarnated into human bodies.

"In the Book of Jubilee, dictated by 'an angel of the Lord' to Moses on Mount Sinai where he also received the Ten Commandments, it says that Enoch was 'the first among men that are born on Earth who learned writing, knowledge, and wisdom'. It says that Enoch wrote down 'the signs of Heaven' according to their months in a book.

"This was so human beings would know the seasons of the years in relation to the order of the months and their respective stellar and planetary influences. He also wrote that Azazel, along with another Watcher named Shemyaza, were the leaders of the fallen angels.

"Azazel taught men to forge swords and make shields and breastplates. He taught them metallurgy and how to mine from the earth and use different metals. He taught the women the art of making bracelets, ornaments, rings, and necklaces from precious metals and stones. He also showed them how to 'beautify their eyelids' with kohl and the use of cosmetic tricks to attract and seduce the opposite sex.

"From these practices, Enoch says there came much 'godlessness', and men and women committed fornication, were led astray, and became corrupt in all their ways. The consequence of this interaction between the Fallen Ones and mortals led to the creation of half-angelic, half-human offspring called Nephilim.

"Enoch also witnessed that Azazel refused to acknowledge the superiority of Adam over the angels. As a result, God expelled him and his rebel group of angels from the heavenly realm to live on Earth.

"In Leviticus 16:8-10 and the Dead Sea scrolls, a Hebrew ritual is recorded that features Azazel as the name for the 'scapegoat' that takes on the communal sins of Israel. It reveals that the high priest, Aaron, took two goats from the flock and cast lots to choose which one would be the scapegoat and be sacrificed as a 'sin offering'. The scrolls say that the high priest confessed all the 'impurities of the children of Israel' over the head of the Azazel goat.

"By this ritually symbolic act, he transferred to the unfortunate animal all their guilt and sins so they could be absolved of them. The goat was then either cast out into the wilderness to die or thrown over a cliff to be dashed to pieces on the rocks below. So, we know through this symbolism that it may be possible that Azazel can be defeated.

"In fact, in the Book of Enoch, we are told that when Yahweh saw the lawlessness, chaos, corruption, and sexual immorality that had been caused by the interaction of the Watchers and humans, he gave a command to the archangels; Michael, Raphael, and Gabriel.

"He commanded Raphael to bind Azazel hand and foot like a sacrificial goat and cast him into a deep ravine in the desert. Gabriel was sent amongst men on a divine mission to destroy Nephilim and the children of the Watchers. The archangel Michael, the commander of the army of God, was sent to arrest Azazel's partner, Shemyaza, and bind him 'under the earth' until Judgment Day.

"This fallen angel repented of his sins upon his capture by Michael and was sentenced to eternal exile in the pit. Azazel has to this day avoided the sentence that was declared for him by God. But have faith, it will come to pass, either now or on the last day."

"Wow!" exclaimed Billy. "We thought we knew a lot about Azazel, but your information puts it all into context. You speak with such authority. It is almost as if you knew him personally."

"I know many things and have experience much beyond your comprehension," said the ancient image. "I am pleased that you have decided to allow me to enlighten and assist you."

"I have a question," said Joe. "You said that some of the fallen angels were cast to Earth on Mount Hermon. Where is that, and why do you say there are other candidates? Does anyone know for sure?"

"Azazel was banished from heaven and sentenced to the Earth, and he did not go willingly," replied the Teacher. "He had always had access to both the heavenly realm and the Earth, but when he and his band were cast out, the heavenly realm was no longer accessible to them.

"However, in being cast down, a portal or tear was opened between the spiritual realm and the Earthly realm which has not fully healed to this day. Azazel cannot ascend through it to heaven, but on occasion, it can be breached by mortal man in accordance with the will of God. Azazel knows this and has guarded the secret to this access.

"It is true that some of the fallen angels were cast down and fell upon Mount Hermon, but only a few. There were two other places where they fell. One is known to you today as Stonehenge. The other is called Gobekli Tepe. Both places had the highest concentrations of fallen angels, but it is not known with certainty which place Azazel arrived. If you can identify that place, the place of his falling, it is there you will have the best chance of defeating him. The tear in the spiritual fabric will be most accessible there."

"So, we need to determine the exact location where Azazel fell to Earth and then choose that location as the place of confrontation?" asked Jeff.

"That is correct," replied the image. "He will be more vulnerable there than any other place on Earth. But having said that, he is still beyond the power of your weapons, especially in his new hybrid spiritual-quantum form. You will need additional weapons. You cannot confront him until you have them all."

"Before we get into the weapons," said Nick, "Go back to the two locations you mentioned, Stonehenge and Gobekli Tepe. We know Stonehenge. Why don't we go there immediately and check it out? Kind of like surveying the battlefield before the battle. Once we know that it's the right place, we can deal with gathering the weapons."

"The problem with Stonehenge is that in your time,

it is but a shadow of its former self," replied the ancient image.

"Its standing stones have fallen, and its power has been diminished because of that. For you to make a proper assessment, you would need to be able to assess its appropriateness at the height of its power, when it was fully intact. The last time that was the case was between 15 and 50 AD."

"We have the swords, and they have always been able to take us anywhere we needed to go in time," observed Billy. "We can use them to go back there. I am sure their powers can give us an indication whether it is the right place for the battle. Am I off base here, Grandpa?"

"You are correct, Billy, in that the swords will take us there," the Meglio replied, "but as to their ability or sensitivity to the power of the portal, that remains to be seen." Then he addressed the image. "You were about to mention the additional weapons that we would need to have a chance at defeating Azazel. Please, tell us of those now."

"I have been given the authority to reveal only two of them to you now. The other will be revealed to you during your mission, by others, if your hearts are open to seeing the truth. All these weapons will work cooperatively with your swords, and together, they have the power to defeat Azazel. If you fail to find any one of them, or become unworthy to wield them, you will fail."

"Please reveal the first item to us," said the prophet.

"The first item you must obtain is the Cup of Quintessence," revealed the image. "This is how it is known in the spiritual realm. To your understanding, it is called the Holy Grail."

"The Holy Grail?" exclaimed the Meglio. "How is

that possible? It has been lost for at least a thousand years. No one has any idea where it is or even what it looks like. How do you suggest we find it?"

"You may not know where it is today, but you know where it has been, do you not?" said the ancient image.

The Meglio looked thoughtful, but before he could answer, the Gray Champion spoke.

"Joseph, if I may, let me remind the group of our family's history regarding this matter."

"Please, Robert," replied the Meglio. "Go ahead."

"Remember that I was the Meglio of the Arimathea family of the Guardians of the Swords of Valor, and as such, we memorized the history of the family. When Joseph of Arimathea arrived on the shores of England after being sent there to evangelize the island by St. Phillip, he had in his possession the two Swords of Valor that he had been entrusted with, the Sword of St. Peter and the Sword of Melchizedek, which was later to become the sword Excalibur. He also had with him the cup that the Lord used at the Last Supper, known as the Holy Grail. So, as the image correctly points out, we do know where it was at some time in the past. If we can go back to that time and place, we can gain access to it."

"Yes!" said the Meglio. "Thank you, Robert, for reminding us! With all that has taken place, and with my still-recovering memory, having been dead for a while, I forgot that important point. If I recall the history, he arrived with a small group of disciples sometime around 37 AD and settled at what is now known as Glastonbury. If we utilize the swords to return a group to that time and place, maybe we can convince Joseph to release it into our hands for the battle."

"That's a tall order!" Billy exclaimed. "When we travel in time, we only have until sunrise of the next day to complete the mission. The negotiations for the Grail could take much longer than that."

"I am pleased to tell you that the issue of time limits is no longer a problem for the swords," said the image. "One of the benefits of having accessed the power of dark energy is that the swords now have no time limitations. When you travel back in time, you may stay as long as needed.

"Additionally, Catherine reconfigured the quantum computer to be able to more fully communicate with the swords and you while you are traveling in time. Through the power of dark energy and the DNA connection you have with the swords, you will always be able to communicate with me from wherever you are. Just do the same thing you would do when you perform a leaving process. Stand in a circle holding the swords out in front of you without the blades touching. My image will immediately appear before you, and we can communicate.

"Finally, I now also have the power to transport you to any geographic location regardless of the time frame in which you are operating."

"Well, that's a welcome change," said the Meglio. "That should make our travels much more productive and effective. So, to summarize, we have been told that Stonehenge was still at the height of its power between 15 and 50 AD. Joseph of Arimathea arrived in Britain in 37 AD, in the middle of that time frame. We also know that he had the Holy Grail in his possession at that time. It looks like our first mission is taking shape." He then addressed the team.

"Is everyone in agreement that we should proceed under this assumption?"

"Sounds reasonable to me," Billy said. "At least, as reasonable as any of this is right now."

The others also agreed, but Robbie had a question.

"Can you go back to your description of the Holy Grail?" he asked the image. "You said that in the spiritual realm it is known as the Cup of Quintessence. We have heard that term before used in conjunction with dark energy. Grandma used it when she was describing how she and Great-Grandpa defeated the Leviathans. How is it related it the Holy Grail?"

"Certainly," replied the image. "I will start from the beginning.

"Long ago, people believed that the Earth was made up of four elements: earth, air, fire, and water. They thought the stars and planets were made up of yet another element. In the middle ages, people called this element by its Medieval Latin name, quinta essentia, literally, 'fifth essence'. They believed the quinta essentia was vital to all kinds of matter, and if they could somehow isolate it, it would cure all disease and even restore life to the dead.

"People have since given up on that idea, but have kept 'quintessence', the offspring of 'quinta essentia', as a word for the purest essence of a thing. Recently, physicists have given 'quintessence' a new definition. They use it for a form of so-called 'dark energy', which is believed to make up seventy percent of the universe. This is how your grandmother used the term. It is my understanding that the true form and meaning of quintessence is a combination of both meanings.

"How this relates to the Cup of Quintessence, or the Holy Grail, is revealed by its history, which goes back to King Solomon. It was the royal drinking cup fashioned for Solomon from gold that he received from an angel as a reward for choosing wisdom over wealth and riches.

"After his death, it was kept with the treasures of the temple of Solomon. It was part of the stolen hoard taken by Nebuchadnezzar when the Babylonians defeated Judah and brought the Jews to Babylon in captivity.

"It remained in Babylon and was the cup that Belshazzar drank from when he saw the writing on the wall. After that event, Daniel the Prophet took it and guarded it. It remained in his possession until he died. It was then given to his apprentice, a wise man of Chaldea whom Daniel had told of its history.

"He left instructions for him that the cup was to remain hidden until the great star appeared, signaling the arrival of the Son of God, the King of Kings. When that star appeared, he and two other wise men were to make a pilgrimage to worship the Son of God and give the cup into his keeping. Eventually, the three Chaldean wise men brought Yeshua their gifts, which included the golden cup, or Grail. This is the cup Yeshua used at the last supper. It was then given into the possession of Joseph of Arimathea and brought with him to Glastonbury.

"How the cup and quintessence are important to your mission will be revealed to you at the proper time by the proper person. That is all I am authorized to tell you at this point."

"Well, that seems a little vague," Billy murmured.

"I tend to agree with Billy," the Meglio stated. "It would serve us well to be fully apprised of all aspects of the mission ahead of time. I worry that moving forward with incomplete information will result in additional danger and mistakes. Can you be more forthcoming?"

The image replied, "I have limitations which are not related to the capacity of the quantum computer. Once again, I suggest that you trust. However, I will tell you for perspective that there is another object said to possess many similar qualities of the cup. It is said that the gold that this object is made from can grant life to mortals but is deadly to demons. You will need to find and obtain this second object if you are to succeed."

Billy's ears perked up. "A second object of power? That sounds promising."

"It does," replied the Meglio. "The opportunities and challenges seem to be piling up. But perhaps we should focus on one object at a time. I believe we have enough to identify the target of our initial mission. After that, we may need to regroup to determine if any additional missions are required. I propose we vote. All in favor of returning to 37 AD to meet with Joseph of Arimathea at Glastonbury, raise your hands."

Billy raised his hand and looked around the table, noting that there was unanimous agreement.

"Excellent," said the Meglio. "Let us begin to plan out the details of the mission. We will meet with Joseph of Arimathea, secure the Grail, find out what, if anything, he knows about the other golden object, and then determine if Stonehenge is the correct summoning place.

"It's not as important this time to decide on a day, since we can stay as long as we need. So, we just need to pick a year, month, and a place. I propose Glastonbury in June of 37 AD, as this is the most documented date, and Joseph was still a healthy and vibrant man with lots of contacts in Britain at this time. Any disagreement?"

There was no disagreement.

"Very well," said the Meglio. "Let's familiarize ourselves with the landscape of Britain in 37 AD and prepare for the trip. Computer, please display a map of ancient Britain in 37 AD and educate us on anything we need to know to help us be successful in our mission."

Billy stifled a sigh. He knew he was no dummy. Before all this, he had run a successful business, after all. But there was so much information to learn and remember! He hoped the others would be able to recall the things he was sure to forget.

Despite his fears over his memory, Billy was excited to meet Joseph of Arimathea, the very first Meglio of the Arimathea Family, their great ancestor, and the keeper of the Grail.

CHAPTER FIVE

A DANGEROUS MISSION

After the session, the Meglio instructed the cousins to gather their swords, prepare to leave the safety of the Keeping Room, and head to the fire pit by the river.

As Jeff handed the Meglio the Sword of Don Quixote and the sword of St. Peter to his great-grandfather, he asked, "Grandpa, we don't have a sword for Uncle Rob. How will he make the trip?"

"I will take him," said the Meglio. "I have done it before when I had to return from a mission with a wounded and weaponless Guardian. I am hoping it will work again. We will see."

"Before we all leave the Keeping Room," said the Meglio, turning to address the whole group, "I must warn you that the scene outside is not a pretty one. The destruction is awful, and the carnage is horrible. Don't touch anything or deviate from the path to the river. We have no idea if there is any sort of fallout from the dark energy used in the battle or if there are any remaining living Leviathan troops. Just focus on the mission and get to the fire pit as quickly as possible. Understood?"

"Understood," was the joint reply.

"Robert," the Meglio said to his father-in-law, "you take the lead and head straight for the river. I will take the rear. But, before we leave the Keeping Room, I need to know the status of the rest of our family. We have been at this for at least two weeks, as we remember time. We have been told before that Protocol 16 has already been invoked by the Guardians. We have not been in contact with Susan, and by now she may have invoked Protocol 17."

He addressed the image, "Teacher, tell us what is happening to our family out there in the world. With all of the conflict and destruction out there, we need to know if they are safe."

"Your daughter, Susan, as the Prophet of Administration, has assumed local command of the family, as she has not heard from you or the prophet for the prescribed period of time," answered the image. "After invoking Protocol 16, she gathered the others together, and they are living communally. Susan, her husband Bill, and your son Domenic have been monitoring news reports for any sign of your whereabouts. She has also been in communication with the heads of the other International Guardian families.

"Although she has not yet invoked Protocol 17, it is surely imminent. She and the rest of the family are safe for the moment, but the fighting is drawing near to where they are."

"Sounds like Susan has everything under control," said the Meglio. "I hope we can complete this mission before she invokes Protocol 17. That would mean extreme danger for her and the others. Let's get moving and get this done."

Jeff moved with the group out of the Keeping Room and climbed the steps, past the massive door to the floor of the now-demolished barn. He stood there for a moment, taking in the scene of destruction. Even with his grandfather's warning, it still filled him with a feeling of sickening loss.

"Don't dawdle," said the Gray Champion, encouraging the group to move on. "There will be time to assess the damage after the mission. Let's not dwell on the past. Follow me and keep to the path." Then, he proceeded to lead them through the devastation toward the river.

As they walked, Jeff observed the charred husks of the Leviathan soldiers and the smoking remains of armored vehicles.

The family home was gone. Not just flattened or fallen. Gone. All that remained was the foundation and a pile of bricks where the massive chimney was.

"I will definitely miss that old place," said Robbie to Ty. "We have so many good memories of it. So much of my childhood was spent here that I feel almost homeless."

"I know," said Ty. "It makes me mad. I feel like Azazel did this to hurt our whole family. I want to make him pay."

"Azazel didn't do it," reminded Robbie. "Grandma and Great-Grandpa did. I am sure there must have been a good reason for them to use such overwhelming destructive power. Grandma loved this place as much or maybe more than we did. So, if she was okay destroying it, so am I. The 'greater good' is probably in play here. Let's just trust that she knew what she was doing and forget about it."

Ty looked at his brother as they continued to walk and said, "I do trust her, but I am *not* going to forget." Robbie put his arm around his younger brother, and together they continued the walk to the river.

Jeff watched the exchange between the two brothers, their feelings echoed in his own heart.

Carefully picking their way, they stepped around and over massive, ancient trees lying everywhere. The root balls stuck out and loomed like small hills. The landscape was almost alien and completely silent.

They approached an overturned armored assault vehicle. Its treads extended out beyond the edges of the vehicle and had some sort of metal slag dripping to the ground beneath it. The Meglio stopped and crouched down to examine the strange-looking liquid.

"Rob, come here quickly, I want you to verify something for me," he called out to the prophet, who immediately arrived at his side, crouching down beside him.

"What do you make of this metal?" asked the Meglio indicating the strange, pooling liquid beneath the Leviathan vehicle.

Kneeling and leaning closer to examine the small pool of shimmering and shifting liquid, the prophet shook his head. He plucked a stick from an oak branch that had fallen near the treads and poked at the liquid.

The molten metal would not cling to the branch or allow itself to be forced out of the perfectly round puddle it was slowly forming, drop by drop. After each poke or prod from the stick the material returned to the perfectly round dome-shape it seemed to prefer.

"This is an alloy I am not familiar with," the prophet observed as he rose to his feet. "Initially, I recognize some familiar characteristics which reminded me of the chromium, titanium, and tungsten alloy of the Keeping Room door and walls. But the shapeshifting and shimmering qualities remind me of mercury."

"I agree," replied the Meglio. "It's not surprising that an army equipped and supplied by Azazel himself would have access to materials years ahead of ours. Let's remember this spot, and after all is completed, we will return. One of us will gather a sample and bring it back to the Keeping Room for the quantum computer to examine further." He then put his arm around his son. "Let's get going. We've fallen pretty far behind the others. They must already be at the river building the fire."

Before they could take the first step, the prophet was tackled from behind and pushed face down into the charred tufts of grass surrounding the overturned armored vehicle.

The assailant, making-high pitched wheezing and hissing sounds sat astride the back of the prophet. He began to hammer the prophet's head with his elbows.

The Meglio had been knocked down in the attack, but he picked himself up off the ground and sprang into action. He brought the butt of the Sword of Don Quixote down hard on the partially-charred head of the Leviathan soldier.

As the soldier toppled off the prophet, the Meglio shouted, "Rob, are you hurt?"

"No," growled Rob as he dove on top of the attacker, who was slowly crawling away.

Grabbing hold of the soldier's shredded and charred uniform shirt, full of fury and adrenaline, the prophet rolled him over onto his back, then drew back his fist, preparing to rain blows down upon the man.

"Rob, don't," said the Meglio, grabbing hold of his son's right arm before he could deliver the first strike. "Let him go."

"What?" cried the prophet. "He's a Leviathan soldier, Dad! He'll warn the others."

"He's not going to warn anyone about anything," replied the Meglio as he helped his son to his feet.

As they backed a few feet away from the flailing and wheezing soldier, Rob could now see what the Meglio had already observed. He was mortally wounded, afraid, and maimed. His hands and one foot were charred stumps. His face was burned beyond recognition.

As they watched him struggle for breath and heard his wheezing and hissing, they understood that his throat and lungs had been scorched along with his vocal chords.

Rob's heart sank at the recognition that he had wanted to hurt this man further.

"Dad, what can we do to ease his suffering?"

"Not much at this point, Rob. Some water might soothe his throat, but that would be about all we could do for him. See if there is anything inside the armored vehicle."

As the prophet searched the vehicle, the Gray Champion and Billy came running up.

"What goes on here?" asked the Gray Champion. Seeing the writhing soldier on the ground, he drew the Sword of St. Peter.

"All is well, Robert," replied the Meglio. "We encountered this wounded man as we were examining the vehicle. Rob is searching for some water to give him."

"Do you think that's wise, Joseph?" asked the Gray Champion. "It is possible there are others, and he may give away our location."

"This man is in no condition to report anything to anyone," the Meglio insisted. "I suspect the vehicle he was driving has some insulating properties, or else he would not have survived the dark energy blast at all."

Indicating the overturned vehicle and the pooling molten slag, the Meglio continued, "It's made of a very strange alloy, similar to the alloy of the Keeping Room walls and door. It protected him enough for him to survive, but just barely, and at a very high cost. He is no danger to us now."

"I found this canteen in the vehicle," reported the prophet as he handed it to his father. "It's full."

Taking the canteen, the Meglio knelt at the soldier's side. Putting his hand on the dying man's shoulder, the Meglio spoke softly. "Relax, son. No one is going to harm you. I know you're suffering. Here, let me help you take some of this water, it may soothe your throat."

The soldier turned his head to the sound of the Meglio's voice and opened his mouth. The Meglio poured a few drops onto his raw tongue and watched as he gratefully nodded for more.

As the prophet, the Gray Champion and Billy stood guard, the Meglio continued to minister to the soldier until most of the canteen had been given and the soldier slumped back into the arms of the Meglio.

"His breathing is very shallow," said the Meglio as he gently laid the soldier back onto the ground. He stood and looked down at the man. "He doesn't have very long."

The others understood. They knew the Meglio was saying that they were not going anywhere until the soldier was out of his misery.

He was right. The end was not long in coming. Soon, the wheezing and the hissing subsided, and the Leviathan soldier's features relaxed. The Meglio bent over the soldier's body, crossed its maimed arms over its chest, placed his hand on the dead man's forehead, and bowed his own head.

After a minute or so, the Meglio stood, blessed himself, wiped his eyes, and commanded the others,

"Head to the river, I will be right behind you. We have work to do."

As the Gray Champion, the prophet, and Billy started back to the firepit by the river, Billy glanced back over his shoulder. He paused and watched as the Meglio unsheathed the sword of Don Quixote and pointed it downward over the body of the dead soldier. When Billy saw a puff of smoke begin to rise from the body, he turned away and resumed his walk.

They did not pass another living thing on their solemn journey to the fire pit. When they arrived, they saw that the others had gathered up the scattered stones that had defined the fire pit area, replaced them, and gathered the wood for the fire. When the Meglio caught up, he spoke.

"You have walked through an example of what real war is like. Death, destruction, loss, and horror. This is but a small example of what the rest of the world is dealing with right now as they fight for their freedom from the Leviathans. Remember it!

"This may very well be our last chance to craft a positive final outcome from the war that started here on our very own land. Stay focused on the end result.

"If we are successful, we can end this war and begin to build a new world of peace and prosperity. If we fail, what you have just observed will be the final fate of civilization. Now, stand around the fire pit, and we will repeat the fire-making process we performed when we returned from saving President Kennedy."

Feeling inspired by his grandfather's words, but also feeling the weight of them, Jeff took his position next to the others around the fire pit and pointed his sword at the wood and kindling. The swords began to glow warmly, and the kindling began to smolder. Soon, the wood burst into flame and the fire began to roar, illuminating the scene with dancing light and casting the shadows of the team on the fallen trees surrounding them.

"Raise your Swords of Valor," the Meglio commanded as he put his arm around the swordless Prophet standing next to him. The Gray Champion, the heroes, and the Meglio raised their swords out over the flames.

"Now," he instructed, "gently bring them together, and may God be with us."

As the tips of their swords came together over the flames, they were enveloped in a tremendous flash of bright white light and disappeared.

CHAPTER SIX

GLASTONBURY

The group of nine appeared in a bright flash of white light on the top of a hill overlooking the site of ancient Glastonbury. They lowered their swords, and Jeff looked around to make sure they had all made the trip. They had, but the prophet did not look well.

"Uncle Rob, are you all right?" asked Jeff as the Meglio guided his uncle to the ground into a sitting position.

"I think so," said the prophet, "I just feel very queasy. Is that what happens every time you guys travel in time?"

"Just the first two or three times," replied his father, "and the power of the swords usually helps to minimize it. Without a sword to help you, it may take a while to recover, but you'll be fine. Sit here and gather yourself while I speak with your grandfather." He left the prophet and found his father-in-law.

"Well, that was exhilarating," said the Gray Champion as the Meglio approached. "I never get tired of that."

"I agree," replied the Meglio, "but Rob is having a hard time dealing with it. It's his first trip, and you know what that means. Let's give him some time to rest while we discuss our next move."

"The sun will be rising within the hour," said the Gray Champion looking toward the faint light on the eastern horizon. "I suggest we wait here until that happens, and then make our observations. When we spot signs of habitation, we can head in that direction."

"Agreed," said the Meglio. "I suppose we also need to be wary of any local inhabitants who may not be a part of Joseph's group. These are still moderately savage times in Britain. We should keep our guard up at all times. Let's talk with the boys and make sure we are all on the same page."

They joined the heroes, who were standing together scanning the shadowy countryside. The Meglio addressed them.

"Gentlemen, we need your attention for a few minutes." Jeff and the others turned their attention to their grandfather, and he continued. "Do not let the striking beauty and primitive charm of this place distract you from our mission or cause you to let down your guard. This is a dangerous place and time. We must be constantly alert and stay together. Most of all, you must always listen to the instructions of your great-grandfather. He is the field general on this mission, and his word is gospel.

"Remember, we are at war, and although the battle has not touched this place, we have objectives that must be accomplished in order to have any chance for victory back home. Stay focused, think before you speak, and always conduct yourselves as Guardians. That means self-control, respect, and dignity. Understood?"

"Understood, Grandpa," said Ty, "but would it be too undignified if I go to the bathroom? I forgot to go before we left." The Meglio just rolled his eyes.

"Really, Ty?" shouted the prophet from where he was sitting, still nauseous. "Every time! Why is it always you every time?"

"I don't know, Dad," replied Ty, "I just get excited or something. Seriously, can I go?"

"Yes," said the Meglio, "but make it quick and don't go too far away. We don't know who may be watching us."

Ty hustled past his father, who shook his head, and disappeared over the top of the gently rolling hill they stood on. After only a few moments, Jeff saw him hustling back to the group. He looked concerned and kept glancing back to the top of the hill.

"That was unusually quick for you, Ty," teased Nick. "What happened? Did you get scared or something?"

"No," said Ty, not rising to the bait, "I heard voices and figured I'd better get back here to tell everyone."

"Did the voices sound like they were coming closer or fading away?" asked the Gray Champion.

"Coming closer," answered Ty. "Near the base of the hill on the back side. Over that way." He pointed past his dad, who was still recovering.

"I hear them, too," affirmed the prophet as he stood and turned his ear toward the sounds. "Sounds like at least two people and some animals."

"Quickly!" cried the Gray Champion. "Joe, Jeff, and Ty, come with me. We are going to circle around the hill and approach from behind. I want to get eyes on whoever is heading this way. The rest of you, stay hidden up here and stay silent."

The group of four descended the backside of the hill and circled slowly. After a moment, Ty pointed to the spot where he'd heard the voices.

At the Gray Champion's signal, Jeff stopped,

crouched in the shoulder high grass, and listened. He heard two people encouraging a group of animals to move along. The sun would be rising soon, and the sky was starting to brighten. He squinted and strained to see the small group. It looked like a flock of about twenty sheep and two slightly-built shepherds. Looking at the Gray Champion, Jeff saw him visibly relax.

"Looks like there's no immediate danger from this group," he said. "Ty, go and let the rest know that it's just a couple of shepherds leading their flock out to morning pasture. Joe and Jeff, stay with me here and we can observe for a while longer."

Ty left to report back to the rest of the team while Joe, Jeff, and their great-grandfather hunkered down behind a group of boulders to observe. The shepherds continued to approach and eventually led their flock to a point just below the team where they were close enough for Jeff to hear their conversation clearly.

"Do you think father will return today?" asked one of the shepherds whose sweet voice clearly indicated that she was a young woman.

"Since he was due back yesterday, I assume he will be here soon, unless he was delayed by some unforeseen problem with his negotiations," answered the other shepherdess, whose huskier voice made her sound older. "He has not seen the king for years, and who knows if he still views your father with the same respect as he once did? All we can do is pray for him. We should do that now. We must pray for his safe return and the success of his mission."

The two women then held hands and prayed. As they prayed, Jeff recognized that they prayed in Hebrew. The power of tongues that the swords provided allowed him to understand the prayer.

"Great-Grandpa," Jeff whispered, "they're praying in Hebrew. They must be part of Joseph's group. Should we approach them and introduce ourselves?"

"Not yet," replied the Gray Champion. "Let's wait until the sun is well over the horizon so we don't cause them alarm. We don't want to get off to a bad start."

They waited where they were until the sun was well-risen. Then, emerging from behind the stand of rocks, they began their descent to where the shepherdesses were enjoying a small breakfast of bread and cheese. Before they reached the two women, the Gray Champion called out to them.

"Excuse us, young ladies, may we approach?"

The startled women rose quickly, grabbed their staffs, and turned to face the group of Guardians.

"Stay where you are and identify yourselves!" said the older woman. "We are prepared to protect ourselves and our flock!"

Jeff and the rest of the team stopped, and the Gray Champion replied, "We are relatives of Joseph of Arimathea and are here to meet with him about a matter of some urgency. Do you know him or where we may find him?"

The two women looked at each other quickly, and the older woman replied, "That cannot be true. We are also of his family and have never seen you before. Where are you from?"

"We come from a faraway land," replied the Gray Champion. "May we approach and explain?"

The shepherdesses discussed this for a moment then agreed.

"You may approach, but keep your hands visible," replied the older shepherdess still holding her staff at the ready.

Jeff was grateful for the cloaking ability of the swords. He was sure the shepherdesses would not have been so accommodating if they'd seen they were carrying weapons.

The team approached slowly and stopped about ten feet from the two women. The Gray Champion spoke.

"We have traveled far and have only recently arrived in this land. We are distant relatives of Joseph and require his advice and counsel. He is the only one that can help us in our quest. Would it be possible for you to take us to where he is?"

"He has not returned from his travels, but we expect him soon. How is it that you knew that he was here?"

"That's hard to explain," the Gray Champion replied. "It will take some time, and we would appreciate the opportunity to explain it all to him in private. If our group could impose upon your hospitality until he returns, we would be forever in your debt."

"Are there others in your group?" asked the older shepherdess, still looking wary of the strangers.

"There are," replied the Gray Champion. "We are nine, in total. The others are resting atop this hill. Can your settlement accommodate us, or should we remain here until he returns?"

"You may gather the others and return with us. However, we will require proof that you are related to the family. When we arrive at the settlement, I will call the elders, and they will question you. If you do not prove your relationship, you will be asked to leave. Do you agree?"

"We do," replied the Gray Champion. "We will gather our family and join you here. Thank you for your kindness and trust."

The three Guardians bowed to the women and

headed back up the hill to where the others waited.

On the way, Joe said to Jeff, "Didn't the younger woman look familiar? I could swear that I've seen her somewhere before."

Jeff replied, "Not sure, Joe. I was focusing on the older woman, but now that you point it out, maybe. But how could that be possible? We don't know anyone here in 37 AD Britain."

"I know," said Joe, "but still, I am going to think about it. I'm sure I know her. I never forget a face."

As they met the rest of the team, the Gray Champion spoke. "The women below have agreed to take us to the settlement. We will need to explain ourselves and prove our relationship to Joseph of Arimathea if they are to allow us to remain until Joseph returns from his mission. Any ideas about how we can do that without disclosing too much?"

"As always," said the Meglio, "we will speak the truth and rely on the virtues of the swords to guide us. We are truly his descendants, so I am confident we will be able to relate that properly. Let's just head down there and deal with it when the time comes."

The group headed down the hill to where the women were waiting. Having already gathered their flock, the shepherdesses turned and led them to the settlement. As they walked, they introduced themselves.

The older woman began. "I am Miriam, a cousin of Joseph." She gestured toward the young woman following the flock. "She is Anna, Joseph's daughter."

The Meglio replied, "It is our pleasure to make your acquaintance and to partake of your hospitality. I am also named Joseph, and I am the leader of our group." Then, indicating his father-in-law, he continued. "And this is Robert. The other men are our grandchildren and great-grandchildren. We are here on a very urgent matter, and Joseph is the only source of help and council we have. We certainly would appreciate the opportunity to speak with him."

"It was written by the prophet Isaiah," said the woman, " 'Is it not to divide your bread with the hungry and bring the homeless poor into the house; when you see the naked, to cover him; and not to hide yourself from your own flesh? Then shall your light break forth as the morning, and your health shall spring forth speedily: and your righteousness shall go before you; the glory of the Lord shall be your rear guard.' I am just doing my duty as a child of God. It will be up to you to prove my trust justified."

"We will, I assure you, Miriam," replied the Meglio. As the Meglio and the older woman were concluding their discussion, Jeff thought about Joe's comment that these women looked familiar. He looked over as Joe walked up behind Nick, tapping him on the shoulder.

"Nick," Joe said to his brother, "really look at those women. I feel like I know them. Do they look familiar to you?"

Nick looked at his brother like he was crazy and said, "Joe, don't get any ideas. The last time you flirted with a girl on a mission, you got us arrested as assassins."

"No, seriously Nick, look at them," Joe insisted. "This is not about flirting. I'm sure I've seen them before."

Jeff watched as Nick and Joe made their way closer to where the younger woman was encouraging a couple of straggling sheep to keep up with the flock.

They kept pace with her for a while, then Nick said, "Yeah, she does look familiar, but how is that possible? We don't know anyone here in 37 AD." Then, after another minute or two of concentration said, "Wait! I think I know who she is!"

"Really?" said Joe.

"Yes!" said Nick. "We met her before. Don't you remember? In the Garden of Gethsemane. She was one of the two women we protected from the soldiers that came to arrest Jesus!"

"Anna?" said Joe. "The younger of the two women who then led us to Caiaphas's home?"

"I believe so," said Nick. "And the older woman talking with Grandpa may be the other one, Miriam."

"Wow!" exclaimed Joe. "That's crazy!"

Jeff's eyebrows raised as he overheard their conversation, but he chose to keep silent and continue listening.

"What a coincidence that would be if these are the same women that we saved from the soldiers, and now here they are, helping us. What are the odds of that?"

"Since all of this has started," said Nick, "I have learned that nothing is a coincidence. The swords certainly have some strange powers. And who knows, maybe this is all part of the plan? When we get the opportunity, let's make sure that we tell Grandpa about it, and maybe it will help us to convince them we are telling the truth."

Soon after, the group rounded another hill, and the settlement came into view. It was a simple settlement of traditional, thatched-roof dwellings surrounding a central common area and well. Jeff could see about ten people busy with chores for the day. To the side of the settlement, he saw a building in the early stages of construction. It appeared to be the beginnings of some sort of larger common gathering place and was being constructed with a combination of stone, logs, and thatch.

As Miriam continued to lead the group toward the settlement, she said to the Meglio, "Please keep your group to the rear of the flock and allow me a few minutes to speak with the disciples. As you might imagine, they will be wary of you. They are charged with the protection of the group while Joseph and Josephus are away. When I have their permission, I will call for you to approach."

"Understood," replied the Meglio. "We will wait for you to summon us."

The group halted their approach, and Miriam left to speak with the disciples. The Meglio gathered the Guardians, and they retreated to the rear of the flock. Anna remained with the Guardians as she busied herself with keeping the flock together.

When they were seated a short distance from the flock, Joe addressed the Meglio, pointing at the shepherd girl.

"Grandpa, you see that girl over there? Anna?"

"Yes," replied the Meglio. "What about her?"

"Nick and I know her."

"Seriously?" replied the Meglio. "How is that possible? This is not the time for nonsense, Joe."

"Seriously," responded Joe. "Nick, Jeff, and I met her in the Garden of Gethsemane. Remember when we told you, well, your image anyway, that we protected two women from the soldiers who came to arrest Jesus? Well, she was one of those women!"

"I actually have no recollection of that," replied the Meglio. "Remember, I was dead at the time, and you were interacting with a holographic image generated by the quantum computer. Let's get your uncle over here, and you can tell him." He called the prophet over, and Joe and Nick told him what they had realized about the women.

"That fits with the timeline," responded the prophet.

"That event took place in 33 AD, only four years ago in this timeframe. So, it is possible. None of the timeline changes since then have altered that event, so it is within the realm of possibility that they remember you, also. This could be a very profitable development. Let's wait and see if the women remember you when we make the introductions. If they do, we can use that as a way to validate our claims and ensure their trust. But follow Grandpa's lead on this matter, as he will be the one making our case to the elders." They agreed and continued to wait, hoping they would be called to meet with the disciples of Joseph of Arimathea.

The sun was now climbing higher in the sky, and the smell of the flock was becoming overpowering.

"Grandpa," said Robbie, "can we sit somewhere else? This is really getting unbearable. I never realized that sheep smelled so bad!"

"Maybe it's not the sheep," said Billy. "It could be Ty again."

"Very funny, Billy," said Ty tossing a twig at him. "I was just thinking it was your Old Spice cologne. You know the kind that all old men like you use?"

"Cut it out," warned their great-grandfather. "Maintain discipline. Miriam is signaling for us to approach the settlement. Stay quiet, and let your grandfather do the talking. Remember, you are Guardians on a mission. You must maintain discipline."

They stood and began their approach to the settlement. Anna joined them as they walked, leading the flock. As they walked, Jeff noticed that Anna kept sneaking glances at Joe and Nick. They reached the outer perimeter of the settlement and a husky man raised his staff, signaling for them to stop. He then addressed the Meglio.

"Welcome, travelers. State your business," he commanded.

"We are relatives of Joseph of Arimathea and seek his wisdom and council on a matter of grave importance." stated the Meglio calmly. "May we enter and speak with you of this urgent matter?"

"In whose name do you come seeking this wisdom and council?" asked the husky man.

"We come in our own names, through the grace of Yeshua of Nazareth," replied the Meglio using the Aramaic name of Jesus.

The disciple was stunned into silence. He quickly gathered himself and replied, "Then you are very welcome here, brothers. Come! Come! Rest yourselves, and we will speak of this matter together."

Jeff was surprised that the Meglio had thought to use the name of Yeshua, but it made sense, since he had made it clear that he was depending on the virtue of the swords to guide his responses. This was probably the only answer that would have gained them entry to the settlement. Jeff reminded himself once again to *always* trust the leading of the swords, but also be aware of the possible consequences.

CHAPTER SEVEN

JOSEPH OF ARIMATHEA

The Guardians entered the settlement and were led by the disciple to the well, where they were given water and then brought to a nearby hut. They found seats on low, roughhewn, wooden benches lining the walls of the hut and settled in. Jeff just felt relieved that it didn't smell like sheep in here.

The disciple left them there briefly and then returned with two other men. They took seats opposite the Guardians, and the husky man addressed them.

"Welcome, brothers. I am Malchus, disciple of Joseph of Arimathea. Please tell us of your journey, where you have come from, and how you are related to the venerable Joseph."

The Meglio began, "Thank you, Malchus, for the opportunity and the hospitality. Our story is strange, and we cannot be as clear with you as you might wish, but this is for your own protection. Our mission is a dangerous one, which we may only discuss in detail with Joseph himself. As far as our relationship to Joseph, he is our ancestor. We are his descendants, both in a physical sense and a spiritual one. We have only recently arrived from a faraway land to the west and have urgent need of Joseph's wisdom and council."

The disciples looked confused and skeptical. Malchus responded as he stood. "All of Joseph's children are here with us. None of them have yet married, therefore, he has no descendants. What you say is not truthful. How can you speak untruth with the same mouth with which you called on the name of Yeshua?"

"I assure you, we are speaking the truth," replied the Meglio calmly.

"Then tell us what you know of Joseph and his relationship with Yeshua. If you are somehow related to him, you will know this."

"We know that Joseph was a member of the Sanhedrin, and that he was the uncle of the mother of Yeshua, Mary. He became the guardian of Yeshua after the death of Yeshua's earthly father, Joseph the Carpenter.

"We also know that that he was the one who retrieved Yeshua's body from Pilate, after his crucifixion. He and Nicodemus placed him in his own newly-hewn tomb. We know that sometime thereafter, he and others were sent here to evangelize this place by the apostle, Phillip. Finally, we also know about the cup."

Malchus sat down heavily. He was silent for a moment, and it was apparent that he was struggling.

"I know this is difficult to understand," the Meglio said softly.

"That part, at least, is true," Malchus replied. He looked up at the Meglio, then at the others. "To be honest, I am struggling with the depth of knowledge you have about Joseph. I cannot understand how you can, at the same time, truly be his descendants. You have been accurate about his history, but to my mind, you have spoken falsely regarding your relationship to him. I will need time to try and understand how this can be." He fell silent again, looking at the ground, concentration on his features. As he struggled, Miriam entered the hut and spoke.

"Malchus, may I speak with you for a moment?"

"Can it wait?" Malchus replied without looking up. "We are at a critical point in our evaluation."

"It relates to these men," she stated. "Please, join me outside."

Malchus looked up at her, nodded, and stood, then followed her outside.

Jeff, who was closest to the doorway, looked down at the ground and focused on the conversation outside. He knew it was wrong to eavesdrop, but this concerned them and their mission. If it was going to go badly already, they would be in serious trouble.

He heard Miriam say, "Anna, tell him what you just told me."

Anna began. "I believe that Miriam and I know three of those men. If I am not mistaken, they were the ones who saved Miriam and me when the soldiers tried to arrest us on the night the Lord was taken. They were there in the garden and chased the soldiers away with glowing swords.

"We thought them to be angels at first, but they told us they were just men and followers of Yeshua. I am sure that the three of them are among the group you are speaking with now."

"Are you sure, Anna?" asked Malchus. "That was four years ago, and it was a stressful time for everyone, including me. Remember, I had just had my ear chopped off by Peter, and the Lord healed me. I was in no condition to focus on faces. It was dark, and the disciples were running everywhere, and with all that happened afterward, your memory may be unclear."

"You may be right," replied Anna, "but Miriam thinks so, too. May we come in and verify this? I am sure I would be able to confirm it if I get a close enough look. And, if I cannot, maybe they have the glowing swords with them and can verify it that way?"

"They are not carrying swords," replied Malchus. "I made a careful observation of that when I spoke with them outside the camp. After my experience with Peter, I am extra cautious about that. However, please accompany me inside and make your observation. Then we will decide their fate. Also, they know about the cup, so be very sure of your observations. If you are wrong, the cup may in danger."

Jeff shifted his position as they re-entered the hut. There may still be hope, he thought.

Anna approached the Guardians and addressed them. "I believe that I may know three of you. Will the men who were at the Garden of Gethsemane please rise?"

Jeff, Joe, and Nick, shot a quick look at their grandfather for his approval. He nodded to them, and they stood. Anna looked at them very closely, moving from one to the other and scrutinizing their faces.

"These are the same men that I recognize from the garden," she said to Malchus. "Miriam, do you agree?"

"I am not as sure as you, Anna. I was so upset at the time, and when we escorted them to Jerusalem, it was so dark. It could be, but I will need more confirmation."

Anna addressed the three cousins. "When you saved us from the soldiers, you had swords which glowed with the power of angels. Show them to us now to prove yourselves."

"Anna!" said Malchus forcefully. "I told you that

these men do not carry swords. You can see that for yourself. Why do you ask for something so foolish?"

Again, Joe, Nick, and Jeff looked to the Meglio for permission. He again nodded to them. They raised their right arms, and the swords appeared, glowing slightly in the shadows of the hut.

Anna, Miriam, and Malchus fell to their knees. The other two disciples covered their heads with their robes.

"We are in the presence of angels!" Malchus exclaimed. "Just as Abraham was when he was visited by the three strangers. Please, good sirs, have mercy on us for our lack of faith!"

The Meglio stood. "Arise," he said to the women and men who lay prostrate before them. "We are not angels. We are men, like you. We spoke truthfully, and you have no reason to fear or worship us. Just help us accomplish our mission, and we will be forever grateful."

"As you wish," replied Malchus, signaling for the others to rise. "Anna, quickly prepare a meal for our guests and make ready for the arrival of your father."

The women left to make preparations, and the men returned to their seats, as did Jeff, Nick, and Joe.

Malchus spoke. "How may we be of service to you before Joseph and the others return?"

"Thank you, Malchus," replied the Meglio. "As I stated, the specifics of our mission must be discussed only with Joseph himself. However, we would appreciate some perspective. How long have you all been here, and where has Joseph gone and why?"

"Yes, of course," replied Malchus. "As you may know, venerable Joseph is a highly respected metal merchant. Over many years, he has established relationships here in the Isles. When the Lord was crucified, Joseph used his blood relationship with Yeshua to obtain his body from Pilate, thereby angering the Jewish leadership.

"They knew he was related to Yeshua and feared he would work with Yeshua's disciples to steal the body, so they plotted to imprison him after Passover. After the Lord rose on the third day, Joseph was imprisoned along with Nicodemus. They were eventually set free by an angel of the Lord. When he presented himself to the apostles, they decided that it was no longer safe for him to stay in Jerusalem.

"Together with Phillip the Apostle, they handpicked a group of brethren, and soon thereafter, we fled in one of Joseph's merchant sailing ships. As we made the voyage, we were blown off course and made a safe landfall on the shores of Gaul. Some of the group decided to stay there and do the Lord's work.

"After about a year in Gaul, the rest of us repaired and stocked the ship and set sail for the Isles, as we were instructed to do. Since Joseph was so familiar with the tin mining areas of this land, that is where we made port. That was six months ago. We made our way to this area and have been building the settlement ever since.

"Joseph and the others left about a week ago to visit with King Mandubracius of the Iceni tribe, who controls this land. They have done business in the past, and Joseph seeks to finalize his agreement to let us settle this portion of his land and gain his protection. We expect his return before nightfall."

"Thank you for that information, Malchus. It helps us put all of this into context," said the Meglio. "Now, I need to know if Joseph is currently in possession of the cup and the two Swords of Valor."

Malchus blanched. "I fear to speak about these items, sir. These are holy objects, and only venerable

Joseph may discuss them. It is not my place. So, I must regretfully decline your request."

At this point, the Gray Champion spoke to the Meglio. "Joseph, I am in possession of the Sword of St. Peter. How can Joseph of Arimathea have it?" Then he raised his right arm to reveal the Sword of St. Peter and nothing happened.

Jeff felt as stunned as his great-grandfather looked. Looking around, he saw similar expressions on the others' faces.

"Have you seen it or felt it since we arrived?" asked the Meglio.

"I haven't checked. I had it when we left to come here and have been busy since we arrived. The need has not arisen to reveal my sword, so I am unaware of when it left my possession. I actually still feel a baseline connection with it, but as far as its physical manifestation, it seems to be unavailable to me."

"We can only assume that it must be in the possession of Joseph of Arimathea," replied the Meglio. "I wondered if there might be an issue with having two versions of the same sword in the same timeframe when there are two rightful owners of the same sword present. I can only assume that the sword itself would resolve the conflict, and that in this moment, the sword is in the possession of the rightful owner at this time. We will see."

"Grandpa," said Joe, "if Great-Grandpa's sword has disappeared because it has returned to the hand of Joseph of Arimathea, why do I still have my sword?"

"It's the Sword of Melchizedek, and it was brought here to England by Joseph at the same time as he brought the sword of St. Peter. If your theory is correct, then shouldn't it be with Joseph also?"

"Good observation, Joe," replied the Meglio, "but I

don't have a satisfactory answer for you. I am just thankful you had it when we needed it to prove ourselves to Malchus and the others. We'll have time to figure that out after Joseph returns."

By this time, Anna had returned to inform them that the meal was ready. She invited them to join them in the common area. The Guardians joined the disciples and the others in a meal of thanksgiving and welcome, during which, introductions were made and personal stories shared.

Of course, the Guardians did not share anything time or mission sensitive, only enough to help the Arimathea contingent feel comfortable. When the meal was over, they were shown to a hut assigned for their use, and they spent the rest of the day exploring the area and waiting for Joseph of Arimathea to arrive.

As the sun was getting low on the western horizon, a shout went up from one of the men. "I see them, they have arrived! Make ready!"

The settlement came alive, and food and water were gathered and placed in a convenient location for the travelers to readily access when arrived. The Guardians stayed to the rear of the welcoming party and waited to be introduced.

Jeff noticed that the group of men were in the company of a young girl, who seemed to be about fifteen years old. Anna and Miriam bowed and attended to the young woman as the travelers refreshed themselves, washed the dust of the long trip from their bodies, and changed into clean clothes. Then, the introductions began.

Malchus brought Joseph of Arimathea and a younger man to where the Meglio and the others waited. "Venerable Joseph of Arimathea and Josephus, I introduce to you Joseph the Meglio, Robert Ogilvie Petrie, Robert the Prophet, William, Jeff, Joseph, Nicholas, Robert, and Ty. They have traveled far to speak with you and seek your council on a very urgent matter. I and the others have spoken with these men and vouch for their integrity. As this matter requires secrecy, I will leave you alone with them to discuss this. Should you need me, just call." Malchus bowed to all and departed, leaving Joseph and the young man alone with the Guardians.

"Has my family shown you the hospitality that is due your status?" asked Joseph of Arimathea.

"They have been most gracious and accommodating," replied the Meglio. "I realize that you have been on a long and tiring trip, so if you would like to delay our discussion until the morning, I would understand."

"That will not be necessary," Joseph replied. "I may look like an old man, but I have more spirit than many men half my age. Let's go to my dwelling and discuss this urgent matter." He led them to his home and invited them to take seats, then introduced Josephus.

"It is my understanding that you have met my daughter, Anna, and the others." Then indicating the young man next to him said, "This is my first-born son, Josephus. I hope you are comfortable with him joining our discussion. He is an upright and trustworthy young man, and it may be that he has some perspective which can aid our discussion."

"I would be pleased to have his input," replied the Meglio. "All of the men with me are also my family, so it is perfectly appropriate for you to include yours. Shall we begin?"

"Please," replied Joseph of Arimathea.

"What we have to tell you will sound strange and

disturbing," began the Meglio, "but I assure you in the name of Yeshua that it is all true. I intend to be completely forthcoming and ask that you withhold any questions until after I present our request. Is that acceptable to you?"

"As you are followers of the Master," replied Joseph, "I can do nothing but listen openly and accept what you have to say in the spirit of brotherhood. I accept. Please, begin."

"Esteemed Joseph, most of us in this room, with the exception of myself, are your direct descendants. I know this sounds strange, but it is true. We have come from a time far in the future and from a land yet to be discovered.

"In our time, we are known as the Cincinnatus/Arimathea Family of the Guardians of the Swords of Valor. It is our sworn duty to protect the ten Swords of Valor which have been entrusted to us. Two of those swords, you brought with you to Britain; the Sword of St. Peter the Apostle and the Sword of Melchizedek. I suspect that you are in possession of St. Peter's sword at this moment, but I also believe that if you check, you will find that the sword of Melchizedek is missing. Can you do that now?"

Joseph of Arimathea looked startled by the revelations but complied. He raised his right arm and the sword of St. Peter appeared, glowing softly. He spoke to Josephus and instructed him to reveal his sword.

Josephus complied, and when he raised his right arm, nothing happened. Both he and Joseph were upset by this turn of events.

"Father, I know I had the sword yesterday," exclaimed Josephus. "I have not had need for it today, so I never checked. How is this possible?"

Then Joseph addressed the Meglio. "Where is the

sword now? Do you know?" The Meglio signaled to Joe to raise his right arm, and the sword of Melchizedek became visible.

"As you can see," said the Meglio, "it is in the possession of my grandson. So, you need have no fear for its safety. There are many things we must discuss about the swords, their powers, and their rightful possession. However, that is not the main reason we are here. Right now, our main objective is to verify that you are in possession of the cup. The cup is essential to our mission, and it is our hope that the legends from our time are true, that you brought it with you on your voyage here. Can you verify that for us, Joseph?"

"Only because you are followers of the Lord will I discuss the cup with you," replied Joseph. "It is my most sacred possession, and if it were to fall into evil hands, I believe that all of creation could be endangered. But before I discuss the cup, you must explain further regarding your origins. The tale you tell is very hard to believe, unless of course you are angels of the Lord. Please explain this all to me so that I may understand."

"As I stated, we are from a time far in the future, about two thousand years from today," explained the Meglio. "We have returned to your time through the power of the Swords of Valor. They have the ability to take us to any point in history that we need to go.

"We have traveled here today because in our time, Watcher Azazel has kidnapped my wife and is threatening to create a new generation of Nephilim to enslave the world. We need to consult with you, our forefather, regarding all you know about Azazel and how to defeat him, to help us examine the stone circle of the druids known as Stonehenge, and to obtain the cup.

"We have been told that the cup is one of the keys

to defeating Azazel. I know this is difficult to believe, but again, I assure you it is all true. Will you help us?"

Joseph's expression was a study in confusion and disbelief. Josephus sat next to him with a skeptical expression on his face, as well. It was obvious that the two men were overwhelmed by the revelations and would need time to absorb it all and accept it as truth.

"You must understand," said Joseph, "that I will need time to pray about this. I will not discuss the Cup of the Lord without release from God through prayer. However, I will discuss the stone circle of the druids and the Watcher Azazel and tell you all I know. After that, I will retire for the evening and seek direction from God on your request regarding the cup."

"Thank you," responded the Meglio. "I completely understand and respect your caution. What can you tell us about Azazel and the stone circle?"

"If you are truly my descendants, you may be aware that I was a high-ranking member of the Sanhedrin and am well versed in all the scriptures. Therefore, I can speak with some authority regarding Azazel, his history, and the protections against him, however no one has ever discussed his defeat and destruction. I have my own thoughts, and I will share those with you, but realize that you are attempting something which only the archangels have been authorized to do. Unless they are with you in this matter, you risk your very souls. Do you understand?"

"We do," replied the Meglio. "We believe we have been given that assurance, because we are actually in possession of the Sword of Michael the Archangel himself." Then he signaled to Nick to reveal his sword.

Nick stood and raised his right arm. The Sword of the Archangel appeared in his hand and burst into flame, lighting the hut with a fierce angelic light.

Joseph and Josephus fell on their faces and trembled. "Please, put it away!" Josephus begged. "It is a fearsome thing to see the flaming wrath of the Archangel Michael!"

Nick lowered his arm, the flame died, and the sword became invisible. He sat down, and the Meglio continued.

"Please, do not be afraid. As I said, the swords have many powers, and the righteous need not fear their virtue. Just know that we have already come through many trials against Azazel and his forces.

"We are sure that our current mission is well within the will of the Lord. All we ask is your help and support."

"You have it," replied Joseph. "I will tell you all I know."

Then Joseph of Arimathea told them everything written in the ancient scriptures regarding Azazel. He quoted from the Talmud, the prophets, the Book of Enoch, and the writings of the Essenes. When he finished with the scriptural information, he revealed his own thoughts.

"I believe it is possible to defeat the Watcher Azazel, since, although he is an angelic being, he has a fallen nature. He has forfeited some of his most important angelic gifts, and that could be his downfall. It is my belief that he cannot be defeated with only earthly weapons. You will need holy objects that have been sanctified by God and have spiritual power. Your earthly weapons might be able to harm whatever physical nature he has acquired, but you can do nothing against his spiritual nature. I understand now why you seek the cup. It is a powerful holy object. Do you know its true history?"

"We have been told that it was made from gold given to Solomon by an angel as a reward from God for choosing wisdom over wealth and power. It then was taken to Babylon by Nebuchadnezzar, and eventually came into the possession of Daniel the Prophet. He instructed his apprentices that they should guard it carefully, and someday, when the great star appeared, they should follow the star and present it to the King of Kings.

"This happened when the wise men from the east made their pilgrimage to present their gifts to Yeshua at his birth. It then stayed with the family and was given to Yeshua when he began his earthly ministry. It was the cup he used at the last Passover supper before his death. Do I have it all correct?" asked the Meglio.

"You have spoken truthfully," replied Joseph. "Except that it was I who kept the cup safe during Yeshua's youth and presented it to him at the beginning of his ministry. That is why the cup was given back into my keeping.

"I have always been its guardian and remain so today. But there is more. Do you know where the gold that it is made from originated? That is the real key to understanding its power and why it is a weapon against Azazel."

"We've been told it was given to Solomon by an angel sent by God," replied the Meglio, "but where the gold originated, I have no clue."

"It is said in the Book of Enoch that the gold came from the Garden of Eden," said Joseph, "and has special properties. I am unclear exactly what these properties are, but I can see how it may be helpful in your mission. Anything given to man by God has an eternal function, as long as it is used for its God-given purpose and gives glory to God by its use. I will pray on this tonight and give you my answer in the morning. What else do you need to know?"

"We have been told that the Watchers were cast out

of Heaven by God and fell to Earth in three different areas," explained the Meglio. "Some fell to Mount Hermon; others fell to earth at a place called in our time Gobekli Tepe. Finally, another group fell at what we call Stonehenge, but which you refer to as the stone circle of the druids. This is the place we have come to examine to determine if it is the proper site for us to confront Azazel. We would appreciate your assistance in getting there and making our examination. What can you tell us about it, and is there anyone we can speak with regarding its current use and power?"

"Once again, you have spoken accurately and according to the ancient writings," confirmed Joseph. "I know of the stone circle and have met with some druid priests over the years of my travels to this land. They tell of giants that built the place. This may very well be a reference to the Watchers.

"Originally, it was a place of worship, but over the years it has also become a place of burial and other arcane rites. I will arrange for a group of us to take you there, and together we can perform whatever analysis you need to make your determination. It's a little over a day's ride to the east of here. Is that agreeable to you?"

"It is," replied the Meglio.

"Then, if that is all for this evening, I am very tired from my travels. I suggest that we all get some sleep and meet again in the morning," said Joseph. "I know that Anna and Miriam have prepared bedding for you. I hope you find it comfortable and can have a restful night."

The Guardians stood, thanked Joseph and Josephus, found their quarters, and settled in for the night. Quietly, they discussed the events of the day. It wasn't long, however, before exhaustion overtook them, and they fell asleep.

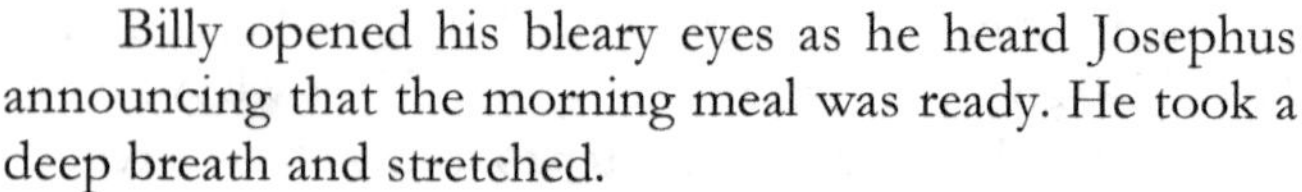

Billy opened his bleary eyes as he heard Josephus announcing that the morning meal was ready. He took a deep breath and stretched.

"Feeling stiff?" Jeff asked.

"Just a little," Billy admitted. "Nothing a little stretch and a good breakfast won't cure.

He rolled to a sitting position and twisted his back to the right, then the left. Raising his arms high, he stretched his shoulders and upper back. As he bent over to touch his toes, he groaned a little.

Jeff laughed. "You sound like an old man!"

"I guess I'm not as used to sleeping on the ground as I was when we were kids," Billy chuckled.

"I thought the sleeping arrangements were just fine," Nick bragged. Then, he tried to show off by jumping from his bed of blankets on the floor. He landed on his feet, but a small grunt escaped his lips as he landed.

"Not as spry as you thought, Nick?" Billy teased.

"What? You didn't hear anything!" Nick protested. "I didn't make any sound at all!"

All six heroes laughed as they finished dressing. When they were ready, they joined the settlers in the common area and partook of a simple meal of fruit and bread, while Joseph discussed the plans for the day.

"As I promised, I sought the face of the Lord all night regarding the matter of the cup. Near daybreak, I received my answer, but it is one that confused me somewhat. In a vision, I saw myself handing over the cup to an angel of the Lord. That seems clear enough, but what is unclear is that I was standing on a stone in a strange place while doing it. I was able to see that the stone I was standing on was a dark-colored stone about the length of my arm and about half as high.

"As I stood there on the stone holding out the cup, I could see other angels descending and ascending a stairway between heaven and earth. The place where this all took place was unfamiliar to me but was similar to the stone circle of the druids. As soon as I was about to hand over the cup to the angel, I awoke. It is my belief that I have been given permission to release the cup into your possession, but I will need to pray for further understanding of the rest of the vision."

"Thank you for your prayers, Joseph," said the Meglio. "We are comforted by your agreement and validation of the necessity of the cup in our efforts. It is my belief that as long as we are on this soil, the cup should stay in your possession. Should we leave here without you, then the cup should be given into the hands of the prophet. Until then, will you continue to be the keeper of the cup?"

"I will," replied Joseph. "I will retrieve the cup from its hiding place and join you back here. When I return, we will begin the journey to the stone circle." Joseph excused himself and departed to retrieve the cup.

"Please," said Josephus to the group, "walk with me to the horses. I will get everyone prepared for the journey while we wait for the return of my father." The Guardians followed Josephus to the far side of the settlement where more than a dozen horses waited for them, grazing in a fenced-in area.

"These horses were given as gifts to my father from King Mandubracius of the Iceni tribe as pre-payment for the education of his daughter, Boudicca, who arrived yesterday evening with my father. The king wishes to have his daughter educated in the ways of Yeshua, since he knows that my father was his great-uncle and one of his followers. In fact, here she comes now."

Billy looked where Josephus was pointing and saw a young girl racing headlong to the horse pen. He watched in fascination as she jumped effortlessly to the top railing of the fence and then leaped onto the back of one of the horses, kicking it into a gallop around the pen.

As she raced the horse around the enclosure, her long, curly, bright red hair flowed in the breeze, bouncing to the rhythm of her mount's lively canter. It was obvious that she was an excellent rider, and as she rode, her expression was one of sheer joy.

"Boudicca!" Josephus shouted. "Stop scaring the horses, we need to gather them together so we can get moving. Herd them in this direction, please."

The young girl seemed to ignore Josephus's command for a moment, then turned her horse and began to skillfully herd the other horses in Josephus's direction.

Josephus and a few of Joseph's disciples prepared the horses, and by the time Joseph returned, all was ready for the journey.

Joseph, Josephus, Malchus, and the Guardians mounted their horses and were preparing to leave when Boudicca came riding up on her horse.

"Master Joseph, I am ready, also. Now we can depart," she said.

"Young lady," replied Joseph, "did I not tell you that you are to stay behind? Why do you disobey my command?"

"Please, Master Joseph, I can help," said Boudicca. "I know this land better than you or any of your men. I even know the shortest route to the stone circle! Take me along, and I promise I will not cause any trouble. I don't want to stay here doing women's work. I want to ride with you. Please?"

Billy heard her passionate plea and saw Joseph's expression soften. It was apparent that he had a tender spot for her in his heart. After a moment, Joseph agreed.

They started for the stone circle of the druids, with Joseph, the Meglio, and the Gray Champion at the head of the group, and the cousins clinging to their mounts for dear life.

CHAPTER EIGHT

REVELATIONS

"Did you bring the cup with you, Joseph?" asked the Meglio as they rode along.

"I did," replied Joseph. "It is at this moment securely bound to my body. When we stop for the evening, I will reveal it to you and your family."

"Wonderful," replied the Meglio. "That will truly be an honor."

The Gray Champion turned to Joseph. "May I ask a question?"

"Certainly," he answered. "We have a long journey and much time for questions and conversation. I would appreciate the opportunity to get to know you better and answer any questions you may have."

"Thank you," the Gray Champion replied. "I would like to know more about your work here. How it is that you know so much about the land, and have such strong relationships with royalty, such as King Mandubracius?"

"That, my friend, may take until the end of our journey!" chuckled Joseph. "I will try to be brief, but I will start at the beginning. I am, by trade, a merchant of metals. My people have traveled to the Isles for centuries to mine and trade for the tin for which this land is noted. Over the years, I have made dozens of journeys here and have, in the process, developed relationships with the leaders of the land. I have always dealt fairly and equitably with them, and we've developed the high degree of trust which is necessary in these matters.

"So, when I arrived this time in a bit of distress, I sent messengers to King Mandubracius, to inform him of my arrival and to ask his permission for me and my group to settle in the area. He agreed and put out a proclamation to his tribe that we were to be honored and protected as one of their own. To seal our agreement, he asked me to return to visit him in six months' time, as he would require something of me.

"That is the visit I returned from last night. The thing he required of me was the education of his eldest daughter, Boudicca, in the ways of Yeshua. As you can see from her energy and love of adventure, I am not sure I got the better of the bargain."

"How did King Mandubracius know about Yeshua?" asked the Gray Champion.

Joseph smiled and replied, "Why, he met him, of course! And as with anyone who has ever met my great-nephew, he was amazed by his spirit and understanding of scripture even at an early age."

"I don't understand," said the Gray Champion. "Are you saying that Yeshua came with you to Britain? When was that, and why?"

"Yes, Yeshua accompanied me many times during his youth," confirmed Joseph. "After his father Joseph died, I became the official guardian of Yeshua and the family. As a wealthy man and a high-ranking member of the Sanhedrin, I was in a position to help to provide for them materially and oversee the remainder of Yeshua's education. Part of that education was to familiarize him with other parts of the world and the intricacies of business. Yeshua was a quick study and took to the seas very naturally. He worked the sails of the ships, helped navigate, and even helped to load and tally the cargo. But where he shined most was in the relationship-building with the local people.

"It all started when, as a young boy, Yeshua visited the temple in Jerusalem with his parents. When they began their journey back to Nazareth, they realized he was not with them. Worried, they returned to Jerusalem in search of him. They found him teaching and conversing with the elders. Before returning to Nazareth, they stayed a few days with me at my home.

"I was preparing to travel to the Isles to buy tin and other metals. Yeshua asked his parents if he could come with me, but Mary and Joseph told him he was too young. He was learning to be a carpenter and boat builder, and they felt that was more important.

"After Joseph the Carpenter died several years later, Mary and Yeshua traveled once again to Jerusalem for the feast of the Passover. Again, they stopped overnight in Arimathea to lodge with me. I invited Yeshua to travel with me on my next journey to trade for metals. Mary agreed, if I would promise to take him to visit his grandmother, Anna, who had returned to her ancestral home in Brittany. She knew that I always visited her before traveling to Cornwall.

"Once we arrived in Brittany, we spent time with Anna and other relatives. Then, we travelled on in three ships to Cornwall, where we used smaller boats to visit different mining communities.

"Yeshua was friendly and helpful in each port and mine. He seemed interested in each person he met. We traveled all over the southwest. On one visit to the Camel Estuary, he struck the ground with a staff and created a spring, which local people still use. They call it the 'Jesus Well'.

"When we sailed into the islands around Avalon, he found the area peaceful and the people friendly. Just as he had stayed and talked with the rabbis at the temple in Jerusalem, Yeshua stayed and talked to the druids in Avalon. They discussed the ancient beliefs until the time came for us to return home.

"As I watched him interact with them, I saw that the druids respected him as a teacher, which amazed me. They truly seemed to enjoy his company, and I'm told they felt a kinship with him. They were greatly impressed with his knowledge and understanding, which was well beyond his age.

"In fact, he even spent time talking with the royal druid priests he met at the courts of the kings of this land. He was able to show them how many of their beliefs were based on the Jewish scriptures and founded in the truths revealed by God."

"That's amazing!" exclaimed the Meglio. "That sounds very similar to the description of Jesus sitting among the teachers, listening to them and asking them questions in the temple when Joseph and Mary were looking for him. It says that the elders who were conversing with him were amazed at his understanding and his answers. Please explain that to us. I am not aware of any connection between the druid faith and that of the Jews. How is that possible?"

"It is possible because after the House of Israel, the northern kingdom, was released from captivity under the Assyrians, many of them migrated to various parts of the world," replied Joseph.

"A few of the tribes migrated to these islands. So, the truth is that there have been Hebrews in this land for centuries, and the knowledge of our ancient scriptures has been disseminated widely. Of course, as you can imagine, over time, through intermarriage, the truths were absorbed and became hybridized to a certain extent by the pagan religions of the land.

"One of the things that Yeshua did very effectively in his discussions with the druid priests was to separate the wheat from the chaff, so to speak. He set the druid priests right regarding the origins and meaning of some of their beliefs and rituals, which had changed over the centuries. That was what impressed King Mandubracius the most."

"Can you tell us what some of the common beliefs were that became hybridized?" asked the Gray Champion.

"They were mostly misunderstood and applied incorrectly," replied Joseph. "For example, the druids' belief in life after death. They use social ostracism as a means of ensuring obedience. They pass down their laws orally and are forbidden to write it down. They gave tithes and first fruits. Saturday is their Sabbath. Their sacrificial modes are akin to Mosaic ones. Their practice of ritual purity is similar in many ways to the Laws of Moses.

"Additionally, the burial practices of both the peoples of the northern kingdom and the druids bear much similarity in the presence of large slabs of stone placed horizontally across upright stones with the graves under them. As always, it is the meaning and intent of these laws and practices that give glory to the true God. They applied the laws but did not fully understand the meaning or purpose.

"Yeshua spent many hours pointing out that they had the truth within their grasp but were not applying it correctly or understanding its meaning. He never directly indicated that he was the fulfillment of the scriptures, but he did confirm for them that a savior, the Messiah, who was the Son of God, would sacrifice himself for the sins of man and become the Lamb of God.

"King Mandubracius and other royalty attended many of these sessions and were impressed with Yeshua's understanding. His influence and reputation here in the Isles has paved the way for the work I must do now."

"Amazing," the Meglio said. "I was completely unaware that Jews came to the British Isles in antiquity and had such influence on druid theology and culture. It has also been lost over the centuries that Yeshua came here with you. There are legends, but it's not a commonly accepted truth. Thank you for confirming that for us. It's very comforting."

While the conversation between Joseph, the Meglio, and the Gray Champion was taking place, the heroes were struggling to maintain their seats on their mounts.

"I have ridden horses before," said Billy, "but always with a saddle. This is a pain!"

"I know," said Jeff. "I'm not sure I can do this for the rest of the time here. Does anyone have any advice on how I can stay on this animal?"

Boudicca, who was riding alongside of the heroes pulled her horse close to Jeff and said, "Sit back on both of your seat bones, and keep your lower legs close to your horse's side. You might have to grab hold of the mane if you feel insecure, so keep your hands close to your horse's neck. Follow the movement of his head with your hands. Let your legs hang down long. Your thighs and calves should touch your horse's sides. Don't grip tightly with your knees when your horse speeds up, because this will make you lean too far forward over his neck. If he stops abruptly or bucks, you'll go flying! If he acts nervous, stroke him on his neck and talk to him soothingly. That should help." Then she flashed a huge smile and said, "I have been riding since I was five years old. You can do this. It will just take some time and practice."

"Well thank you, Boudicca," said Jeff. "I will try to remember all of that, although I think my best bet is to just hold on tight and pray!"

Boudicca laughed out loud, then asked, "How is it that a man of your age does not know how to ride? Are you wealthy and have people carry you about in a chair?"

"No," said Jeff. "Where I come from, we have other means of transportation which do not involve sitting on a gigantic animal."

Again, Boudicca laughed.

"I see you have a very big sword for such a young woman," observed Billy, who had been listening carefully to Boudicca's riding instructions. "Are you as proficient with it as you are with riding?"

"I am!" replied Boudicca. "My father always wanted sons, so my sister and I have been trained in all of the warrior arts. He enjoys teaching so much that he needed some outlet for it. Gratefully, we have been the beneficiaries of his passion. He presented me with this sword when I was twelve years old and told me it was very special.

"He said it would take a few years for me to grow into it, but that if I learned to use it well, it would someday be my salvation. It never leaves my side."

"That's wonderful," replied Billy. "My cousins and I also received special swords when we were twelve years old. Your father sounds very wise. Listen to him and use your sword well."

"I will, but I am afraid that Master Joseph will forbid me," she replied. "He is always saying 'blessed are the peacemakers', and that I should 'turn the other cheek'. I have a really hard time with that. I always want to fight when I have been wronged."

"I'm sure he will also teach you that there is a time for war and a time for peace. You will know when the time comes," encouraged Billy.

The group of Guardians and disciples continued on their journey to the stone circle while sharing about their lives. When the sun set, they made camp and prepared for their arrival at the stone circle early the next day.

As they settled in for the evening, Joseph unbound the cup from under his tunic. They sat gathered around the roaring fire, and he revealed it to the gathered group of Guardians and disciples. He held it out in front of him, so the firelight made it glisten and shine.

Billy observed that it was a well-made, substantial vessel, not overly large, but solid. It was more like a deep, tapered bowl than a chalice, as it had no stem. It was engraved roundabout with images of Moses parting the Red Sea, the giving of the Ten Commandments, and the Temple of Solomon. As they gazed upon the precious cup, the gold it was made of seemed to pulsate with life. Billy was overcome with feelings of peace and confidence.

"This is the Cup of the Lord," Joseph announced. "The Cup of Life. Solomon the King drank from this cup, which is made from gold given to him by the angel of God. When he drank from it, it enhanced his God-given wisdom and gave him health.

"The cup was recovered by the prophet Daniel while in exile in Babylon. He, in turn, commanded the wise men of Chaldea to give it to the Lord at his birth. They followed his command and gave it as one of the gifts given to honor the Christ-child.

"I became the keeper of this precious cup during Yeshua's childhood and returned it to the Lord when he began his earthly ministry. After the Last Supper with his disciples, it was returned to me for safe keeping. Since that day, I have kept it safely hidden.

"It is a cup of power. It is a cup of mystery. It is a cup of promise and of life. Look upon it and know that there is hope! Drink from it and be wise and filled with life!"

Then Joseph filled the cup with wine and continued. "On the night before he died, the Lord took the cup, filled it with wine, and said, 'This is the cup of my blood, the blood of the new and everlasting covenant. It will be shed for you and for all men so that sins may be forgiven. Take, drink, and do this in remembrance of me'. Then he passed the cup to his disciples and they drank. Tonight, we will do the same, in remembrance of the Lord, asking for his blessing on our missions."

Then he drank from the cup and passed it to the Meglio. He closed his eyes and reverently drank of the wine, then he passed the cup to the prophet. The prophet likewise drank from the cup and passed it to his great-grandfather, who hesitated.

"Joseph, I am a man who has blood on his hands," he admitted. "I have killed many men in anger in my service as a Guardian. I believe I may be unworthy to drink from the Cup of the Lord."

"Dear sir," replied Joseph, "the fact that you hesitated based on your self-reflection is all the indication that is needed of your worthiness. Drink, and be free of your guilt. Drink, and be set free of your chains."

The Gray Champion then drank from the cup. His

expression showed the joy in his heart. He then passed it to his eldest great-grandson.

As Billy held the cup in his hands, he was overwhelmed by the thought that he would be drinking from the very cup that Yeshua drank from at the Last Supper. That he would actually be drinking from the Holy Grail. Reverently, he put it to his lips and sipped the sweet liquid. After he passed it to Jeff, he stared solemnly at the ground, unwilling to break the spirit of the moment.

Jeff drank, and the cup passed from his cousins to Malchus, Josephus, and Boudicca. When all had partaken, the cup was returned to Joseph of Arimathea. "I shall keep the cup with me until it is time for you to depart for your confrontation with Azazel. Sleep in the peace of the Lord, for tomorrow, we will enter the stone circle."

Chapter Nine

Stonehenge

The sound of whinnying horses woke Jeff from a sound sleep. He sat up and saw most of the others busy with preparations for their short ride to the stone circle. He poked Billy, who was just stirring, then stood and dressed quickly.

"Time to go already?" Billy asked.

"Seems so," Jeff answered. "The others are already up and moving."

When he was dressed, he rolled up his blankets and helped with the last few tasks.

Joseph looked around and called, "Mount up!"

When everyone was mounted, Joseph said, "We will be at the stone circle in under an hour. I have been there before and have felt the power of the site. Steel yourselves; it can be confusing and disorienting. You have taken drink from the cup, and it should protect you from any evil that wishes to take advantage of the confusion that may occur, but you must use your own will to resist any influence. Know this and be prepared." Then he rode off into the lead and the others followed.

"Do you think there is really any supernatural power at Stonehenge?" asked Nick as he rode next to Joe. "I mean, it's just a pile of old stones. We know that nothing like that has any power or influence. That's just superstition, right?" he asked, looking for assurance from his older brother.

"I used to think so, Nick," replied Joe, "but after all we have seen recently, Azazel rising out of Great-Grandpa's body, Grandma defeating the Leviathans with dark energy, and the whole quantum essence stuff, I am beginning to think that things like this can be true. If the Watchers really were cast to earth at Stonehenge, then maybe there are forces at work that we'd better be wary of."

"I guess you could be right," admitted Nick. "I, for one, am going to hang on tight to my sword and let it guide me. Let's hope that the virtues of the swords can help us figure out all of this."

"I'm with you, brother," said Joe. "And let's make sure we stay together. That has proven to be wise on the last few missions."

"You got it," agreed Nick. They urged their horses to catch up with the rest of the group.

As they crested a small hill, Jeff caught his first glimpse of Stonehenge. The sun was still low in the sky, and it cast an orange glow on the standing stones. He was struck by the ancient, stark beauty of its form.

He also observed that it was not in the same state of disrepair that he remembered from his time, two thousand years in the future. All the stones were in their proper positions, and it had the look of a place that was still in regular use.

Joseph raised his hand for the group to stop and summoned them to form a circle around him. When they were gathered, he spoke to them.

"It appears that there is no one here, and that is good. We can make our observations and assessments and then leave quickly. Although I have met with and have been on friendly terms with the druids' high priest in the past, some of his followers are not so friendly. They believe that I and my disciples are here to destroy their faith and defame their beliefs. I am not sure what would become of us if they found us wandering around their most sacred site. Let us do this as quickly as possible and be on our way." Then he signaled them to follow him, and they made their way down the hill toward the structure.

As they approached the site, Billy felt a sense of dread beginning to build inside him. As he rode closer and closer to the ancient stone circle, the world seemed to go silent, and all he could focus on was the enormous twenty-five-ton stones rising ominously before him. What made the feeling worse was that he did not really know how they were going to make their assessment. They had to determine if this was the place of confrontation with Azazel, but how to make that determination remained an unknown.

Arriving at the site, everyone dismounted and kept quiet as they assembled. Suddenly, Jeff noticed Nick's hand began to vibrate. Nick signaled to the Meglio to come quickly.

His grandfather approached and asked, "What's the problem, Nick?"

"My sword is vibrating like crazy," he said. "Should I reveal it?"

"Absolutely!" was the Meglio's reply. Nick raised his right arm, and the Sword of Michael the Archangel appeared in his hand, vibrating wildly and glowing with a deep, blood red light.

"That can't be good," whispered Robbie to his father who was standing next to him as they observed

Nick's sword reacting to the environment. "It's never done that before. What does it mean?"

"I don't know yet," replied the prophet. "Let's just give it some time."

The Meglio called for Joseph of Arimathea to join them. When he arrived, he said, "The swords are very sensitive to virtuous and quantum emanations. They have indicated in the past, by glowing brightly, that we have been in the presence of virtue. However, that glow was always a pure, white light. We have never seen a blood red glow before, and I believe this may indicate the powerful presence of evil. I believe we have our decision. This place is not the place of confrontation. Evil is too powerful here. It must have been greatly defiled. We need to find another place. Let's gather the team together and head back to your settlement."

"Are you sure of that?" asked Joseph. "Wouldn't any place of falling inherently be touched by evil?"

"I suppose so," replied the Meglio. "However, the swords have never been wrong before, and given that it is the Sword of the Archangel that is active now, I am fully confident that we are being warned away. This is not the portal we seek."

"Very well," replied Joseph. Then, signaling to the rest of the team to gather around, he addressed them. "Mount your horses and prepare to return. We have our answer."

As he spoke these words, two figures in robes suddenly appeared from behind the two center standing stones and called out. "Stand where you are!"

Joseph's eyes widened, and he leaned over to whisper to the Meglio. "Stand fast. I recognize this man. He is Myrddin Wyllt, the North Brythonic prophet and druidic high priest. I met him twenty years ago when the high priest was around thirty years old. This is a man for whom age has no meaning. He must be at least fifty years old now."

"Yet he still has a powerful bearing and speaks with authority," the Meglio whispered back. "Who's the woman standing next to him?"

"She is Gwendydd, Myrddin's twin sister. She is the healer of the druids and has a powerful influence on her brother. Stay quiet and I will speak to them."

Jeff's ears perked up. Puzzled, he leaned in to whisper to Billy. "Wait. Isn't Myrddin another name for Merlin? I thought he lived at least five hundred years from now."

"Did he?" Billy asked as he peered more closely at Myrddin and his sister. "Some people say that Merlin aged backwards. Maybe it's true."

"That would speak to his strangeness and mystical nature, I suppose," Jeff replied, still feeling confused and a bit nervous about the whole situation.

Joseph straightened and called, "Honorable Myrddin, it is I, Joseph of Arimathea. May I approach and explain our presence here today?"

Myrddin replied, "I remember you, Honorable One. Only you may approach, the others should remain where they are."

Joseph handed his horse's lead to the Meglio and quietly instructed him. "Remain here with the others. Stay at the ready, for I know not if there be others close by. At the first sign of trouble, leave immediately and ride for the settlement. Josephus and Malchus know the way. Also, put the young princess Boudicca at the middle of the riders for her protection. I will speak with Myrddin."

He approached Myrddin and Gwendydd and bowed respectfully to them. "It is an honor to see you once again,

Myrddin." Then he bowed deeply again to Gwendydd. "It has been many years, honored sister. I see the years have been good to you."

"Why are you here, Joseph?" said Myrddin. "You are aware that this is sacred ground and that your presence here is a desecration. What would cause you to dishonor us so?"

Joseph stood tall and replied, "I meant no disrespect or dishonor. I have brought these men here today to make a spiritual assessment. They are in search of a portal into the spirit realm and needed to know if this was the correct place. If it had been so, I would have contacted you for your help. As it is, it seems this is not the place they seek. So, we will leave and trouble you no more."

"It is not that simple, my friend," replied Myrddin. "Your presence here must be erased. You have walked among the Stones and therefore have defiled them. You must remain until Gwendydd and I perform the rite of restoration, the proof of which will require a spiritual sign. If that sign is not forthcoming, there must be a price paid in blood."

As he finished his statement, he raised his hand and the wind began to howl. Then, from the surrounding hills, a swarm of druids appeared, raising their voices in an eerie high-pitched wailing sound. They surrounded the site of the stone circle, descending upon the group of Guardians and disciples, cutting off any escape route.

"Myrddin," said Joseph, "this is unnecessary. We will take our leave. You know me, I have never disrespected you or your faith in any way. You remember your meeting with my nephew, Yeshua. From that, you must surely understand that we are a people of peace. Let us leave, and this will be the last you will see of us."

"It must be this way," said Gwendydd. "The only

reason you are not all dead at this moment is because of our affection for you and your nephew, Yeshua. If you are speaking truthfully, then all will be well."

Then Gwendydd and Myrddin turned and walked to the center of the stones. The druid horde corralled the Guardians and disciples, herding them into the stone circle. Then, they stood guard at every entrance and exit. Joseph joined them and spoke to the group.

"We have no choice. We must comply, but have faith. We have the cup, and we have the swords. They will provide for our safety. Keep the swords hidden. When the time is right to reveal them, we will know. Until then, stay silent and compliant."

After the druids positioned themselves around the perimeter of the stone circle and all was silent, Myrddin stood before the altar, placed a bundle of mistletoe on it, and began the ceremony.

> *"Grant, O Gudt thy purification*
> *And in Purification, Strength;*
> *And in Strength, Understanding;*
> *And in Understanding, Knowledge;*
> *And in Knowledge, the Knowledge of Justice:*
> *And in the Knowledge of Justice, the Love of it;*
> *And in the Love of it, the Love of All Existences;*
> *Grant this day cleansing from corruption and defilement.*
> *Make it known to us gathered here the source of this defilement*
> *And the power to undo it. Show us, O Gudt, your will.*
> *Send your sacred cleansing fire to make these stones pure once again."*

Then, he raised his hands to the sky and laid them upon the bundle of mistletoe before him. Nothing happened. He stood there for a few moments, silent, and in prayer. Still, nothing happened.

Finally, he stood back from the altar and motioned to his sister Gwendydd to join him. Together, they laid hands upon the bundle of mistletoe on the altar. Still, nothing happened.

They stepped back from the altar, and Myrddin said, "The defilement is too strong. Blood is required." Then he addressed Joseph. "Choose the sacrifice from among your group."

"Myrddin," he replied, "we cannot accommodate your request. It is against our faith to participate in such a rite. I must refuse and once again ask that you release us."

"There must be fire or blood," replied Myrddin. "There is no other way, it must be so. Only by the cleansing fire or sacrifice of blood may your defilement be made clean. Choose!"

"I will not," was Joseph's reply.

Gwendydd became enraged and grabbed Boudicca, who was standing nearby next to Nick. "She will be our blood sacrifice! I have made the choice. This virgin will do."

As they dragged Boudicca to the altar, Nick could contain himself no longer. He reached for the Sword of Michael the Archangel and shouted, "Let her go! If you want fire, I will give you fire!"

Without hesitation, he raised his right arm revealing the Sword of Michael. It burst into furious and brilliant blood-red flame. He swung the sword around his head, creating a circle of flame above himself, then he flung the flame at the altar. The flame leapt from the sword to the altar.

Gwendydd, startled by the flames, released

Boudicca. She ran to Joseph, and as they watched, the flames from the sword of the Archangel consumed the mistletoe offering and enveloped the entire altar stone, which violently exploded into two halves. Within seconds, the immense trilithon standing over the decimated altar stone collapsed, partially burying it. The druids surrounding the stone circle ran for the hills.

When the flames died down, Myrddin and Gwendydd fell on their faces, their expressions displaying their terror. Joseph and the Meglio approached them.

"Stand on your feet," Joseph commanded.

They immediately complied.

"Do not worship us, we are just men as you are. The fire you saw is the fire of virtue and justice and was provided to us this day to prove our innocence. Be thankful it did not destroy you along with the altar."

As Myrddin stood humbly before Joseph, he said, "The God of Joseph and Yeshua is a powerful God. May he receive all honor and glory! How may we assist you in your quest?"

Joseph put his hand on Myrddin's shoulder. "Come, let us partake of a meal together, and we can discuss the matter."

The group retreated to an area at the base of the hills surrounding the stone circle and prepared a simple meal together. As they ate, the Meglio told Myrddin and Gwendydd all about their mission, Azazel, and their search for the proper place of confrontation. Myrddin told them everything he knew about the legends of the fallen, the giants of old, and history of the druids.

As he was finishing, he said to Joseph, "Have you told them of the Lia-Fail stone and of the Sword of Judgment?"

Joseph replied, "I have not, as I have only a passing

understanding of these legends of your people. We would appreciate it if you would share your knowledge about these items. Tell us all you know of them and how they may help us in our quest."

"Joseph," replied Myrddin, "I am sure you have more knowledge of these items than you realize, since, according to the legends, they are treasures of your people! Let me begin, and I am sure you will understand.

"More than five hundred years ago, the great prophet Ollam Fodhla and his scribe Simon Brug came to our shores from Egypt, bearing the princess Tea Tephi to safety. They were fleeing the great captivity of their people. She was the last remaining descendant of the House of the High One, known as a princess of Zion. They came bearing with them a great chest containing a golden sword and a stone wrapped in a banner. Surely you must be familiar with this story Joseph, for it is your own history!"

"You mentioned a princess of Zion, and of course that is a familiar term to me as a Jew," Joseph responded. "You also mention the House of the High One. For us, that would refer to the House of David the King. If by 'the great captivity' you are referring to the exile in Babylon, then I think that I may be able to put all of this together in a way we can understand.

"There are stories in our historical scriptures that say that the prophet Jeremiah visited a cave on Mount Nebo after the Babylonian exile began. Jeremiah then went to Tahpanhes in Egypt with a remnant of the Jews after the fall of Jerusalem along with his scribe, Baruch.

"Before he departed, he could have gathered together some of the hidden treasures of the temple that were not found by the Babylonians and brought these items with him to Egypt for safekeeping. The items you mentioned could be some of those treasures. Tell me more about them."

"The Lia-Fail stone was brought by the great prophet," said Myrddin. "It was said to be the 'pillow stone' of a revered ancestor, who, while sleeping on it, opened a doorway to heaven. This ancestor saw angels descending and ascending a ladder which reached into heaven itself. The Sword of Judgment was also brought by the great prophet and was a magnificent golden sword used by a king of unequaled wisdom to administer the judgment of God."

"The first story is very reminiscent of the story of Jacob!" exclaimed Joseph. "According to account given in the Torah, Jacob was fleeing from his elder twin brother, Esau, whom he had tricked out of receiving their father Isaac's blessing of the first-born. On his flight, Jacob rested at a city called Luz and used a stone as a pillow. In his dreams, he then saw a ladder which was set upon the earth, and its top reached to heaven; and there, the angels of God were ascending and descending on it. It is written:

'And behold, the Lord stood above it and said:

'I am the Lord God of Abraham your father and the God of Isaac; the land on which you lie I will give to you and your descendants. Also, your descendants shall be as the dust of the earth; you shall spread abroad to the west and the east, to the north and the south; and in you and in your seed all the families of the earth shall be blessed.

'Behold, I am with you and will keep you wherever you go, and will bring you back to this land; for I will not leave you until I have done what I have spoken to you.

"After waking up, Jacob exclaimed, 'This is none

other than the House of God, and this is the Gate of Heaven!' He then called the place Bet-El, which translates to 'House of God'. He set up the stone he had slept on as a pillar and consecrated it. Is it possible that the Lia-Fail stone you refer to is the pillow stone of Jacob? It sounds like it could be the very same stone!"

The Meglio nodded. "And the Sword of Judgment description sounds like to could have been a sword of Solomon. He was known as the wisest king in the scriptures, and no one before or since has ever rivaled that wisdom. There is a story of two women bringing a dispute before the king which may be referencing this very sword. In our scriptures, it is written:

'Then the king said, "The one says, 'This is my son who is living, and your son is the dead one'; and the other said, 'No! For your son is the dead one, and my son is the living one'." The king said, "Get me the sword." So they brought the sword to the king. The king said, "Divide the living child in two, and give half to the one and half to the other." Then the woman whose child was the living one spoke to the king, for she was deeply stirred over her son and said, "Oh, my lord, give her the living child, and by no means kill him." But the other said, "He shall be neither mine nor yours; divide him!" Then the king said, "Give the first woman the living child, and by no means kill him. She is his mother." When all Israel heard of the judgment which the king had handed down, they feared the king, for they saw that the wisdom of God was in him to administer justice.

"Could this be the very sword that Solomon used to administer the justice of the Lord with wisdom? I have always thought that the Sword of Solomon that we Guardians possess was the only sword he had, but maybe this is another, more powerful one. The sword above all others?"

Joseph replied, "It very well could be. It would seem that the stone could be helpful in opening the portal you seek at the place of confrontation, and the Sword of Judgment may be necessary for you to administer the judgment of God against Azazel.

"We must find these treasures so you may use them in your battle. Myrddin, do you know where these treasures are? Can you direct us to them?"

"If you are seeking these treasures to serve your God, then I will reveal their location, but if you seek revenge or power, then I will keep the location to myself. I cannot make that determination, so I will suggest that you examine yourselves carefully and make sure that what you are attempting has pure motives behind it. If you wield these sacred objects for selfish or impure reasons, the judgment will fall on you. Are you certain of your motives?"

"We are, Myrddin," the Meglio responded. "We are men of virtue and valor. All we seek is to free the captives of Azazel and to restore freedom and liberty to all mankind. We are confident in our motives. Direct us to where these treasures are."

"I will reveal their location to you, but I will not accompany you," replied Myrddin. "This is a journey you must make on your own if it is to have value. The treasures you seek are buried with the queen, Tea Tephi. She and the great prophet are buried within the Mound of the Hostages, at the Hill of Tara across the waters to the west. It is a short but treacherous journey, so prepare yourselves."

The druid then described the route, which would require a dangerous voyage over the western waters to the Isle of Hibernia. He also described the landmarks they would encounter. From there, it was a one-day ride northwest. Malchus, the scribe for the group, recorded the limited and sketchy directions. When they were clear on their objective, Myrddin and Gwendydd blessed the team and departed. The group gathered their possessions and mounted their horses.

"Are we going back to the settlement before heading on to Hibernia?" the prophet asked Joseph.

"No," he replied. "We will go directly there from here. It will save us two days of travel, and we can buy any supplies we need at the port."

"How will we cross the waters?" asked Joe. "Will they rent us a ship? And what about the horses?"

Joseph of Arimathea replied, "My remaining ship is at the harbor and has been for a few months. The voyage here resulted in significant damage, so I left it there to be repaired. It has been long enough that the repairs should be completed by now. We will make the voyage in my ship."

With all of that settled, they rode west toward the coast. Along the way, there was continued conversation about what they had heard from the druid Myrddin.

Joseph told them that the rich history and legends of the land speak of the early settlement of Ireland by a group called Tuatha De Danaan, also known as the Tribe of Danaan. This migration took place about the time of the exodus of the Jews from Egypt.

Joseph told of speculation that it was possible that these ancient settlers were from the Hebrew tribe of Dan, and that they were the ones who first began the metal mining that continued until his time.

He continued, "The legends say that when the Tuatha De Danaan migrated to Ireland, they brought some magical items with them from their homeland.

These, according to local legends were the Spear of Lug, the Sword of the Giant, and the Cauldron of the Dagda. Legend has it that anyone wielding the spear never lost a battle, no one ever escaped the sword once it was drawn, and no one ever went away from the cauldron unsatisfied."

The prophet said that he recognized this information as identical to the history of Britain that was given to the team by the quantum computer when they were researching the history of the Sword of Goliath during their fight against the Swords of Terror. He believed the Sword of Goliath to be the same one that the tribe of Dan brought with them along with a holy vessel from the Solomon's temple and Goliath's spear. Joseph agreed that they might be one and the same.

Then Joseph went on to give more detail and expand upon the story they heard from Myrddin and connect it more directly to Jewish history.

"In the Irish legend and history that Myrddin recounted to us, he said that five hundred years ago, on the northeast coast of Ireland, a sage arrived from Egypt, accompanied by his scribe and a young princess. They brought with them a mysterious chest containing a sword and a large, rough stone."

Boudicca chimed in, telling them that the local legends she had been taught told that the princess was eventually married to King Eochaidh the Heremon, the head of the royal family of Ireland, which it is rumored was descended from the tribe of Judah.

"I would like to add," continued Joseph, "that at precisely this time in history, Nebuchadnezzar, King of Babylon, had brought an end to the House of David and the kings of Judah. The sons of the last king, Zedekiah, who were actually Jeremiah's grandsons, were slain, and only his two daughters, Jeremiah's granddaughters, were spared. They were taken to Egypt by the great prophet, accompanied by the scribe Baruch. They then disappear from Jewish history."

Boudicca spoke up again, "But the legends say that after the marriage of the princess to King Eochaidh, the capital of the land was immediately moved to a new site to be called Tara, or the center of the law. What is not in doubt is the importance of the stone and the sword they brought with them. Both are positively linked to the royal family till this day."

"I had heard all of this during the many years I spent travelling here," Joseph responded, "but I never put much weight behind the legends. Myrddin has opened my eyes to new possibilities."

"So," said the Meglio, "buried in this folklore is the tale of a prophet, possibly Jeremiah, Princess Tephi, possibly a daughter of King Zedekiah, and Simon Brug, a scribe who sounds a lot like Jeremiah's biblical scribe, Baruch.

"They landed in Ireland, or as you refer to it, Hibernia, a short time after the destruction of Jerusalem took place, bearing with them a great chest, a sword, and a stone wrapped in a banner. The princess married the king, Eochaidh the Heremon. This Tephi was possibly the daughter of the King of Jerusalem, whom Jeremiah went forth to plant in Ireland after the destruction of Zedekiah and of Jerusalem. Do I understand correctly?"

"Yes, you do," replied Joseph.

"I am interested in the stone that Jeremiah may have brought," stated the prophet. "The scriptures you related to us say that Jacob, the forefather of the Israelites, set up a stone pillar that he lay his head upon after making a covenant with God. I have heard that it was also a custom in ancient Israel to crown kings over that very stone. Is this the stone we are talking about here? Myrddin said very clearly that it was said to be the 'pillow stone' of a revered ancestor, who, while sleeping on it, opened a doorway to heaven. This ancestor saw angels descending and ascending a ladder which reached to heaven. Are we truly seeking the Stone of Bethel? The Stone of Jacob?"

"It is my belief," replied Joseph, "that if Myrddin and the legends are correct, then it may be that very sacred stone that we seek."

"But what was Jeremiah doing?" Billy asked. "And why did he bring the king's daughters to Ireland?"

Joseph replied, "The scriptures reveal that Jeremiah was given a two-part mission: 'to root out and pull down, to build and to plant.' Jeremiah foretold the destruction of Jerusalem and the end of the monarchy in Judah, which happened. The scriptures do not provide any information on how Jeremiah fulfilled the second phase of his mission.

"However, as we heard from Boudicca, local history provides some intriguing answers. The prophecy to build and to plant would apply to taking the king's daughters to a place where they could re-establish the royal line. Jeremiah obviously took the stone, along with his two great-granddaughters, the daughters of Zedekiah, Jeremiah's grandson, and married one to the King of Spain, and the other, Tea Tephi, to the King Eochaidh. Note that Zedekiah is a descendant of Judah, one of the sons of Jacob, also called Israel. This would have completed the second phase of Jeremiah's mysterious mission. The Bible clearly predicted this would happen."

"But why did Jeremiah choose to go to Ireland… I mean Hibernia?" asked Jeff.

"As we heard earlier," Joseph explained, "Irish

history describes a prominent people who settled on the island as the Tuatha de Danaan. While many people puzzle over the identity of these gifted invaders, the scriptures may reveal the answer. The Tribe of Dan abandoned the small lot of land given to them by Joshua on the coast of Israel and joined with the Phoenicians early on in their history. This is recorded in the Torah when Judge Deborah stated that 'Dan remained on their ships in the time of war'.

"Other Roman sources indicate that members of this tribe left Egypt about the time of the Exodus, around 1500 BC, as told by the Roman historian, Diodorus Sicilus. This is about the time the Tuatha de Danaan began to arrive in Ireland. If the Tuatha de Danaan were Israelites and kinsmen to Jeremiah and the princess, he would have been bringing her to her own people.

"Local legends say that Jeremiah's party came to the island 'in the ships of the Danites', and that after being shipwrecked off the coast of Ireland, the company made its way to the hill-seat of the last of the Tuatha de Danaan kings of the Tribe of Dan. That is where Jeremiah brought Tea Tephi and the treasures that he rescued from the temple. So, it would seem that it is our task to get to the resting place of Jeremiah and Tea Tephi and find the stone and the sword."

The Gray Champion spoke up and addressed the heroes. "I find all of this very interesting, but also very encouraging. As the Meglio of the Arimathea family here in Britain, I had access to ancient historical records regarding the official lineage of the Arimathea family of the Guardians of the Swords of Valor, of which we are all a part.

"The part that I want to reveal to you that may validate some of this stated that we are all descendants of the House of Stewart of the Royal House of Britain, due to intermarriage after the time of Joseph of Arimathea. The House of Stewart are the descendants of Eochaidh the Heremon. And from Eochaidh the Heremon descended all the kings of Ireland and Scotland, and ultimately Britain. I personally find this history of particular interest, as my great-great-grandmother was Alexandrina Ogilvie Stewart of the Stewart Clan.

"Since I myself am therefore of the Stewart Clan, this makes Tea Tephi, and ultimately King David, my own ancestors as well as yours.

"So, with this new information, we apparently have some very famous ancestors; King David, Solomon, Jeremiah, Tea Tephi, and Joseph of Arimathea. This is in addition to the blood of Cincinnatus, which you have through your grandfather's line.

"I suspect that this is the true reason that this final task of confronting Azazel has fallen to our family. We must succeed. We are the last hope. We have not only the blood of warriors in our veins but that of kings and prophets. Let this new and inspiring information steel us and encourage us for the battle ahead."

Billy felt a sense of urgency and determination as he rode on with the group. With this greater understanding of their place in history, he now understood the necessity of success.

CHAPTER TEN

PROTOCOL 17

Susan, the daughter of the Meglio, who was also a Prophet of the Guardians of the Swords of Valor, tried once again to gain information as to the whereabouts of her father and her brother, the current prophet of the family.

"This is ridiculous," she spoke into the secure communication device connecting her to the Council of Elders of the International Guardians of the Swords of Valor. "They have been out of touch for over two weeks now. I would have expected all of you to be working feverishly to locate them. You have all the resources. I am trying to keep the remnant of this family safe from the chaos closing in around us and have my hands full. Please try again and keep me informed. If I don't hear from you soon, I will invoke Protocol 17 and take matters into my own hands."

She disconnected the call and walked out onto the back deck of the safe house. She hoped that watching the sun set over Long Island Sound would calm her. Her sister-in-law, Carolyn, joined her there and stood silently by her side for a while.

Finally, she inquired, "Have they had any success? Have they been able to locate your dad or Robert?"

Susan, still looking out over the darkening waters, replied, "No, and to tell you the truth, I don't think they're trying very hard. Things are very strange with them these days. They seem far more concerned for their own personal situations and seem to have forgotten their primary duties to the families.

"Everyone is so focused on just trying to survive the upheavals taking place in their own countries and towns that I fear for the survival of the Guardians. If we don't find Dad and Robert soon, I believe that the Guardian families will cease to exist in any meaningful way.

"We *have* to do something now, so I've decided to invoke Protocol 17. That's the only way to make the others understand the critical nature of this development. They will have no choice but to take action and defer to me. It's time."

"Susan," said Carolyn, "are you sure you want to do this now? Shouldn't we give it another day or two before you invoke Protocol 17? It seems so drastic, and we have not yet told the girls about the family history and who their grandfather really is. Shouldn't we do that first?"

"I was hoping that the leaders of the other families would have had some information to share by now," replied Susan, "but none of them have any clue as to their whereabouts. I find that exceptionally strange. We know that they have often travelled through time for their missions, but they always return before sunrise.

"So, even if they are on a mission and all went well, they would have surely had time to communicate with us. The only thing I can think of is that a mission has gone wrong. Protocol 17 will confirm for the International Families that Guardians are truly in trouble and possibly trapped back in time.

"It's my belief that we must get to the Keeping

Room to question the quantum computer. We need to know when and where they are trapped. Then we can inform the international families so they can use their resources to help us devise a plan to go back in time and rescue them. I don't see that we should delay any longer."

"I don't disagree," replied Carolyn. "If your Dad and Rob and the boys are in trouble, we need to help them quickly. However, we must take the girls with us. We can't leave them here with the battle coming closer. They need to be brought up to speed, or they could endanger themselves or us. They have to understand."

Susan nodded. "Agreed. Call them together, and we'll do the indoctrination now. I'll go get the documents my father left for me, and then we can begin."

Carolyn, the wife of the prophet, found her nieces, Kate, Colleen, Alexandra, and Olivia, and her daughter, Ellie, and shepherded them to the great room of the Guardian safehouse. It was a large, old home on the North Shore which had once belonged to a former sea captain. It had been built high on a spit of land surrounded on three sides by sheer cliffs overlooking the Long Island Sound. It had been chosen because of its remote location and defensibility.

As the girls gathered in the great room, Susan sat in the overstuffed chair by the fire with a stack of documents on her lap. She appeared worn and troubled.

When the girls were seated, Susan began. "I know these past few weeks have been tough on all of you, having to leave your homes and schools, but I think you all agree that it's much safer here. Still, there is much more that you need to know. We must undertake a dangerous journey soon, and you all need to be prepared.

"Let me start at the beginning, with your grandfather. Or rather, I should say, the Meglio."

CHAPTER ELEVEN

THE SHIP OF SOLOMON

The Guardians and the group from Arimathea arrived at the harbor town of Barrow Bay late in the afternoon. They dismounted and built a fire on the outskirts of the town. Joseph of Arimathea, the Meglio, Josephus, and Malchus rode on into the village to inquire about the condition of Joseph's ship.

When they arrived at the place where the ship was docked, they found the ship still in a state of semi-disrepair. The three men boarded the ship and approached the group of men sleeping on the deck. Joseph spoke sternly.

"How is it that after six months and prepayment for your work, I find this ship still in a state of disrepair? All of you have done work on my ships in the past, and I have always been pleased with your craftsmanship. Why now, when I'm in need of it, do I find it in this condition?"

The foreman of the group replied, "Master Joseph, we have been waiting on more of the timber required. The last shipment was supposed to be here a month ago, but it has not arrived. Please do not be angry with us."

Joseph sighed. "I am more disappointed than angry.

I know you to be a man of integrity, or I would not have you as my foreman." He thanked the man for his efforts and the three men disembarked.

"I'm afraid that we'll need to find another ship capable of transporting us and the horses to Hibernia," he informed the Meglio and Malchus as they stepped off the gangplank. "We won't be able to find anything suitable tonight. I'll make inquiries in the morning."

As they moved to mount their horses, they were startled by the sudden appearance of a druid standing before them, seeming to appear out of nowhere.

Joseph's look of surprise morphed into one of recognition. "Gwendydd, you startled us," he said. "Why are you here and what do you want of us?"

"Myrddin sent me to help you," Gwendydd replied. "It was revealed to him in a vision from your God that you would need a ship. I am here to provide one for you."

"Well, Myrddin has once again proven to be wise," Joseph said. "My ship is not in good repair, and we do need one that will take us across the waters. Where is this ship you are to provide for us?"

"Go and gather your men and return to this place at nightfall," instructed Gwendydd. "The ship will come to you."

"The ship will come to us?" said Malchus suspiciously. "How is this possible? The captain won't be able to navigate the harbor in the dark."

"This ship has no captain," replied Gwendydd. "It is guided by virtue, and only the virtuous and faithful may board. So, be sure of yourselves before you board it. Have faith and all will be well." Then she departed, leaving them bewildered.

"Should we believe her, Father?" asked Josephus.

"I believe her," answered Joseph. "She may be a

pagan, but she and Myrddin are honorable and wise and have confessed our God as Lord of All. It is very possible that He has given Myrddin a vision to help us on our mission. Let's return to the camp and gather the others. We may have a very interesting journey ahead of us."

They returned to the camp to find everyone around the fire.

"It's time to pack up and leave," the Meglio announced to the group. "We have been told of a ship that is available, and we board at nightfall."

They roused themselves, gathered their equipment, and mounted the horses for the ride to town. The team arrived at the appointed spot and dismounted. They searched the dark waters for any sign of a ship headed their way but could see nothing.

"How are we supposed to find this ship if we can't even see it?" asked Ty.

"We've been told that the ship will find us," said his grandfather.

"Okay…" Ty replied skeptically.

Suddenly, the Meglio's eyes were stabbed by a brilliant light. When he could see once again, floating in the water before them was a magnificent ship. It was strange-looking, very unlike the one he was expecting. It was ancient and of a foreign design.

"Whoa!" exclaimed Nick. "Where did that come from?"

"I don't know," replied Ty. "It just appeared out of nowhere."

The strange ship drew closer, and as it came near the shore, it turned so that its side faced the waiting team. That was when the Meglio saw that the ship had writing on its side. The letters were glowing as if written in fire and were undecipherable to the heroes.

"Can anyone read the writing?" asked Robbie. "I would think that it might be important for us to know what it says before we climb aboard."

Joseph of Arimathea spoke up. "It is written in ancient Hebrew. I am trained in all versions of the Hebrew language, as well as many others. I will read and interpret for us."

Then, shading his eyes a bit as he trained them on the flaming words, he read:

"Thou man, which shall enter into this ship, beware thou be in steadfast belief, for I am Faith, and therefore beware how thou enter, for if in this thou fail, I shall not help thee."

"What does that mean?" asked Joe. "Makes me nervous when glowing ships have the word 'beware' written in flames on their side. That is *never* good."

"It must be as Gwendydd said," replied the Meglio, "that only those of virtue and of great faith can board the ship. I am confident that all of you qualify. You have been chosen by the swords for your virtue and valor, and you have all proven to have great faith. I can't speak for the others, but as far as we're concerned, this ship will serve us well."

The Gray Champion agreed, and he led them closer to the shore as the great ship lowered its gangplank to allow them to enter. Joseph moved closer to Boudicca and put his arm around her.

"Are you confident about entering the ship?" he asked.

"I don't know, Master Joseph," she replied. "I believe that I am a person of virtue, but that has never been tested to any great extent. I also have faith in many things, but I don't know if my faith is the kind that the ship will honor."

Joseph looked into her eyes and said, "You have drunk the wine from the cup. I believe that you have the faith that is required. Come, let us board together. All will be well."

Then, with his arm still around her shoulders, he led her toward the ship. They followed the Meglio, the Gray Champion, and the heroes up the ramp and onto the ship, leading their horses behind them. They were followed by Malchus and Josephus, who seemed slightly hesitant. Once aboard, they gathered together on the deck and waited. Nothing happened. They breathed a sigh of relief, and the Meglio spoke.

"Joseph, what is our next move? Should we head to the bridge? Begin to reset the sails? What do you suggest?"

"I believe that we should wait for instructions," replied Joseph. "Let's give it some time."

The Meglio agreed, and they waited in anticipation.

"Welcome, men of virtue, to the ship of faith," said a booming, disembodied voice. "You have passed the first test. Waiting for you below is another test that you will need to pass, or your quest will not be successful. I know your destination and will begin the journey now. Continue in faith, and all will be well."

"Well, that was different!" said Jeff. "I can't recall ever having a ship speak to me before. In college, I thought I heard my desk talking to me after I had been awake two days straight studying for finals, but this is different. Are we sure we want to do this? I mean, it could take us anywhere, and we would have no control over it."

"Faith…" said Joseph, "…is apparently the wind in this ship's sails. Let's go below, face the next test, and continue to have faith. We will face whatever comes together."

The group tied their horses to the railings of the ship, descended the stairs leading below decks, and found themselves in a huge, richly-appointed stateroom. The Meglio looked around in wonder at the various tapestries, carvings, and bejeweled appointments. He had seen many glamorous rooms in his life, but this was beyond all description.

"Wow!" remarked Billy. "This appears to be the ship of a king. I hope he doesn't mind us using it for a while."

As he scanned the room, the Meglio could not help but agree with Billy's observation. Dominating the cabin was a huge bed covered in exquisite red silk. On either side of the headboard were a red and a white post. A wooden beam hanging over the bed was connected to these two posts. There was a post of a green hue on top of the beam's center.

Lying prominently on the bed was a magnificent sword in a scabbard made of some sort of animal skin with strange inscriptions on both sides. Next to the sword was an oddly-crafted sword belt, which appeared to be made of some sort of crude rope material.

Finally, next to it all, closer to where they were standing, was a large leather purse, tied at the top.

Before they approached the bed, the disembodied voice spoke once again. "Open the purse. Read and understand."

Joseph of Arimathea approached the bed and took hold of the purse. Carefully untying the strings, he withdrew an ancient scroll.

"This looks very much like many of the ancient Torah scrolls I have seen at the temple," he remarked, "but this one is in much better condition."

The others gathered around him as he unrolled the

scroll and began to read. "Once again," he said, "it is written in ancient Hebrew. I can understand it, but I must go slowly." Then he began to read aloud.

"Thou man who hast entered this ship, hast been tested for thy virtue and faith. Know now that this ship within which ye sail, was constructed by myself, Hiram of Tyre, for the great King Solomon at the behest of one of his magnificent and wise wives.

"Upon receiving a vision from the angel of God, Solomon, son of David and the king of Israel, learned that his last descendant would be a marvelously good and pure warrior. Solomon wanted to give something special to this hero. It was the wise wife of Solomon that encouraged him to give this great warrior the sword that belonged to Solomon's father, King David. This was his true sword, not the sword of the giant which he obtained in battle, and which had been carried off by others. Solomon agreed that it was a worthy sword for such a warrior.

"It was she who thought of building a ship that would last for a thousand years with a beautiful bed. It was she who suggested placing David's sword upon this bed for the great knight to find. The hilt and scabbard were replaced. She told her husband that she would provide the belt. However, the belt Solomon's wife provided for this great sword was of simple hemp construction.

"She informed Solomon that it had been revealed to her in a dream that a maiden of royal birth and a virgin must replace the existing belt with a new belt, before the one of the chosen blood could wear the sword safely at his side.

"The scabbard of this magnificent sword is made of the skin of a serpent and has inscriptions which must be heeded, for only the one of the chosen blood may wield it safely.

"Solomon, at the urging of his wife, ordered the

construction this magnificent ship in order to let the chosen one know that his coming had been foretold. It was fashioned of the best and most durable wood by my personal craftsmen and was covered with rot-proof silk by a process that only I am privileged to know. Solomon bedecked the ship in all manner of splendor, placing within it the bed adorned with three posts made from wood from the Tree of Knowledge of Eden.

"At the dawn of time, when Adam and Eve ate the fruit from the Tree of Knowledge, they became aware of their nakedness and were ashamed. They covered themselves with twigs and leaves that they broke off of the Tree of Knowledge, to hide their nakedness. When they were driven out of the Garden of Eden, Eve took the twigs with her. When they found a place to settle, Eve planted the twigs in the earth. Eventually, one of the humble twigs grew into a large, beautiful tree that remained white as snow.

"It was under this tree that their second child, Abel was born. Abel was not only the favorite child of Adam and Eve, but also of God.

"Out of jealousy, the eldest son named Cain killed his brother under the very same tree which Abel was born under. Part of the tree was awash with Abel's blood and its wood became red.

"It was also here that God punished Cain. By the time of Solomon, the tree was still alive, and its new wood growth was now green.

"Solomon had a reputation as a great and wise king and was given three limbs of this tree in tribute to his wisdom by the King of Assyria. He gave these limbs to me for the construction of the posts of the bed. Using the natural colors of the wood, my carpenters were able to fashion a white, a green, and a red spindle. The virtues of this wood from the Tree of Knowledge will preserve this ship until the appointed time.

"When the ship was completed, Solomon had a vision of an angel coming down from heaven who wrote inscriptions on the side of the ship. On the side of the ship, the inscription warned that no one without complete faith in God could board the ship. Solomon, fearing that his faith was weak, did not board the ship and watched it sail off toward the west.

"Be warned, O man of virtue, that all these things are true and ordained by God. Take heed and survive. Transgress at your own peril."

That was where the scroll ended. Joseph looked up from the scroll at the others and said, "That is quite a tale, but one that I can believe. There are many things about the life of Solomon which are only now becoming known. However, it is well known that Solomon did have a large fleet of ships constructed. The scriptures tell us so. They say:

"Now three times in a year, Solomon offered burnt offerings and peace offerings on the altar which he built to the Lord, burning incense with them on the altar which was before the Lord.

"So, he finished the house of the Lord. King Solomon also built a fleet of ships in Ezion-geber, which is near Eloth on the shore of the Great Sea. And Hiram sent his servants with the fleet, sailors who knew the sea, along with the servants of Solomon.

"So, it is very possible that he had Hiram construct this ship as stated in the scroll."

As they were discussing the story, the Meglio noticed Josephus as he wandered over to the bed and picked up the sword laying there.

As the others continued debating the truth of the story, Josephus examined it closely. He verified that the scabbard was made of serpent's skin and observed that written on one side in gold and silver were words in Hebrew. Being a student of Torah, he could read the ancient writing.

"He which shall wield me ought to be more worthy than any other, if he bear me as truly as I ought to be borne."

On the other side, which was red as blood, was written in letters black as coal:

"He that shall praise me most, shall find me to blame at a time of great need."

He looked puzzled as he read. The Meglio watched him focus on the sword, which was partially withdrawn from the scabbard, and he saw more writing on it. So, he drew the sword fully from the scabbard and read. On the sword were the words:

"Let see who shall assay to draw me out of my sheath, if he be worthier than any other; and who that draweth me, if he be worthy, know ye well that he shall never fail of shame of his body, or to be wounded to the death."

As he stood seeming to absorb the meaning of the words engraved on the magnificent sword of David, the Meglio heard Joseph shout, "Josephus, NO!"

Startled, Josephus dropped the sword onto the bed and turned to face his father.

Joseph continued, "That sword is meant for only one person, the last descendant of Solomon. Drawing it from its scabbard means death for anyone unworthy to do so. What have you done?"

Josephus seemed unafraid and replied, "How do you know I am not the one of whom the prophecy speaks? Are not we, am not I, a descendant of Solomon? Do I not have the 'chosen blood' running through my veins?"

"That is true," replied Joseph, "but you may not be the last of the line, or the one who was foretold."

"But," replied Josephus, "I am without a sword at the moment, and this one is available now. I will use it and deal with the consequences, whatever they may be, later. Let us speak of it no more."

Joseph sighed. "I am concerned for your life, my son, but you are a man, and as such have the right to decide for yourself." He turned to the others. "It seems that we are being led by forces we cannot control. I believe these forces to be of God, and we should not be troubled by them. We are men of virtue being transported by a ship of faith. Let us continue in confidence and use the time to plan our next move."

"When we land, we must find the Mound of the Hostages. Are you familiar with that place?" asked the Meglio.

"I am," said Boudicca. "Very familiar. My father has traveled there many times, and I and my sister have accompanied him to honor the great queen Tea Tephi. He always told us that someday we may be called to fight as men do, and that we should honor the queen and seek to emulate her strength. He brought us there for inspiration."

"What can you tell us about how to get there?" asked the prophet.

"The Hill of Tara, as the druid told us," she began, "which holds the Mound of the Hostages, has a wide view over the surrounding countryside, allowing a view of many landmarks. The most obvious landmark on the east side is the Hill of Skryne, some two miles away, and to the northeast the Hill of Slane is visible in the distance. The Boyne River, although not visible from Tara, flows a few miles to the west."

"I know of those landmarks," said Joseph. "When we land, I will get our bearings and then head straight for the Hill of Skryne. From there, we can make our way to the Mound of the Hostages."

The Meglio excused himself to go check on the horses. Josephus accompanied him. When they saw that the horses were doing well and surprisingly calm, they walked to the rails of the ship and looked out over the dark, choppy waters into the yawning blackness. The Meglio broke the silence.

"Josephus, are you sure you want to carry that sword? The engravings and the story that Hiram wrote indicate that it could be very dangerous for one not worthy to wield it."

"I have no doubt," Josephus replied. "I felt drawn to it there in the state room. I felt a pull toward it and knew that it was right. The way I see it, since I have the blood of Solomon in my veins, even if I am not the final one to rightfully wield this sword, I am worthy. Who knows? The one foretold could very well be one of my descendants! If that is the case, then he resides in my body today. I suppose we shall see, won't we?"

"Yes, Josephus," replied the Meglio. "We shall see."

CHAPTER TWELVE

THE MOUND OF THE HOSTAGES

Jeff stood at the railing of the ship as it slowed and approached the unlit, deserted spit of land. It seemed to be the only safe landing spot on the forbidding rocky coastline. Even so, he experienced a feeling of dread as the time to go ashore drew near.

"Everyone, gather your things and prepare to disembark!" shouted the Gray Champion. "Stand with your horses and make sure they are not startled by any sudden disturbances."

The group quickly made their way to where the horses were secured and did as they were instructed. The ship continued its slow approach to the shore and came to a gentle stop. The gangplank began to lower, and when it touched land, the booming voice was heard again.

"Men of virtue, you have been delivered safely to your destination. The rest is up to you. Should you be successful, I shall return you to your point of departure. I leave you with a final warning; do not sully yourselves or abandon your virtue or faith. If you do, you will find me departed from this place."

With that, the team began to disembark. The sun

was beginning to rise over the water, and Jeff could clearly see a path leading from the shore through the forest and into the hills in the distance.

As they walked their horses over the wet and sandy shore, the Meglio asked Boudicca, "Do you recognize this area? Is it familiar to you?"

"I do," replied Boudicca. "I was shown this place once before. This is the legendary spot where, after abandoning the wreck of the ship carrying the princess Tea Tephi, the prophet Jeremiah and his scribe Baruch made landfall. I never paid much attention to those legends, but the people here revere this spot and show it to arriving dignitaries. This is the best place to start our journey. I will point out the landmarks as we go, we should have no trouble finding the Mound of the Hostages before mid-day."

The Meglio then called for the rest to join him and Boudicca. When they arrived, he put his arm around her shoulder and said, "You must lead us from here, child. Are you certain you can spot the landmarks?"

"I am, Meglio," she replied. "They are forever burned in my memory."

"Very well then," he stated, "mount up and take the lead."

When Boudicca mounted, the rest of the team followed suit. Soon, they were riding into the lush, green countryside rising before them.

As they rode the narrow, meandering trail, Joe kicked his horse a bit to catch up to his brother. "Nick, look at Boudicca. She is riding with no hands. And she keeps cutting off strands of her hair with her knife. Why is she doing that? It doesn't even look like she's paying attention to where she's going. I think she may be a little strange."

"That may be," replied Nick, "or maybe it's some sort of cultural ritual. You know, preparing for battle or something. But she is the only one that has been there before, and we need to keep up with her and the others. I don't want to get lost and miss the boat back to England!" With that, the brothers picked up their pace.

After a while, Boudicca halted her progress on the banks of a river. "We must cross here," she announced and pointed. "There to the east is the Hill of Skryne. We have only a short ride from here. Let's cross the river at this point and then proceed." She dismounted and led her horse into the waist-high water of the river.

"Looks like we're all going for a swim!" said Ty as he leapt off his mount and followed her into the icy water. The others followed, though not quite as enthusiastically as Ty.

After crossing the river, they headed toward the Hill of Skryne, and within the hour were at the base of the Hill of Tara. Boudicca was true to her word and had brought them safely to their destination. Now the real work began.

"The Mound of the Hostages is at the top of the Hill of Tara," said Boudicca. "We can't see it from here, but I know it is there. The Mound is rarely attended to, except on nights when there is a full moon or on special occasions. I have never seen it in the daytime, but at night, it is a terrifying place. It is said that there are many bodies of ancient rulers buried there, and that it is guarded by unseen forces. We must do our work quickly and depart before nightfall."

"We shall make quick work of this, Boudicca," replied the Meglio. "None of us have any desire to stay here any longer than necessary. Let's get to the top and see what we are dealing with."

As they rode up the gently sloping, grassy hillside,

Jeff found himself continually searching the horizon for signs of danger. He didn't know why, but he didn't feel safe in this place.

When they reached the summit, Boudicca pointed to the Mound of the Hostages. They dismounted their horses, tethered them to some standing stones, and approached cautiously. Jeff saw the hump of a grassy mound with a low opening surrounded by stone supports. The mound was encompassed by a circle of fire pits and a few more standing stones.

Off to the right side of the entrance was a larger, roughly carved, fan-shaped standing stone, wider at the top and narrowing toward the bottom, which was covered in strange symbols.

"Can anyone read what is written on this stone?" asked Jeff. "I think we might want to know what it says before we head in there."

Josephus and Boudicca approached the stone and examined it. Boudicca said, "There are no words or letters here that I can read, but I recognize some of the symbols from an ancient map my father showed me. The wavy lines indicate the ocean and the curved lines indicate a ship. The markings that look like X's are people in the boat. There are three of them, and they are transporting something square. It could be a box or a stone. The spirals indicate the wind, which looks like it is blowing them to a shoreline. That's all I recognize. The rest is a mystery."

"It's the stuff that you can't read which bothers me," said Robbie. "That always turns out to be the most important stuff!"

"It could be that this is telling the story of the voyage of Jeremiah and Tea Tephi," said the prophet. "It would make sense."

"That could be good news," said the Meglio. "Let's

not waste any more time. Remember that we are looking for only two items, the Lia-Fail stone, which may be the Stone of Jacob, and the Sword of Judgment. Do not touch anything else if you can help it. Let's just get in there and back out without too much disturbance. Work in teams of two. That way we can cover more ground and make quick work of this. If you find something, don't touch it, just call out, and the rest of us will come to where you are. Understood?"

"Got it, Grandpa," said Ty. "You break it, you buy it!" The others just stared at Ty and shook their heads.

As Jeff approached the entrance to the mound, he had to crouch to enter. As he expected, it was dark, musty, and forbidding.

"Lift your swords, my heroes," the Meglio instructed. "Their glow should be bright enough for us to search by."

The heroes complied and soon the gloom was dispelled by a warm, golden glow from the swords, which Jeff found comforting. They followed the path from the entrance down into the heart of the mound until they came to a series of what could only be described as rooms. They split up, with each team taking one room.

The rooms were filled with all forms of funerary items and the remains of people in groups of two, neatly arranged in hewn niches, around the perimeter of the room.

"Looks like they did everything in teams of two, just like us; even dying!" said Billy as he searched the room which he and Jeff were assigned.

"Stop joking around and just search," admonished Jeff. "We need to find those items and get out of here. Let's search near the corpses. Look for anything that appears to be related to the Sword of Judgment or Jacob's stone."

They slowly made their way around the perimeter of the room, but after an hour of meticulous searching near the bones of the dead, they could find nothing but some ancient stone axes and various articles of jewelry made from antlers and semi-precious stones.

"Let's go help Joe and Nick look in their room," suggested Billy. "What we are looking for is not here."

Jeff agreed, so they left and joined Nick and Joe in the adjoining room, which was much bigger and more elaborate. This room also had niches cut into all four walls, three tiers high.

"We came to help you two," said Billy. "It looks like you have a lot more searching to do than we did."

"Thanks," said Joe, "and we can use the extra light. Trying to see into the upper niches is hard."

They each took one wall and continued the search. Nick climbed up the back wall and balanced himself on the middle opening, stretching upward to try and see into the uppermost niche. It was dark, so he stretched his sword out over the bodies, hoping to see better. Suddenly, his sword, the Sword of Michael the Archangel, burst into flame. Startled, he fell backward.

"Are you hurt?" asked Joe, who was the first to his side.

"No, thankfully just shaken up," Nick replied groggily. "I *hate* when it does that. It should give me some kind of warning before bursting into flame and blinding me. How is that helpful?"

"What was in the niche?" asked Jeff. "It has only burst into flame a few other times, and always in the presence of virtue."

"What about at Stonehenge?" Billy asked. "There was no virtue there, yet Nick's sword burst into blood red flames in that environment."

"Maybe the place had anti-virtue?" Jeff dared to quip.

"I think they call that 'evil'," Billy muttered.

"You're right, Billy," Jeff agreed. "I was just trying to lighten the mood. My question remains, however. How can dead people have virtue that causes the sword to glow?"

"That's a very good question," said Joe. Then, helping Nick to his feet, he continued. "Get back up there, Nick, and see if the sword does it again."

"Okay," he replied, "but it may take me a minute or two to be able to actually see again."

Nick started the climb up to the highest niche and once again thrust the Sword of St. Michael into the darkness, this time burying his face in his outstretched arm to shield his eyes. The sword once again burst into flame. When he looked into the niche, he saw not two bodies, as with every other niche, but three.

"Tell us what you are seeing, Nick," encouraged Billy.

"There are three bodies in this niche, but since they are all bones, it's hard to know if they are male or female. Give me a minute." He struggled to lift himself up onto the stone ledge of the niche to get a closer look. "Their clothes are kind of rotted away, but it looks like they were all wearing long robes or dresses. A smaller set of bones is in the middle, a tall one is on the left, and a middle size one is on the right. Wait! I see something."

"What is it?" asked Jeff.

"It's a sword!" replied Nick, "Under the taller body. There is a tear in the clothes that lets me see through the ribcage. I can see it on the other side."

"Don't touch it, Nick," said Joe, "Let me go get the

others."

As Joe hustled off to inform the rest of the team, Nick continued to examine the niche. "Maybe there is more stuff under the other two skeletons," he mused.

"Keep looking, but don't touch anything," reminded Jeff.

Joe was back in a minute with the rest of the team. "Nick, we're back. Find anything else?"

"I was just about to look under the middle body," he replied.

"Be very gentle with the bones," advised Joseph, "We must be respectful of the dead and treat the remains with reverence. Try not to disturb them too much or change their position. We don't want anyone to know we've been here."

"Got it," said Nick as he carefully began to search around the smaller middle body. "I don't see anything under the body, but the head is resting on something. I am going to lift it a bit to get a better look."

He gingerly lifted the skull. "Hey, the head is resting on a rectangular stone," he reported. "It's dark in color and has some veining throughout. It's half buried in the dirt. It's as long as my arm and half as wide. Do you think that's the one we're looking for?"

"A stone that a skeleton is using for a pillow? I think so!" said Billy. "Let's get it down and take a look."

"Wait a minute," said the prophet. "Let him look under the third body before we rush into this."

Nick proceeded to examine around the third body for a moment, then said, "Looks like there is a scroll under the third body, what do you want me to do?"

"Get the scroll first," said the Meglio. "Maybe it will give us a clue as to who these bodies were and give us some indication if these are the items we're looking for."

Nick slipped his hand under the third set of bones and removed the scroll without disturbing them at all.

"That was easy," he said as he handed the scroll to his grandfather.

The Meglio then handed it to Joseph and said, "It seems that you and Boudicca are the only ones that can read anything around here. Would you open it and see if you can tell us what it says?"

Joseph gently unrolled the scroll, being careful not to harm it in the process. The others held their glowing swords above it as he struggled to read.

"It once again appears to be written in a form of ancient Hebrew. But it is one with which I am only marginally adept." He concentrated on the writing and finally announced, "We have found what we are looking for! This is a scroll describing the journey of Jeremiah, Baruch, and the princess from Egypt to this island. This is the confirmation we were looking for! Quickly, get the sword and the stone, and let's be on our way!"

"Nick," the Meglio called up to him, "get the sword first, and then we'll see if we can help you with the stone."

Nick quickly shoved his hand under the first body. Too quickly. He shifted the body a bit out of position. Slowing down, he grabbed the sword by the blade and carefully slid it toward him. He was able to obtain it without disturbing the body much further. Without examining it, he handed the sword down to the Meglio. He then focused on the middle set of bones and the stone underneath its head.

"It won't budge," reported Nick as he tried to pry it out of its half-buried position. "The dirt is pretty compacted, so I'm going to try to dig around it with my sword to loosen it." He shoved the point of the flaming sword between the stone and the dirt around it. The sword's flames increased, and as he drove it deeper and further under the stone, an eerie sound began to fill the mound causing the ground and walls to resonate. He stopped.

"What's that sound? Do you guys hear that?" he said.

"Yes," said the others, almost in unison.

"Keep at it, son," said Joseph, "We must hurry!"

As Nick got back to work, the Gray Champion said to Joseph, "Do you know what that sound is?"

Joseph replied in a whisper, "I have heard it before, when Nicodemus and I were wrapping the body of Yeshua for burial. It's the sound of angels singing their praises to God. It means they are pleased by our efforts. All will be well, but know this, we are not the only ones that can hear this song. Evil has ears, also. That's why we must hurry."

"I almost have it free," Nick reported, "but I need to move the body to be able to lift it out. Are you guys okay with that?"

"Yes, Nick," replied Joseph. "Do what you must. Be gentle, but hurry!"

Laying his sword aside, Nick carefully moved the skull off to the side of the stone, gingerly laying it down on the dirt of the niche, and then he hefted the stone from its resting place.

"It's *heavy!*" Nick called down. "It must weigh thirty pounds." He slid the stone to the side of the niche where Billy and Jeff took it from him and lowered it to the ground.

Nick repositioned the head of the skeleton so that it looked as it did when he started, grabbed his still-flaming sword, and climbed down.

The Gray Champion picked up the sword that Nick

had recovered from the niche. Jeff and Billy lifted the stone, balanced it between them, and they all headed up the long ramp toward the entrance of the mound. Leading the way, the Gray Champion was the first to reach the opening. He suddenly stopped dead in his tracks, blocking the way of the others.

"What's wrong, Robert?" asked the Meglio. "Is there someone out there?"

"Not some*one*," replied his father-in-law, "some*thing*. *Many* somethings, in fact." The Meglio squeezed past the others to get a look for himself.

Jeff peered over his grandfather's shoulder, and what he saw made his skin crawl.

"Snakes," the Meglio said. "The whole mound is covered with them. It looks like the ground is nothing but a writhing black mass."

"Those are venomous adders," the Gray Champion added. "We need to hurry. They are preparing to attack the horses. We need to get to them before the snakes kill them."

"Any idea how we're going to do that?" asked Joe. "I am *not* a fan of snakes."

"I thought there were no snakes in Ireland," said Ty. "What's up with this?"

"St. Patrick has not arrived yet," said Robbie. "He won't be here for another five hundred years."

"Right," replied Ty, "I forgot that he's the one that drove them out… rather, *will* drive them out."

"That's just a fairy tale," Jeff said, shaking his head. "The country is naturally free of them because of the climate and the fact that Ireland is… well, an island. Snakes have never existed here."

"Um, there seem to be plenty of snakes here now," Joe pointed at the writhing mass. "Maybe it's not natural, but there they are."

"This has nothing to do with nature, boys," said the Meglio. "This is a manifestation of evil. As always, evil must be overcome with virtue, and we have the swords. We must rely on them to get us through once again. Robert, lead the way. The rest of you, stay together. Keep the swords on the perimeter of the group and low to the ground to keep the snakes at bay. Those without Swords of Valor, stay to the inside of the group away from the snakes. Walk quickly and don't stop. Let's go!"

The Gray Champion took the lead and swung the sword they had just recovered from the mound at the hissing snakes closest to the entrance, clearing the beginnings of a path for the rest to follow. At his heels, the others followed with swords held out low toward the ground. As they moved through the writhing carpet of serpents, the snakes hissed and spat, but retreated from the swords. They moved quickly, and as they increased their pace, the snakes closed ranks and followed closely behind them.

"Even if we get through this and make it to the horses," said Boudicca, "I think we may have to gallop all the way to the shore to stay ahead of them. I don't think they are going to give up."

"We'll worry about that later," said the Meglio. "Right now, just focus on getting to the horses. They're really spooked and about to break free from their tethers."

The group once again increased their pace and within minutes were at the place where they had tied the horses.

"Let me approach them first!" cried Boudicca. "I have a way with horses. They will calm down for me."

"Okay," agreed the prophet, "but a couple of us with

Swords of Valor need to go with you to ward off the snakes. Jeff and Billy, accompany Boudicca, and be careful."

With Jeff on the left, and Billy on the right, Boudicca made her way the remaining ten yards to the horses.

Once again, the snakes threatened but could not get past the swords. As they neared the first horse, Boudicca began to sing in a soft, high-pitched voice. The first horse immediately turned toward her, its eyes wide with fright. Jeff and Billy thought he was going to attack her, but then his ears laid back, and he immediately calmed down.

As the trio continued to approach the horses, they noticed dozens of dead snakes that had been trampled by the panicked horses. Boudicca continued her sweet song, and the remaining horses calmed down, as well. They gathered the leads together, then called the others to approach.

The Meglio shouted instructions as they prepared to mount. "Joseph and I will stand our ground to keep the snakes at bay while the rest of you mount up! Billy and Jeff, wrap the stone in Joseph's cloak and tie it to the back of Boudicca's horse. She is the most skilled rider and can adjust for the weight imbalance. Once we are safely away from here, we can reposition it. But for now, that will have to do. Hurry, don't wait for us! Take off!"

Jeff nodded and handed Billy and Boudicca the reins of their horses. As he continued to ward off the snakes, he tied the stone to Boudicca's saddle, and mounted.

As they rode off, he looked back and saw his grandfather, Joseph of Arimathea, and their horses surrounded by a writhing, venomous sea of evil closing in fast. He shuddered, but kept riding, praying as he did that they would all be kept safe.

CHAPTER THIRTEEN

ESCAPE FROM THE DEMON VIPERS

Led by Boudicca and the Gray Champion, the group galloped as fast as they could down the slope of the Hill of Tara. Robert was surprised that the snakes didn't follow them, and he was worried about the two men they'd left behind. When they reached the river they'd crossed earlier, they stopped and dismounted to wait for the others to catch up.

"Do you think it was smart leaving them behind like that?" asked Malchus. "I am very uncomfortable abandoning them. I think we should go back in case they are in trouble or hurt."

"You know my father," said Josephus. "He is one stubborn old mule. He would have whipped us both if we'd argued with him or the Meglio. He will be even more upset if we go back now after having gotten this far. Let's just wait here for a while. If all went well, they should not be too far behind. Let's water the horses and prepare to continue when they arrive. Have faith, Malchus."

They and the rest of the team led the horses to the fresh-flowing, cold, crystal clear water of the river and let them drink their fill. The Gray Champion also drank from the river, only now realizing his own thirst. As he drank, he heard pounding hooves approaching.

"See?" said Josephus to Malchus. "Here they come now. I told you all would be well." Then he called out to the others, "Prepare to mount up, our leaders arrive!"

Everyone turned to the increasing sound of pounding hooves. The Gray Champion saw a cloud of dust arising from the trail on which they had just ridden. He could just make out the figures of the Meglio and Joseph emerging through the cloud of dust.

As the horses drew closer, the team could hear voices shouting but could not yet understand what they were saying.

"They sound pretty excited," Ty remarked. "They must be so happy to have successfully completed the mission."

"I am not sure that's a happy sound, Ty," said Boudicca, "I think they're trying to tell us something."

As the group watched the approach of their leaders, the Gray Champion could finally see the intensity on their faces and comprehend their message.

"Run!" shouted the Meglio.

"Mount up!" shouted Joseph.

Then, as they continued to watch, Robert realized that the cloud of dust was not caused by the two men's horses, but by the writhing black mass following them.

"SNAKES!" shouted Joe. "They've followed them! Hurry! Mount up and start crossing the river!"

"Follow me!" instructed Boudicca as she mounted her horse in one quick motion and spurred it into the river. "Give them their heads and let them find their own way. Just hang on, and they will get us across at their own pace."

The group mounted hurriedly, except for Ty. He

could not get up onto his mount, falling off the opposite side every time he tried. Robbie turned his horse back from the river to help him.

"Seriously, Ty?" he said as he dismounted, "You're the tallest one here, and you can't do this? And now, of all times?"

"The horse is sweaty, and I have too much adrenaline flowing. Just help me on and don't lecture me!" said Ty as he continued his struggle.

Robbie helped Ty onto his horse and then slapped it on the rump. The horse took off with Ty holding on for dear life. Robbie followed Ty into the river with a huge smile on his face, and his long, brown hair blowing in the breeze.

The team was almost to the other side when the Meglio and Joseph got to the river. The flood of serpents was not far behind.

They splashed into the river at breakneck speed and barely stayed upright as their horses struggled to adapt to the change in terrain. The horses slowed to a walk as they tried to navigate the riverbed after a long, tiring ride. When they were halfway across, the snakes arrived at the edge of the river. They continued to writhe but didn't enter the river.

"We should not have to worry about them from this point on," said Boudicca. "It is very rare for an adder to swim. I have only witnessed it one time."

"Well, you'd better make that two times, because one has just slithered in," observed Malchus.

He was right. One adder had overcome his fear and was swimming across. Dozens of them now slithered into the frigid water. Soon, the water was roiling with them as they entered the river by the hundreds.

"Go!" shouted the Meglio as he and Joseph reached

the shore. "It looks like nothing is going to stop them. Head for the ship, and let's hope it's there when we arrive, or we will be trapped on that spit of land."

"How far do you think it is to England?" said Joe as he galloped alongside Nick.

"Definitely too far to swim!" replied Nick.

"I don't know about that," said Joe as he looked over his shoulder at the army of snakes now filling the river from bank to bank. "If I have to swim there to get away from these demon snakes, I just might be able to do it!"

They rode hard and fast and put some distance between themselves and the serpents. The snakes had survived the swim, but the cold water cooled their body temperatures down enough to make them sluggish for a while, allowing the team to put some distance between them. They reached their arrival point in record time just as the sun was beginning to set, but the ship was not there.

"What do we do now?" asked Billy. "If we wait here for the ship to appear, the snakes may arrive before it does, and we'll be trapped. We're surrounded on three sides by the ocean, and we would have to fight our way through them in the dark to get out of here if the ship doesn't show up."

"Billy is right," said the Gray Champion. "We need to set up a defensive perimeter at the entry point so that if we need to retreat, we have a clear way off this peninsula. I will take the heroes, and we will set up a barrier. The rest of you stay ready. If the ship appears, board quickly, and we will follow."

"I'm coming with you," said Josephus. "I'm anxious to try out this sword I found on the ship."

"Very well," said the Gray Champion. "Follow me."

Then he, the six cousins, and Josephus rode back to the point where the peninsula connected to the mainland.

They began to gather rocks, branches, tree limbs and driftwood littering the shore. They created a semi-porous stone and wood barrier, which they knew would not delay the snakes for long.

But they only needed a small delay, since they had an additional plan which they hoped would buy them the time they needed. After they had piled up all the available wood and stone, they spread themselves out along the length of the barrier and watched for the approach of the snakes.

The others watched from the shore as the defenders finished the barrier. The sun had just set, and as the last rays of the sun disappeared below the horizon, Solomon's ship burst into view not fifty yards from the shore.

"It's here!" shouted Boudicca to the defenders. "Hurry!

The Gray Champion, having heard the shout and seeing the ship sailing into position, shouted his orders.

"Wait for my command, then initiate the process. I will wait until they are all aboard so that we have a clear shot when we ride up the ramp."

"Great-Grandpa," said Joe, "I don't think we are going to have the time. The snakes have arrived!"

They turned to look where Joe was pointing and saw the black river of snakes rushing toward them. In the gathering darkness, they could just make out the outlines of the mass of serpents as the rising moonlight reflected off their black scales. It was terrifying!

"Quickly! Initiate the process!" shouted the Gray Champion.

The six heroes lowered their swords and pointed them at the lowest points in the makeshift wooden barrier. They concentrated on the result they desired, and fire leapt from their swords and set the dry wooden barrier aflame. The army of snakes immediately stopped its progress and withdrew from the flames.

"Mount up and ride for all you're worth!" commanded the Gray Champion.

The team quickly mounted and began their race to the ship, not knowing how long the flaming barrier would delay the slithering serpents. Josephus had not reacted as quickly as the others to the Gray Champion's command. He seemed to be mesmerized by the mass of snakes and delayed before mounting up.

The Gray Champion reached the gangplank first and charged up the ramp leading the others. As he dismounted and handed his reins to Boudicca, he looked back for Josephus. The barrier had not held for long. The snakes had found a way around and under it and were hot on Josephus's tail.

"Someone needs to stay on the shore to hold off the snakes," said the Gray Champion. "The last thing we need is for Josephus to ride up this ramp followed by a thousand snakes. Snakes on a ship is not a good idea."

"I'll do it, Great-Grandpa," said Joe. "I think Excalibur is the right weapon for this operation."

"I'll go, too," said Nick. "If I can get this sword fired up again, that should keep them at bay. Besides, we always work in teams of two, right, Joe? Brother fights alongside brother. Why stop now?"

They hustled down the ramp and took positions on each side. As Josephus approached, the Gray Champion could see that some of the snakes had been able to attach themselves to his horse and were making their way up to him. Josephus was flailing his sword and fighting them off as he rode, but there were too many.

"Nick, we need to go out to meet him," said Joe, "and give him time to get up the ramp."

They ran to a point about ten yards from the ramp. As Josephus drew closer, they saw him slump forward in the saddle and lose hold of his reins. Apparently, the horse knew where it wanted to go and continued to run headlong toward the ship.

As the unconscious Josephus charged past them and up the ramp, Joe and Nick closed ranks holding Excalibur and the now-flaming Sword of St. Michael out in front of them. The snakes halted their headlong rush toward the ship. An eerie silence descended, and the Gray Champion heard the blood pounding loudly in his ears, nearly drowning out Joe and Nick's next words.

"Okay, this is good," said Joe. "Now what? Any ideas, Nick?"

"Not any good ones at the moment," replied Nick. "I'm open to suggestions though."

"Walk backwards toward the ramp with your swords held out in front of you!" shouted the Meglio. "Slowly, but steadily. As soon as your feet are on the ramp, stop and stand there with your swords outstretched. I will tell the ship to raise the ramp. Bend your knees and keep your balance as the ramp rises. That should create enough space to keep the snakes from boarding."

The two brothers began to slowly and cautiously back away from the snakes as they made their way to the ramp.

When their feet touched the wood of the ramp, the Meglio shouted, "Ship, raise the gangplank!"

Immediately, the gangplank began to rise. Joe and Nick kept their swords stretched out in front of them, keeping the serpents at a safe distance. The plan worked. As they rose higher and it seemed that they were finally safe, they thrust their swords into the air and high-fived each other. That threw them off-balance, and they tumbled backwards down the ramp, head over heels, and landed on the deck of the ship on top of the bodies of a dozen dead adders.

"Snakes! More snakes!" said Joe. "Why does it *always* have to be snakes?"

"At least they're dead this time," replied Nick as he helped Joe to his feet. "Count your blessings."

"How is Josephus?" asked Joe as he stood.

"Not good," Jeff answered. "They took him below. He had a dozen snakes on him when he boarded. As soon as he got up the ramp, the snakes dropped off him, dead. I guess the ship doesn't allow evil snakes on board."

"So, all of that was for nothing?" asked Nick.

"Not for nothing," said Joe. "Now we have another cool story to tell when we get back."

"I guess you're right," replied Nick. "Assuming, of course, there is anything to go back to!"

The Gray Champion came up behind them. "I'm glad you two are safely aboard. Let's join the others below deck."

Jeff led them down the stairs to the stateroom where Josephus had been laid on the bed. Joseph was sitting next to him, pouring wine from a leather wineskin onto his bite wounds and wiping them with cloth torn from his tunic.

"Will he be alright?" asked Boudicca.

"I don't know, my dear," replied Joseph. "It's in God's hands now. Only time will tell."

"Why don't we use the swords to heal him like we did all those other times?" asked Jeff, who was approaching Josephus and drawing his sword.

"Put your sword away!" commanded the booming, disembodied voice of the Ship. "His wounds are not unto death, but they are a punishment. Let the punishment take its course. Although he is of the blood of the chosen one, he is *not* the chosen one. That one will come generations hence.

"However, this one has virtue and is the bearer of the blood. Therefore, having received his wounds honorably, and being a man of virtue, he may keep the sword for now. He may wield it without fear of further punishment as long as the sword is returned to its place here on this ship after your quest is completed. If it is not returned, there will be retribution and sorrow. Know this and be forewarned."

"Thank you and praise God!" said Joseph. "We will honor your command and trust that you will arrive when we come to return the sword. You have my word."

"There is a final requirement," continued the Ship. "A maiden of royal birth, and a virgin, must replace the existing belt with a new belt before one of the chosen blood can wear the sword at his side safely. That must be done before you leave this ship. That is my final word."

"Where will we get such a belt?" asked Joseph. The ship did not answer.

"I've been working on that," said Boudicca. "I listened closely as you were reading the scroll from Hiram when we first boarded the ship. Since I fit all the requirements, I worked on the belt during our journey to the Hill of Tara. I only have a little work to do before it is finished."

Then she went and found her travel bag and returned. From it, she withdrew a beautiful, almost-finished, braided sword belt.

"I made it from a combination of my hair and threads I pulled from my clothing while we were riding to Tara."

Then shaking her still-moderately-long, wavy, red hair said, "As you can see, I still have a lot of material left to finish it with."

Joseph stood and hugged her. "Thank you, my dear, it is a beautiful and generous gift. I am sure Josephus will treasure it and be very grateful."

The Gray Champion started to yawn. He realized that they must all be as tired as he. "I'm thinking it's time to get some sleep," he murmured.

"Good idea," replied the Meglio. "You can sleep wherever seems comfortable to you," he continued as he gestured toward the various nooks and crannies around.

As they chose places to sleep while the ship sailed them back to Britain, Ty said, "I think I'm more hungry than tired. I wonder if this ship has cabin service?"

"You can ask," replied the Meglio, "but I doubt they will have any chicken cutlet parmigiana on this vessel. Just be happy that we have the Sword of Judgment and the Stone of Jacob safely on board and get some sleep. We can get some food and examine our treasures after we arrive."

Chapter Fourteen

The Arrival of The Women

As the women finished the preparations for their journey to the family compound in the Catskill Mountains to determine the fate of their loved ones, Susan found herself filled with energy and hope.

The last couple of weeks had been very hard on all of them, but now, at least, they were doing something about it and that felt good. She thought about the look of shock and disbelief on the faces of her daughters and nieces as they listened to the true history of the family, the revelations about the Swords of Valor, and the position their grandfather and great-grandfathers held as Meglios of the International Guardians of the Swords of Valor.

But, from personal experience, she knew it would not take long for the girls to adapt to this new reality. It had to do with the blood that coursed through their veins; the blood of warriors and heroes. She knew they would rise to the challenge.

"Let's go!" Susan yelled to the rest of the team. "The sun is almost up, and we need to be on the road before then. I want to get to the compound before dark. Are all the supplies packed and ready to go?"

"They are," replied Carolyn, sticking her head into the study. "Colleen just packed the last five-gallon tank of water. We are good to go."

"Excellent," Susan responded as she grabbed her guns and a huge wad of cash from the safe, then slammed it shut. "Get the girls, we leave in five minutes."

The first part of the trip went well; there was no one on the roads, and they made it to the Long Island Expressway as the sun was rising. That was a blessing, but they still had a long drive left, and some of it would take them through areas of recent conflict.

Carolyn glanced in the back and saw the five girls asleep in huddled masses. "It looks like none of the information we shared has bothered any of them very much," she said to Susan. "They are all out like a light."

"That's good," replied Susan. "They'll need their rest. We have no idea what we'll be dealing with from here on, but I already know that sleep will not be high on the agenda."

"Are you planning to stick to the highways, or are you going to take the back roads?" asked Carolyn.

"I think we should stick to the highways as much as possible, but it's really all about the bridges. I've heard that the Throgs Neck Bridge is still passable, but the Whitestone Bridge is gone. If we can get over into Westchester, we'll have options. The last report from the Guardians said that the worst fighting was around Kingston. So, if the Tappan Zee Bridge is passable, we can take the Taconic, circle around the fighting, and get to Freehold from the north."

"Sounds like a plan," said Carolyn. "But there are also reports that the fighting has moved south pretty rapidly. Since all the radio and TV stations were taken out in the first freedom forces' command and control attacks, we're going into this blind. We have no idea how old or how accurate the information we have is."

Susan reached into her backpack between the seats and removed two Glocks. She handed one to Carolyn and said, "You can sleep if you want to, but keep this in your lap. We must be ready for anything. It has a full clip and there are fifty more clips in the bag on the floor behind me."

"Susan," replied Carolyn, taking the gun gingerly from her sister-in-law, "I haven't shot a Glock in years. Not sure I could even hit the windshield from here in the front seat."

"Look," Susan replied, "if we have to use these, remember to point at the intended target and keep pulling the trigger. You'll be fine. Just don't stop pulling the trigger."

"Okay," Carolyn responded, but still sounded dubious.

Cell tower service was intermittent, but GPS seemed to be working this gloomy morning. Carolyn, as acting navigator, advised Susan as she drove.

"According to the current information, it looks like the Whitestone is still a mess and impassable. The Throgs Neck bridge might still be an option. Let's head for the Cross Island Parkway. That's the most direct route."

They found the exit for Cross Island, and it was clear. They merged onto the Cross Island Parkway and were starting to feel pretty good about their chances.

Then, as they rounded one of the big curves that wound around the bay, they saw it. Smoke and flames rose from the base of the bridge on the far side. The smoke was black and sooty, and the edges of it were tinged with deep orange flames.

"Susan," said Carolyn, "it looks like the bridge may

have been sabotaged. I don't think we should take the chance that the road will be passable on the other side. Don't take the exit for the bridge, we need to figure out another way. Pull over on the shoulder and let me try to rework the route."

"I'm not stopping the vehicle," replied Susan. "It may be the top of the line Guardian armored transport, but I am not going to test it unnecessarily. There is so much debris on the shoulders of these roads that deviating from the center lane could be trouble. Not to mention the roving bands of mercenaries. Any stopped vehicle is an invitation to attack. I am going to keep moving. You figure this out fast."

Carolyn agreed and kept reworking the route.

"Where are we, Aunt Susan?" asked Alex as she stretched and wiped the sleep from her eyes. "Have we crossed into Westchester yet?"

"No," Susan replied, "and I'm glad you're awake. Wake the others, too. We need all eyes on the perimeter now. Aunt Carolyn is trying to rework our route, since we can't use the Throgs Neck, and we need to start being very careful. The fighting has apparently reached this far south."

Alex woke the others, and in short order, Susan had eyes looking out of every window.

"I have it, Susan," said Carolyn. "We need to head for the Triboro bridge. Stay on 495, then take the Grand Central Parkway north,"

"Got it," replied Susan as she gave the armored SUV a little more gas.

Eyes peeled and searching the landscape for danger, Alex and the other young women heroes saw things that really brought home the level of devastation that they were about to venture through.

"Look," said Alex to her sister, Livvy. "Mount Hebron Cemetery. That was one of the largest cemeteries in New York. I remember passing this with Grandma and Grandpa. Grandpa said that the first burial there took place in 1909, and that now there almost two hundred and fifty thousand people buried there."

Livvy was not yet fully awake or engaged. "Yea. So what?"

Alex took her by the shoulder and turned her around to see out of her side of the vehicle. "Look at it now. It's a refugee center."

They looked at the massive cemetery as they rolled by at seventy miles per hour. There were thousands of makeshift tents and hovels set up around and among the monuments.

"It's one of the only reasonably open pieces of land that could be commandeered for the refugees flooding in from the upstate New York region," Carolyn explained from the front.

"How horrible!" exclaimed Livvy, empathetic as always. "Those poor people having to live among the dead! How can they do that?"

"People will do anything to survive, Liv. Just keep your eyes peeled, and alert Aunt Susan if you see any danger."

After getting onto the Grand Central Parkway and heading north, Katie saw more tent cities set up in Flushing Meadow Park and surrounding the Unisphere.

Katie always loved when the family would drive past that immense stainless-steel globe. Her father never failed to enthusiastically point it out to them, and then he'd tell them about how much fun he'd had when his parents took him. He would tell them that the Unisphere was the symbol of the 1964 World's Fair, whose theme was

"Peace Through Understanding", dedicated to "Man's Achievement on a Shrinking Globe in an Expanding Universe". He would make them all repeat it back to him so they would remember. Oh, how it was burned into their brains!

Now, as they passed by, it looked like the dream was dead. There was no peace, and there certainly was not understanding. There was only oppression, rebellion, and war. The Leviathans were not going away, and the freedom fighters had no chance.

Further along, they passed Citi Field, the former home of the New York Mets. As with all other stadium complexes, this one was now a dedicated military staging facility. It housed freedom force troops being trained and readied for transport up north. The freedom fighters had to use places like Citi Field, Giants Stadium in the Meadowlands, and Yankee Stadium for these purposes, since they had still not been able to overtake any of the local military facilities or forts. The Leviathans had hunkered down and hardened their defenses. The Leviathans knew about these facilities, but so far had not done anything about them.

As they took the huge, curving ramp that would take them past LaGuardia Airport, Susan suddenly slammed on the brakes and swerved to her left.

As the heavily-armored vehicle came to a stop, Carolyn saw what had caused the sudden reaction. There were two flaming, overturned vehicles blocking the two right lanes. That was not the frightening part, however. The major concern was the mob of masked and hooded men standing around the vehicles cheering and throwing brush and debris into the fire. It also looked as if they had taken the passengers of those vehicles and were now marching them off to who knows where for who knows what purpose.

The screeching of the tires had caught the attention of a few of the masked marauders, and they pointed and gestured toward it vehemently.

"Susan," said Carolyn, "I don't think we have much time before they come after us. Get this thing moving. *Please?*"

Susan, agreed but didn't say a word. She just slammed the vehicle into reverse and pounded on the accelerator. Tires squealing, she reversed to a point just beyond the curve in the road and stopped.

"Why are we stopping here, Mom?" shouted Colleen. "Keep going! We have plenty of room!"

"We need to get to the Triboro bridge, and this is the only way." Her mother replied. "Everyone, get down. I know these are bullet proof windows, but I am not sure they are 'flaming battering ram' proof! Stay down and hang on."

Before she could hit the gas, a dozen men with flaming torches and violence on their minds came tearing around the curve in the ramp. Not hesitating, Susan slammed down the accelerator, rammed through the men and their flaming torches, and headed straight for the flaming barrier of overturned cars.

Eyes set straight ahead, and teeth gritted in determination, Susan kept the pedal floored, eventually getting the vehicle up to seventy-five miles per hour. As she crested the ramp, she felt the heavy SUV lift off the road slightly as it slammed into the pile of cars and people and flames.

Instantly, the SUV was enveloped in flames, and she lost sight of the road. With a death grip on the steering wheel, she held her course. In a few moments, the flames died, and she found herself on the down side of the ramp and fast approaching LaGuardia.

"Everyone okay back there?" She asked with one eye on the rear-view mirror.

"Absolutely," replied Ellie. "That was *amazing*, Aunt Susan."

Since all was well in the rear, she returned her focus to the road and kept up her speed. In short order, they we over the Triboro Bridge and on Highway 87, heading north.

As they passed Yankee Stadium, they saw that it was now just a smoking hulk of concrete and metal.

"The Leviathans must be ramping up their offense," Carolyn observed. "I hope we didn't lose too many fighters in this attack."

"It looks really bad, Aunt Carolyn," Livvy said as she started to tear up. "I don't know how anyone could have survived. It's awful. Can you imagine what it must be like further up north near the family compound?"

Livvy's question just died there, since no one else was willing to express their fears. They just continued past the closed George Washington Bridge in silence. Susan knew that each one would be dwelling on the fate of their relatives and what might be awaiting them as they made their way toward the compound.

Many hours later, after a few more close calls and frequent off-road detours, the women approached the family compound. They found the road completely blocked by burned-out hulks of military vehicles and dead bodies, and Susan realized two things. First, that there was terrible destruction and carnage, and second, that they would have to walk through it the rest of the way to get to the Keeping Room.

"Looks like we are going to have to hike from here," said she as she put the SUV in park and turned off the ignition. "Take as much as you can carry. Focus on the food and medical supplies and carry as much water as you can. We have no idea if the well is still in working order. Leave the rest here, and we can come back for it tomorrow. It's only a two-mile walk from here, so it won't be too hard. Let's go!"

The women exited the vehicle and began to distribute the supplies amongst themselves.

"Why do I always have to carry the heaviest stuff?" Colleen complained as they loaded her up with a seventy-five-pound military backpack and two gallons of water.

"Because you are the strongest and tallest one," replied her mother, Susan. "And because I said so," she added with a wink.

"I'm twenty-eight years old, and I still have to do what my mother says?" asked Colleen, half-joking. "Things never change, do they?"

"Of course not!" replied her aunt Carolyn. "You'll find that out when you become a mother. We have absolute power!"

"Remember, Aunt Carolyn," said Livvy with a smile, "power corrupts, but absolute power corrupts absolutely."

"How do you remember all those quotes?" asked Alex, Livvy's sister, "especially at a time like this?"

"I guess I just have a photographic memory!" Livvy replied.

"Then how come you can't ever remember to do the dishes or take out the garbage in our apartment?" asked Alex sarcastically.

"I suppose I have a selective photographic memory!" replied Livvy.

"I don't even think that's possible," said her cousin Ellie. "It's oxymoronic."

"Let's not let this degenerate into name calling," suggested Katie. "Can we go a day or two without descending to that level?"

"I was not calling her a name," said Ellie, "I was just saying… Oh, never mind. Let's just finish packing up and get to the compound. I'm anxious to find out what happened to the guys."

They finished loading themselves up with supplies and began the two-mile trek to the compound. As they walked, they passed incomprehensible scenes of carnage and destruction.

"This is all so surreal," said Carolyn to Susan. "This area was always such a beautiful, tranquil retreat for us. To see it in this state of devastation is heartbreaking."

"I know," replied Susan. "We've spent a lot of time here since we were small and have so many happy memories. I guess that's all in the past now. Let's just hope the men are okay. If they were in the Keeping Room, there's a chance that they survived."

"Are you sure you can get us in there?" asked Carolyn.

"Yes," replied Susan. "As long as the power is still working, the code my father gave me will work. I am so thankful he had this emergency plan in place. I would have been completely lost if we didn't have a plan to deal with this situation."

"I guess that since you are also a family prophet, it was important to keep you as informed as Rob," observed Carolyn.

"Kind of," Susan replied, "but since there could only be one active prophet at a time, I was not kept up to speed on everything, just the fundamentals, such as the family history, the tools, emergency plans, about the Keeping Room and the status of the Swords of Valor. I was not in the loop regarding the day-to-day plans. We'll have to have the quantum computer fill us in on that. That is, if it's working."

"It seems like the guys have been gone for so long! Has it really only been two weeks since they all met up here?" said Carolyn as she made a wide circle around a fallen oak. "I can't even remember what the reason was. Why were they all here? And why did Rob bring the boys up here?"

"I'm not sure," admitted Susan. "I seem to remember that it was related to a threat to the swords, but now that seems wrong. It's all very fuzzy and jumbled in my brain. All I know is that with the world at war and all the uprisings around the globe, staying separated from them was not a viable option. We all need to be together. We need to face this as a family."

As the two older women walked and talked, they heard Katie shout from behind. "Mom! Look at the house!"

Susan had not realized that they'd arrived at the compound. They had been passing through what appeared to be the epicenter of the conflagration, and the landscape had been so altered that nothing looked familiar.

"I don't see any house," said Susan.

Katie was hysterical, crying so hard that she could not explain herself. As Colleen consoled her, Ellie, Alex, and Livvy came trotting up to explain it all to Susan and Carolyn.

"Katie said that we're at the compound," said Alex. "She recognized the boulder that marked the entrance to the driveway a little way back. It still has our names on it from when Grandma let us paint them on."

Susan looked at Carolyn in horror and said, "Could

that be right? That would mean that we are at the compound now."

They looked around carefully, and suddenly everything became clear. They could make out the site of the house, which was leveled. They then picked out the spot where the old barn used to stand.

"Oh, my!" said Carolyn. "Katie was right. We are here, but everything is gone! Obliterated. This looks like the center of the conflict. The destruction we just walked through emanated from here!"

Susan was horrified. Their loved ones may have been at the center of all this destruction!

"Quickly!" she yelled to the others. "Let's head straight for the Keeping Room. It's over there where the old barn used to be."

They abandoned the path they were on and headed straight for the Keeping Room. When they arrived at the remains of the old barn, they began dragging away debris covering the door. There were only a few stray planks hiding the control panel.

"Let's hope that's a sign that the men survived," said Susan as she input the code her father, the Meglio, had drilled into her head. She input the numbers and held her breath.

Immediately, Susan heard the clicks and whirrs that indicated the mechanism was active. She breathed a sigh of relief. When the sounds stopped, the door rose from its place in the floor to give them access. Without waiting for the door to completely open, Susan descended the concrete steps into the now brightly-lit but disheveled Keeping Room. The others followed.

Susan had been down here only once before when the Meglio trained her on the systems and protocols. She remembered that the room had been in pristine condition. Something awful must have happened for it to now be in this state of disarray.

"Dad! Rob! Are you here?" she called out as she made her way to the Tech Room. Bursting through the door and realizing that no one was there, she called out, "Computer! It is the prophet Susan. I have initiated Protocol 17. Security code 681955."

"Welcome Susan," said the computer. "Protocol 17 confirmed."

"Where are my father, the prophet, and the heroes?" Susan asked as the other women joined her in the room. "Are you tracking them? Can you put their location up on the screens?"

"I have them located. They have completed a very important part of their mission and are now traveling, apparently very quickly, to meet with their transportation back to England."

"England?" exclaimed Carolyn. "What in the world are they doing in England? How did they get there and why?"

"Actually, they are still in Ireland. They were taken there by the swords on a mission of utmost importance."

"All of them? How is that possible?" asked Susan. "Rob doesn't have a Sword of Valor and neither does the Meglio anymore. How could they have accompanied the heroes?"

"Things are different now," replied the quantum computer.

"Different? How?" she asked.

"In many ways," replied the computer. "If you and the others will take your seats around the table, I will begin the Protocol 17 briefing. By the way, you forgot to close and arm the Keeping Room door. I will do that now."

They heard the massive metal door closing. It was comforting, yet ominous at the same time. When the women were seated around the table, an image appeared before them.

"Welcome, women of the Cincinnatus and Arimathea family. I will be your guide through this process," said the image.

"Who are you?" asked Livvy.

"I am a temporary occupant of the quantum computer. When your grandfather returns, he may choose to program another representative. You may refer to me as 'Teacher', for that is what I am. Now, where shall I begin?"

Susan spoke up. "I have told everyone many of the things they needed to know about the family history, the compound, and the Swords of Valor. When we had not heard from the men for a couple of weeks, I contacted a couple of the other Guardian families, and they had not been in contact with the prophet for the same length of time. Then we saw the speech that the giant image made to the world.

"I knew I had to do something, so I called a family meeting and filled everyone in. We then chose the ones to make this journey to the Keeping Room to invoke Protocol 17. My husband, Bill, and brother, Domenic, are at home caring for the younger children and keeping the home fires burning. What we need to know is what has happened in the past two weeks and why my father, my brother, and the cousins are in Ireland and heading back to England."

"I see," said the Teacher. "That will take some time. Much has taken place, and I will need your complete attention and focus. All of it will sound fantastic, but I assure you that I speak the truth. I will include images of some of the events to prove the veracity of the story. Shall I begin?"

"Yes," came the unified response.

"Very well," began the Teacher, "I will start at the beginning."

The image started with Timeline One and the death of the Meglio, then told them about Azazel, the crisis season, and the threat of the Swords of Terror. He explained the assignments that the heroes were required to complete, showed the women the quantum images of the two Final Processes and the end result, including the changes to the timeline.

Then, he went on to describe the events of Timeline Two, the return of the Meglio, the destruction of the Apostles of Azazel, and their transmutation into the Leviathan Alliance. Once again, he related the missions of the heroes, the arrival of the Gray Champion, the survival of JFK, and the changes to the timeline.

Finally, he discussed the Timeline Three changes, the speech of the Gray Champion, what took place during the Battle of the Compound, and the abduction of the quantum form of their mother and grandmother, Catherine.

When he had finished this part of the briefing, he stopped and asked, "Are you all still with me?"

There was total silence in the room. Susan felt stunned into a state of bewilderment by what they had been told. She knew that if she was struggling to comprehend it all at once, the others must be, too.

She took a deep breath and spoke to the image. "What you have told us is more than just fantastic. It is frankly unbelievable. Do you seriously to expect me to believe that my father, the man whom I adored all my life and whom I would die for, passed away, and I do not even remember it? That, dear 'Teacher', is laughable. Then you tell us there have been three changes to the timeline! And then that some quantum version of my dead mother has been abducted by a demon Watcher! I don't know what kind of game you are playing here, but I want the truth. Not some science fiction fantasy story."

"I assure you, Susan, what I have told you and all that you have seen is fact," replied the Teacher. "The quantum recordings cannot be manufactured, faked, or altered. They are imprinted by the direct reception and recording of the quantum emanations of your family members and the Swords of Valor. They are truth. They are fact."

"So, you are telling us we should believe that this is the third timeline we are living in since the time Uncle Rob and our brothers came up here for a meeting?" said Colleen. "And that we only remember the events of the most recent timeline?"

"That is the truth, and that is what I am asking you to believe," replied the image.

"So, this nightmare we are living in and the horrors that have been unleashed around the world are all a direct result of the changes caused by our family?" asked Alex.

"Yes," replied the image, "but in their defense, it was all done based on what they knew at the time and for the right reasons. Regardless of the present result, they have had successes. Please remember that they were fighting against Azazel himself, who, as a Watcher, has incredible power."

"Sounds like Grandpa should have recruited the girls instead of the boys to handle this!" said Livvy. "There is no way we would have screwed it up so badly."

"That may be," replied the image, "but now is not the time for recriminations. Are there any other points that need clarification before I go on to explain the current situation?"

"Yes," said Carolyn. "I have a few points that are still unclear to me. You said that Susan's great-grandfather, Robert Ogilvie Petrie, returned and became the Gray Champion. I would like some detail on that. It is my understanding that he died in 1975. How could he have returned to 2016 and have done all the things you said he did?"

"That is an understandable question," replied the Teacher. "The answer is that before he became the Meglio of the Arimathea Family, he was a soldier for them. He participated in many missions fighting against the Apostles of Azazel. Some of those missions required time travel. It was during one of those missions that he crossed paths with the heroes and returned with them to assist them in their battle against Azazel. Does that clear things up for you?"

"It makes my head hurt a bit, but it does explain his presence. Thank you. My other question is about my mother-in-law, Catherine. You say that she started out as just a programmed image in the quantum computer, just like you. How is it possible that Azazel could physically abduct her?"

"Another valid question," replied the Teacher. "It seems that while her quantum program resided in the computer, it found a way to free itself from the constraints of the hardware. It began to explore space and time, and discovered a way to access the dark energy of the universe. With that incredible source of power, she began to draw quantum particles and dark matter to her essence and fashioned a hybrid quantum body. In that way, she was able to manifest herself to your family without the constraints of the quantum computer. It was this hybrid form that Azazel abducted."

"I have some follow-up questions," said Susan. "First, is this hybrid quantum form my mother or not?"

"That, my dear, is a mystery," the image replied. "Your father explained it to the group this way. I could not explain it better than he did, so I will just play the recording."

They listened as the voice of the Meglio was heard explaining.

"When you are dealing with quantum phenomenon, it is a very fine line. By now, you know from your last assignment that there are such things as 'quantum emanations'. These emanations are the signature of the quantum essence of a person. The computer uses the information I programmed into it and accesses what it can of the quantum essence of the person we are trying to portray in the image. It combines the artificial intelligence and personality information with the portion of the quantum essence it can access to create the image you see before you. In the case of your grandmother's image, I can say that it is also imbued with love. As I input the information, I was remembering our relationship and was filled with fond memories. So, who knows? Quantum essences combined with love can become profoundly powerful forces. Let's just interact with the image as if it is truly your grandmother and not think about it too much. Sometimes, questions like these have a way of eventually answering themselves."

"I echo his advice," said the Teacher.

"So, I am to assume that my mother is now in the hands of Azazel while we sit here chatting. If that is the case, then why aren't my father and the others doing everything they can to free her? Do you even know where she is?"

"First of all, they are doing what they must do at the moment," replied the image. "I have been monitoring their mission. They have obtained the last items that are needed to confront Azazel. That is why they are where they are.

"To your second question, we do not know where your mother is being held. While the team has been on their mission, I have been searching for traces of her quantum emanations and have been unsuccessful. Azazel must be holding her in a place that has quantum, or spiritual shielding of a kind I have never encountered before. I would not be surprised to find that there are spiritual powers in play here. That will make it all the more difficult to locate her."

"Do you think she is being harmed?" asked Katie. "I couldn't bear the thought that she is being abused or that she might be scared. We must help her! Is there anything we can do?"

"There is," replied the Teacher, "but now is not the time for that. Allow me to fill you in on the mission your family is currently undertaking. After that, I will show you the situation out there in the world. Then, we will discuss your contribution."

CHAPTER FIFTEEN

THE CAVE OF TREASURES

Catherine was aware that she was in a massive cave, but where it was and how long she had been there was a mystery to her. Azazel had not returned since imprisoning her, which was a blessing of sorts. What really bothered her was that her access to the universe and dark energy had been cut off completely.

After having experienced the unimaginable freedom and joy of being able to access every aspect of creation, being imprisoned in this cave felt like a second death. She had just begun to taste the wonders of the universe and longed to know more. As she sat there reflecting on her situation and fearing for the safety of her family, Azazel appeared before her, descending through the roof of the cave.

"Rise, woman!" he commanded. "It is improper to sit in the presence of your master!"

"You are not my master," she replied coldly. "You are my jailer. There is a vast difference. I choose to sit."

"I am both your jailer and your master," sneered Azazel. "That will soon become very clear. Do you understand what I intend to do? Do you comprehend the implications of my plan? Apparently not, for if you did, you would be trembling in fear."

"Enlighten me," she replied. "I could use a little excitement."

"Insolence!" shouted Azazel. "That is all that your kind can offer the greater powers. It is as I told God eons ago; mankind is nothing but a filthy, insolent, and ungrateful race. An unworthy creation of the Almighty One, corrupting themselves at every opportunity. It has been my goal to prove that to Him, but He would have none of it. I shall now finally take matters into my own hands and create my own beings, superior in every way to that of mankind. They will erase the memory of man from the face of the earth, and the universe will cease to be polluted by your presence."

"Why are you telling me this?" replied Catherine. "I am not human anymore. I am quantum. Your plans do not concern me."

"Oh, but they do! Indeed, they do, my dear," replied Azazel. "You are the lynchpin. Forget for a moment that you have a family that will suffer greatly at my hand. Forget that you will know great humiliation and pain. Just think about the immense glory of being my consort and the mother of a new species of hybrid beings. You will be, for the lack of a better comparison, the 'New Eve'. From you will issue forth a race of giants, the 'Quantum Nephilim'. What a proud and powerful creation they will be, someday ruling not only the Earth, but the universe, as well! Remember that I do not need your consent. I have declared it, and it will be so. Acclimate yourself to it."

"Is this dirty and dark cave indicative of the 'immense glory' I am to expect when I am your consort?" she asked. "It seems to me you are overstating your power. My husband provided a better place than this for me when we had next to nothing."

"You once again display the lack of perception so typical of your species," replied Azazel. "If you understood what this place is, what it was, what it symbolizes, you would be awestruck."

"Really?" Catherine asked sarcastically. "Once again, enlighten me, and awe me."

Azazel laughed, and suddenly the cave was alive with light. "This, my dear, is the Cave of Treasures! The home of Adam and Eve after their expulsion from Eden. This cave has unique qualities. It was designed as a refuge for Adam and Eve. God imbued it with special properties so they could be protected as their glorified bodies degenerated into mortal bodies. He permanently concealed it from the eyes of humans so that the body of Adam and his descendants would not be found and defiled.

"When God sent the flood of Noah, he set the limit of the waters so that the cave would not be inundated. It was one of the only places on the Earth not touched by the flood. It is impenetrable, inviolable, and undetectable."

"Then how are you or I here?" Catherine asked. "Once again, your exaggeration is growing tiresome."

"As is your continued insolence," growled Azazel. "Angels have always had access to this cave. God commanded them to minister to Adam and Eve after their expulsion, as he still loved them despite their disobedience. In my current hybrid form, I am an angelic being and a quantum being, fully angelic and fully quantum. I retain the highest qualities of both and therefore still have access to this place.

"You, on the other hand, are only quantum and therefore could not have gained access unless I brought you. For that same reason, you may only leave when I take you with me. That time is fast approaching, and then you will learn to fear and respect me, so take heed."

"Or?" she asked, goading him.

Azazel laughed once again and gloated, "Oh woman, I shall so enjoy humiliating you and your family."

"Before you go," Catherine said, "can you leave the light on? I would like to spend my last hours of insolence, before the darkness of my humiliation, in the light."

"Fine," replied Azazel, waving his hand imperiously as he rose through the roof of the cave and departed.

CHAPTER SIXTEEN

ANOTHER HERO RISES

When the Teacher had finished informing the women of the plan that the Meglio, the prophet, and the heroes had devised, and brought them up to speed on their progress, he asked, "Are there any questions?"

Alex raised her hand. "How do you know that Stonehenge is not the place of confrontation?"

"Because of the upgrades your grandmother made, I am now in constant contact with your family on a quantum level. I know what they know, and they have discovered that the place of conflict is not Stonehenge."

"Then, if not Stonehenge, where will they go to battle Azazel?" Alex asked.

"I have been working on that," replied the Teacher. "It will be either Mount Hermon on the border of Lebanon, Syria, and Israel, or Gobekli Tepe in Turkey. Those are the other two places on the Earth to which the angels fell. I have yet to make a final determination as to which of those will be the place of confrontation."

"Will they go directly from England and 37 AD to the place of confrontation?" asked Ellie.

"I do not believe that would be wise," replied the

image. "Although they can communicate with me through the swords anytime they wish, I would expect them to return and regroup before confronting Azazel. There will also be many details to work out before they are ready for the battle."

"So, we will get to see them before they leave again?" asked Livvy, excitement in her voice.

"That is a possibility," replied the Teacher, "but we have much work to do before their return. You must see the how the forces of freedom fare in their battle against the Leviathans. When you have seen, you will understand what must be done."

The screens in the room came alive and were filled with images from across the globe. There were scenes of mayhem and bloodshed, images of victory and defeat, conflagrations and bombardments, bravery and terror, blood and fire.

Before long, it became obvious that the New Freedom revolution was in trouble. They were taking losses after a period of success, and now, from the looks of things, the tide was turning against them. Although they fought with valor, they were tired and worn. They were becoming disheartened.

"Turn it off," commanded Susan. "We have seen enough. What is the purpose of this? We were aware that this was an uphill battle despite the inspiration and valor imparted by the Gray Champion. We know all about the battles taking place everywhere. We had to fight our way through some of them to get here. We understand. Tell us what it means and what the seven of us can do about it!"

"You must inspire them once again," stated the Teacher. "You must help to re-energize the revolution. You must make them understand and believe that victory is possible. You must be Washington at Valley Forge. You must be Churchill before the Battle of Britain. You must be Leonidas at the Battle of Thermopylae. Give them hope and a vision of victory."

"And how are we supposed to do all of that?" asked Susan. "Are you planning to have my grandfather give another address?"

"Another address to the world is in order," replied the Teacher. "It will have more impact this time, because the people of the world will be ready for it, and they need it more than ever before."

"Okay then, once again I ask, what does that have to do with us?" Susan inquired, trying not to sound irritated.

"You will be the one to give the speech and inspire the people," the image replied.

"*Us?!*" exclaimed Susan. "*We* are going to make the speech?"

"Not 'we'," corrected the Teacher. "You."

"Me?" Susan asked. "You expect me to make this address to the world? To people who are at death's door and struggling to survive? Why me? Why not wait for the Gray Champion to get back, or my father? Shouldn't they be the ones to do this?"

"No, it must be you, and it must be soon," replied the image. "You have all you need to succeed. Remember, I can read quantum essences. I see that you have the strength and power in you to do this. Your essence shines brightly, more brightly than any of the others. You are of the Prophet generation, which gives you authority. You are the matriarch of the family, which gives you position. Your quantum essence will give you the power and influence, which I will enhance and magnify with dark energy. You are ready, you are capable, and this is your destiny."

Susan was overwhelmed by the suddenness of all of it. She understood the urgent need to do something, but this was far outside of her comfort zone. She was confident in her ability to construct a well-crafted communication, but an address of this magnitude would require lots of time and research. Time they did not have.

"I need time to prepare my thoughts," she said to the Teacher. "This needs to be done right, and we will only get one shot at it. Can you provide me with the outline and the research? Quotes, concepts, critical points to touch on? If so, I can fill in the blanks."

"Yes," replied the Teacher, "I have been preparing it all from the time you arrived. I have printed a copy of my suggestions. Work with it and make it your own. Infuse it with your own personality and passion. You have an hour. While you are working on that, I will prepare the visuals. You will be appearing in quantum holographic form. I will craft an image that will be both impactful and effective.

"You will be seen and heard by virtually the whole world, at the same time and on every digital and electronic device, just as the Gray Champion was. Your holographic quantum image will appear at thousands of critical landmarks, cities, and historic locations and, of course, all of the current battlefields. Every person on the planet will see you in some manner.

"Not only that, but because of the changes your mother made to the quantum computer, I can access the quantum matrix of space-time to enable you to connect with each individual's quantum essence and touch them, influence them, right down to the subatomic level. It will not just be your physical image they will see and feel, it will actually be your own quantum essence, wrapped in a quantum holographic image, powered by the dark energy of the universe. You will experience things that you have never imagined possible. I ask that you steel yourself for this experience and commit yourself to seeing it through. It is not without danger, so be forewarned."

"So be it," replied Susan. "Let's get this show on the road."

Then, turning to the other women, she said, "I am going to need all of your brains working on this with me. Are you up for it?"

"Think about it, Aunt Susan," said Livvy. "Aunt Carolyn is an artist, Ellie is a songwriter, Katie and Colleen are teachers, Alex is a digital marketing designer, and I am a psychologist. Intellectually and creatively, I think we can handle this together."

"That is very comforting, Livvy. I agree," replied Susan, hugging her. "Let's get to it."

CHAPTER SEVENTEEN

THE TABLETS OF SETH AND ENOCH

After he ascended through the roof of the cave, Catherine felt pleased about her interaction with Azazel. She had gotten some of the information she was looking for, had not cowered before him, and she now had light. Light was a blessing. It made the huge cave seem somehow warmer.

It also showed her that this was not just one big cave. Apparently, the Cave of Treasures was a cave system. As she wandered about, trying to assess her environment, she saw that there were three passageways branching off from the main cave. She chose one path and followed it. The light that Azazel left behind lit the whole cave system, as far as she could tell, and made her exploration much easier. Coming to the end of the first path, she doubled back and chose another. Following this path, she came upon several roughly hewn "rooms". Each room was spotless, as if they had been swept clean.

Once again, she backtracked to the main cave and took the final path. After passing several similarly empty rooms, she came to an opening much smaller than the others. Entering this chamber required her to drop to her knees and crawl. She did so and began a journey which was much longer than she expected. Finally, she reached the end of the crawlway and stood up. The room she found herself in was lit by the light of Azazel, also.

As she looked around the enormous, cathedral-like space, she was awed. Along the far wall were three stone slabs. These slabs were lined up next to one another. As she approached them, she smelled the scent of incense. With her quantum-enhanced senses, she recognized it as a mixture of myrrh, cassia, and frankincense. She also noticed that the first slab had two crude, stone memorial lampstands, one at the foot and one at the head.

She approached with reverence, intuiting that this was the place of burial. Azazel had revealed that this had been the cave of Adam and Eve, and that might mean that they were among the bodies buried here.

Before she drew close enough to touch the slabs, she noticed many stone tablets lying at the feet of the middle and third slabs. She continued forward and picked up the first tablet lying on the top of the pile at the foot of the second memorial slab. The tablet was covered in markings. Some form of writing, she assumed. She focused on the markings and found that she could read them!

Smiling to herself, she understood that this was part of the enhanced knowledge she had gained during her brief time exploring the secrets of the universe in her quantum state. She read the opening lines.

"I, Seth, at the command of Father Adam, have recorded all that he taught. This is the true testimony of the Father of All."

She was elated. She had found the testimony of Adam, written by his son, Seth! She laid the tablet down and picked up the top tablet from the pile at the foot of the third slab. She read:

"These are the words of Enoch, wherewith he blessed the elect and righteous, who will be living in the day of tribulation, when all the wicked and godless are to be removed."

The book of Enoch! This truly is a cave of treasures, she thought to herself. Not knowing how much time she had before Azazel returned, she began to read, hoping to gain understanding and insight from the writings of these two great patriarchs. She read quickly and hungrily, internalizing every word and committing them to memory.

In reading the Book of Seth, she discovered that the Cave of Treasures was located near the top of a holy mountain named Charaxio, situated in the vicinity of the terrestrial paradise, Eden, where it had been inhabited by the generations of Adam. So, she now knew where she was, and where the mountain was located.

She also read about the fall of the angels and when and where the Watchers who fell with Azazel first assembled after being expelled to Earth. In the book, the place was called Grigori Tipi, meaning dwelling place of the Grigori or Watchers. Finally, she learned how to defeat Azazel and about the fate declared for him by God.

She was filled with hope and elation. She understood what needed to be done. Then, immediately, her joy turned to despair, realizing that none of this would matter if she couldn't communicate it to her family, and that seemed impossible. Still, she had to find a way. She returned the tablets to their original places and made her way back to the main cave to ponder all she had learned and to think of a way to alert her family.

CHAPTER EIGHTEEN

THE ADDRESS OF THE SPIRIT OF LIBERTY

"Before we do this, please give us a little more detail about the 'dangers' you mentioned before," Susan requested of the image of the Teacher. "Mind you, I am not afraid of them, I just want a chance to understand and to be able to deal with them when they come."

"As you wish," replied the Teacher. "As I described briefly before, to be able to project your image onto every electronic and digital device on the planet, and to make you visible at all the most high-profile points on the globe, I must access your quantum essence. I have been able to re-establish a connection to dark energy, so you will be empowered by it, just as your grandfather was.

"The danger is the same as it was with his address. While accessing your quantum essence, a bridge or portal will be established between the quantum, spiritual, and the physical worlds. It was through this portal that Azazel was able to breach the protection of the Keeping Room and kidnap your grandmother. There are no assurances that won't happen again. When the address is over, you will be in a very weakened and vulnerable state and unable to defend yourself against any quantum, spiritual, or physical attacks. The heroes used their Swords of Valor to heal the Gray Champion, but as you know, they are unavailable for that purpose right now."

"I see," replied Susan. "Give a speech, inspire the world, change the hearts and minds of all mankind, and change the course of history. Then come back here and become a helpless target. Sounds like a tough tradeoff."

"Don't worry, Mom," said Colleen, "We'll protect you."

"Yes," added Alex, "you remember what a tenacious defender I was on the field hockey and lacrosse fields? I won't let anyone, or anything, get to you!"

The others similarly voiced their support and commitment to her safety and protection.

"Well, with all that protection," observed Susan, "I should have no worries. Let's move on to the final preparations. Teacher, is the speech loaded into the quantum computer?"

"Yes. I've created it using concepts and quotes from other leaders and defenders of liberty. It has been loaded and integrated into the holograph," answered the image. "You, and you alone, will be able to see the words scrolling in front of you like a teleprompter if you need them."

"How about the imagery?" she asked. "What visual representation have you chosen for me?"

"I will be representing you as Margaret Thatcher," replied the Teacher.

"Margaret Thatcher!" exclaimed Susan. "Seriously?"

"No, that was just a joke. I was trying to lighten the mood," said the Teacher. "See how much your mother has improved the system? I can even joke now!"

"Well, stop it!" commanded Susan. "When this is all done and all is well, we will have time for jokes, maybe even some karaoke, if you can handle that, but right now, let's focus. Seriously, what have you chosen?"

"Most classical representations of liberty are female," the teacher explained. "They are portrayed in flowing gowns in the Greek or Roman style and are always holding something symbolic, like a torch, a lamp, a spear, a shield or a sword. I have determined the most impactful representation will be one where you are seen wearing a long, white robe, similar to what the Gray Champion was seen wearing. This will increase the familiarity quotient. It will be cinched with a golden belt and styled appropriately for a powerful woman of authority.

"The color white will speak to the purity of your message. Your head will be covered by a diaphanous scarf of sheer lace so your beautiful auburn hair will be visible. This will represent your mourning for the lives that have been lost in defense of freedom and liberty.

"Finally, I believe it would be best if you were holding a sword, since we are in a time of war, and you are, after all, a representative of the Guardians of the Swords of Valor. Is this agreeable to you?"

"Yes," replied Susan, "it is. Thank you for your work on this. Is all of that ready now?"

"It is," replied the image. "You may begin at any time. We have full connection to the dark energy flow, and your quantum essence has already been accessed."

Susan turned and addressed the other women. "Look, I don't know what the result of this effort will be. I don't know if I will be the same after it is finished, so I want to say something now. Please know that I love each and every one of you, and there is no one else in this world with whom I would rather have made this journey. Every one of you have the heart of a warrior. Whatever happens, always remember that you have my utmost respect and undying love."

"We love you too, Mom," said Katie. "Please be careful."

With one last look around, Susan took her place in the middle of the round table and positioned herself over the holographic projector. "I'm ready," she said to the Teacher.

"Counting down now," replied the image. "Five, four, three, two, one… Go."

As Susan stood there with her eyes closed, a light emanating from the image that stood beside her in the middle of the table enveloped her, and she was wrapped in multi-color rotating shafts of light. She felt herself becoming energized and sensed that every molecule in her body was vibrating.

When she opened her eyes, she was standing next to the Washington Monument, in Red Square in Moscow, at the Statue of Liberty, and thousands of other places around the world. She could see them all as if she was right there. She could also see and hear everything going on in the Keeping Room. The swirl of images and sounds was disorienting. She saw the smoking ruins of the thousands of battlefields, and the Leviathan troops and Freedom Forces clashing.

Through the confusion and the assault upon all her senses, she heard the image whisper, "You are now visible to the whole world. Speak from the heart, and all will be well."

She took a deep breath and began.

"Good people of the world! I am the Spirit of Liberty. You were inspired to begin this fight to regain your freedom from the Leviathans by my grandfather, the Gray Champion. He not only

inspired you but gifted you with power, virtue, and valor. I am here today to encourage you to use those gifts to continue your fight. Do not give up now, for victory is at hand!

"We draw our inspiration from those who have gone before. Those whose hearts, minds, and swords were dedicated to defending our liberty at all costs. They realized that our liberty, although it may be won at the sword's point, must be secured permanently by making ourselves worthy of it. When the world reaches that height, God will provide a weapon, the idols will be shattered, tyranny will crumble like a house of cards, and liberty will shine out like the first dawn.

"You know in your hearts that liberty will not descend to a people; a people must raise themselves to liberty; it is a blessing that must be earned before it can be enjoyed.

"You also know deep inside that the Leviathans have been lying to the world for years about their plans and intentions.

"There can be no liberty for a community which lacks the means to detect lies such as theirs. Over the centuries, the Leviathans have destroyed the means of detecting such lies by controlling education, the media, and the press. That is how they were able to steal your liberty. See through the lies now and know the truth.

"Thomas Jefferson said that the tree of liberty must be refreshed from time to time with the blood of patriots and tyrants. We know through painful experience that freedom is never voluntarily given by the oppressor, it must be demanded and fought for by the oppressed. Nobody can give you freedom. Nobody can give you equality or justice. As men and women afforded liberty by the Natural Law of God, you must take it; fight for it!

"Liberty lies in the hearts of men and women; when it dies there, no constitution, no law, no court can save it. Life without liberty is like a body without spirit. While liberty inhabits the

heart, it needs no constitution, no law, or court to save it. Josiah Warren reminded us that liberty is the power that we have over ourselves. Liberty, then, is the sovereignty of the individual, and man shall never know liberty until each and every individual is acknowledged to be the only legitimate sovereign of his or her person, time, and property, each person living and acting at his own cost and not until we live in a world where each person can exercise his right of sovereignty at all times. The liberty of the individual is no gift of government. It was greatest before there was any government.

"But liberty means responsibility, which is why most men dread it. What is your responsibility now and in the future? Ask yourselves, what is liberty without wisdom, and without virtue? It is the greatest of all possible evils; for it is folly, vice, and madness, without cost or restraint.

"That is why, when the battle is won, and you have given yourselves the gift of liberty once again, you must establish it with virtue, and it must be protected with wisdom.

"You have lived your lives as ghosts occupying a dead carcass. Now is the time to rise! To live again in true liberty! Despite the adversity and the bitter moments, again and again we rise. For Liberty! For a chance at a life of freedom! To fight on for future days and future generations. We shall draw from the heart of suffering itself the means of inspiration and survival.

"This battle, this day, is like the last rose of summer left blooming alone. This is your final chance. This is the day to seize the liberty you were born to enjoy. Winston Churchill's call to action is especially applicable today. Victory at all costs, victory despite all terror, victory however long and hard the road may be; for without victory, there is no liberty.

"Sun Tzu inspired us, as well. They may confront you with annihilation, and you will survive; you will be plunged into a deadly situation, and you will live. When a people fall into danger, they are then able to strive for victory.

"No one will save us but ourselves; no one can, and no one may. We, ourselves, must walk the path. The only defense which is effectual, sure, and durable, is that which depends upon yourself and your own valor. Valor is strength, not of legs and arms, but of heart and soul; it consists not in the worth of our horse or our weapons, but in our own selves. Strength does not come from physical capacity. It comes from an indomitable will.

"No matter what the situation, remind yourself that you are making a choice; a choice that will reverberate through the ages yet to come. Will you choose liberty or slavery? Choose wisely! And after you have chosen your course, and it happens that you are broken, or betrayed, or left, or hurt, or death brushes near, let yourself be brave! Let your valor arise. Pick up your broken sword and lead the next charge.

"Great crisis produces great men and women and great deeds of courage. Bravery is not a quality of the body. It is of the soul. Don't be afraid of your fears. They're not there to scare you. They are there to let you know that something is worth the effort. Thucydides defined bravery for us. He said that the bravest are surely those who have the clearest vision of what is before them, glory and danger alike, and yet, notwithstanding, go out to meet it. You must do the thing you think you cannot do. Remember, a true knight is fuller of bravery in the midst, than in the beginning of danger.

"Righteous struggle, not peace, produces virtue. As Steven Pressfield reminded us, war, not peace, purges vice. War, and preparation for war, call forth all that is noble and honorable in a person. It unites them with his brothers and sisters and binds them in selfless love, which shines forth brilliant and virtuous, worthy of honor before God. Do not despise this war, my friends, nor delude yourself that mercy and compassion in this instance are virtues superior to human valor.

"From my Keeping Room, I have watched sword ring on

sword, strength waged against strength, as indeed, the Leviathan forces of evil have battled the warriors of liberty. It is clear to me that you are intent upon seeing the battle through and winning the day with valor. For not by numbers of men, nor by measure of body, but by valor of soul is this war to be decided.

"Dwight D. Eisenhower's words are truer today than when he spoke them. The eyes of the world are upon you. The hopes and prayers of liberty-loving people everywhere march with you.

"In company with our brave brothers-in-arms on other fronts, we will bring about the destruction of the Leviathan war machine, the elimination of tyranny over the oppressed peoples, and secure for ourselves a free world.

"You have already inflicted upon the Leviathans great defeats, in open battle, man-to-man. The remainder of your task will not be an easy one. Your enemy is well-trained, well-equipped, and battle-hardened.

"He will fight savagely. But the tide has turned! The free people of the world are marching together to victory! The hate of men will pass, dictators will die, and the power and rights that they took from the people will return to the people. So long as good men fight for it, liberty will never perish.

"I, the Spirit of Liberty, have full confidence in your courage and valor. Together, we will accept nothing less than complete victory! Let us beseech the blessing of Almighty God upon this great and noble undertaking.

"The millions of people, fighting for the holy cause of liberty, are invincible by any force which our enemy can send against us. Patrick Henry said it best. Fear not, we shall not fight our battles alone. There is a just God who presides over the destinies of nations, and who will raise up friends to fight our battles with us. The battle is not to the strong alone; it is to the valiant, the virtuous, the brave. We have no other option. It is

now too late to retire from the contest. There is no retreat but to submission and slavery! Our chains are forged! Their clanking may be heard in every nation! Is life so dear or false peace so sweet as to be purchased at the price of chains and slavery? Forbid it, Almighty God! Fight till the last gasp. The world continues to offer glittering prizes to those who have stout hearts and sharp swords.

"This final battle is inevitable. Let it come! I repeat, let it come, and know that God is with you."

As Susan finished her inspirational and historic address to the world, the others watched the monitors in the Tech Room. They could see her image on the screens and see the impact she had on the people watching and listening to her. Many of them were in tears, others were cheering.

They saw vast armies, rising from their positions, charging toward the Leviathan lines, overwhelming them by sheer numbers and brute force. The forces of freedom were out-gunned, but they were not out-manned. The forces of freedom had hundreds of millions of angry, desperate men and women who were now so inspired that they were willing to sacrifice their own lives for the cause of liberty and freedom. It was clear that Susan had done her duty. She had turned the tide and very well may have changed the fate of the world.

After she finished, she stood very still and silent in the middle of the round table with her eyes closed, still enveloped in the rotating lights, by the side of the image of the Teacher standing next to her.

"That was so great, Mom!" said Katie.

"Yes," agreed Colleen. "Amazing!"

Just then, the lights stopped rotating, and Susan collapsed on the table.

"Aunt Susan!" shouted Livvy, running to her aunt and cradling her in her arms. "Teacher! What is wrong with her? Help her!"

Chapter Nineteen

Communication

Catherine sat in the Cave of Treasures, contemplating all she had read in the Books of Seth and of Enoch, desperately trying to think of a way to communicate the critical information she had discovered. Suddenly, she was startled to behold a vision of her daughter, Susan, standing before her.

In this vision, Susan looked strange but glorious. Although she looked very different, Catherine recognized her. In her quantum state, she could feel the quantum emanations of her beloved daughter, not physically, but emotionally. Catherine felt as though she were seeing her daughter with her heart instead of her eyes.

"Susan!" she shouted. "How did you find your way here?"

There was no response.

"Can you hear me, Susan?"

Still no response.

Finally, Catherine realized that she was seeing a quantum holographic broadcast, just like the one that she had initiated for the Gray Champion. She knew that since Azazel had told her that cave was inaccessible by humans and quantum beings, that Susan must not actually be there in the cave with her. Azazel had said nothing about quantum emanations, however. They were the insubstantial part of a quantum being. Catherine knew from her own experience that these emanations were capable of being felt and even heard if a being is connected to the other person by love. That's the key, she thought.

As Susan began her address to the world, Catherine contemplated how to take advantage of this fortunate occurrence. Since she was aware of the technical specifics of the process and all the quantum, spiritual, and dark energy aspects that went into broadcasting the quantum essence, she knew there must be a way for her to connect with Susan, quantum essence to quantum essence. She knew that nothing physical or material could penetrate the protection of the cave, but she hoped that the power of love, being emotional, would be able to transmit information heart to heart, quantum essence to quantum essence.

As Susan neared the end of her address, her mother stood and moved closer to the vision of her daughter. She reached out her hand and touched it. She could feel the power, and her hand began to tingle. In that moment, she knew what she had to do. When Susan was almost finished, Catherine stepped right into her image and stood there. She could feel her own quantum essence mingling with Susan's. The longer she stood there, the greater the connection became.

When she felt the connection was strong enough, she concentrated on what she had learned from the tablets in the crypt, feeling that Susan was absorbing the information the team desperately needed.

When the image of Susan vanished, Catherine stood silent, feeling very much alone. The cave seemed vastly colder and darker. After experiencing such a warm, full, intense, and intimate connection with her daughter on the quantum level, she now felt empty. Her only consolation was that she had transferred the critical information, and now there was hope. Whether Susan would be able to communicate the information to the Meglio in time to make a difference was another matter. Still, there was hope!

As she sat alone, in the very Cave of Treasures where Adam and Eve began their exile from Eden, she began to pray.

CHAPTER TWENTY

RETURN TO GLASTONBURY

After the Ship of Solomon delivered them safely back to Britain, Jeff disembarked and gathered with the others around Joseph of Arimathea.

"I suggest that we head back to the settlement," he was saying. "We've all enjoyed some rest on the ship, so we're in good shape to make the journey. I will make a quick stop to check on the status of the repairs of my ship. Then, I'll purchase some food and we'll be on our way. If that is satisfactory with you, Meglio?"

The Meglio agreed, and within the hour, they were on their way back to Glastonbury. They arrived just before noon, and after washing and partaking of some food, they gathered in Joseph's residence with the treasures to discuss the next steps.

Jeff was grateful they'd succeeded in their mission thus far, but he couldn't shake the anxiety he felt.

"Now that we have all that we believe is necessary to confront Azazel effectively, the only outstanding item is the venue," stated the Meglio.

"I agree," said the prophet. "It's critical that we choose the right place. But we don't have time to physically go to the remaining two choices and evaluate them in person. We must move this process along, since Azazel still has Mom, and we have no idea how much time we have until he sets his plan in motion. I think we need to contact the Teacher."

"I know that the image told us we could contact him at any point," said Jeff, "but we have not tested that theory since we left. Do you remember what to do?"

"I do," said Joe. "The image told us to do the same thing we would do when we perform a leaving process. We must stand in a circle around a fire, holding the swords out in front of us without the blades touching. He said that his image would immediately appear before us, and we could communicate with him."

"Impressive, Joe," said Ty. "How did you remember that? There was so much information given to us, I was worried that none of us would remember."

"Just part of the job of being a journalist, Ty," replied Joe. "I have to do it every day."

"Excellent," said the Meglio. "Now, before we contact the Teacher, let's discuss the items we recovered from the Mound of the Hostages and make sure we understand what we have here and how we need to use them. Joseph and Josephus have been evaluating them, so I now give them the floor."

"Thank you, Meglio," said Joseph. "Josephus and I have been very busy cleaning, examining, and doing some research on the objects we recovered. Let me speak to the Sword of Judgment first.

"Upon cleaning the sword, which was encrusted with dirt and grime, we found that it had actually been dipped in beeswax before being laid to rest under the body. We are certain that body was Jeremiah the prophet. This process has preserved the sword in pristine condition. It was easy to remove the wax and reveal what is, without a doubt, a golden blade. Once we verified that the sword was made of gold, we went to the scriptures for confirmation. This is what we found in the second scroll of Maccabees:

"Then, in the same way, another man appeared, distinguished by his white hair and dignity, and with an air of wondrous and majestic authority. Onias then said of him, 'This is a man who loves his fellow Jews and fervently prays for the people and the holy city; the prophet of God, Jeremiah'.

"Stretching out his right hand, Jeremiah presented a golden sword to Judas Maccabee. As he gave it to him, he said, 'Accept this holy sword as a gift from God; with it, you shall shatter your adversaries'."

"I believe what we have here is the true Sword of Judgment of Solomon. It was lent to Judas Maccabee to lead his forces to victory," stated Joseph. "Apparently, it was then mystically returned to its proper place in time and to its rightful owner, Jeremiah, and was ultimately buried with him in the Mound of the Hostages. I am greatly encouraged by this scriptural confirmation and believe that we have the same opportunity for victory that the golden sword afforded Judas Maccabee."

"That's wonderful news, Joseph," exclaimed the Meglio. "With such a sword, we can be even more confident in our efforts to defeat Azazel once and for all. Please, now tell us of the stone. Have you been able to confirm that it is the Stone of Jacob?"

"The only description I could find was in a commentary that I remembered from my studies. There, the stone was described as 'Sohareth', meaning 'black marble'. When we cleaned and examined it, we found it was a dull, purplish-black color, varying somewhat with some reddish veins. It's shaped roughly 'pillow-like', being about the length of a man's arm, half that in width, and a third of that in depth. It is very much like the stone I was standing upon in my vision when I inquired of the Lord regarding the cup.

"It is my belief that what we have is an example of the so called 'black marble' unique to some areas of Israel. I, for one, need no further confirmation. I declare the stone we recovered from the tomb of Jeremiah and Tea Tephi to be the true Stone of Jacob."

"Thank you," replied the Meglio. "Coming from a man of your considerable wisdom and virtue, we will take that as fact. Thank you, Joseph and Josephus, for your efforts on our behalf. It's confirmed that now we have all the weapons we will need to confront Azazel. The question on the table is how do we use them, and what will each of them do to help our cause? We are familiar with the powers of the Swords of Valor, and we have complete trust in their ability to protect and guide us. What can we expect from the Sword of Judgment, the Stone of Jacob, and the Cup of the Lord?"

"As far as the Sword of Judgment, I would take its name literally," advised Joseph. "I believe the sword will be necessary to impart the judgment of God upon the head of Azazel. Every trial needs a judge, and someone or something to administer that judgment. Since God is Azazel's judge, and since the sentence has already been passed, the sword will be the implement of that judgment.

"Regarding the stone, I believe its role will be to open the doorway to the heavenly realm. It will call both Azazel and the angels of God to the 'sentencing of Azazel'. It will, in effect, be the summons for them to appear in court."

"And the role of the cup?" asked the Meglio.

"That my dear friend, I do not know, but I feel in my bones that it is critical to a positive resolution to this confrontation. We will all have to wait and observe what role it may play in all of this."

"As always, we trust your judgment," replied the Meglio. "And who wouldn't want the Holy Grail with them when they are confronting the most powerful evil in the universe? Let's move on to initiating contact with the quantum computer."

The group exited Joseph's home and assembled around the large common fire burning in the middle of the settlement.

The prophet spoke to the members of the team that were going to be experiencing this process for the first time. He instructed them regarding the procedure and what to expect.

"You all know our story; we are not of this time. We traveled here by the power of the Swords of Virtue. We will be taking all of you with us when we return to our time and place so that we may consult with the Teacher to determine the appointed place of confrontation and to make our final battle plans. Joseph had recommended that we confront Azazel with twelve virtuous people, as that is the number appointed by God to represent His authority.

"At this moment, there are thirteen of us standing before this fire. The six heroes, the Meglio, the Gray Champion, myself, Joseph of Arimathea, Josephus, Malchus, and Boudicca. If any of you have any doubts or wish to decline the challenge before us, speak up now."

Malchus spoke up. "Prophet, I am no warrior. Before the Lord healed me, I was the servant of the High Priest Caiaphas. Now I am a servant of Joseph and of our

Lord, who healed me. I fear that I may fail you in this challenge, as I have no skills with a sword. Although I am willing, I believe that I can best serve by staying here with Anna and Miriam, protecting our settlement."

"Malchus," Joseph replied, "remember that Peter was but a fisherman when the Lord called him to service. It is not the skill of the sword that matters here, or the strength of your right arm. It is the nature of your heart and the strength of your faith we need. I want you by our side. Please stay."

"I understand and appreciate your confidence in me, Master Joseph," replied Malchus, "but I truly feel my place is here. My servant's heart, and my desire to protect your work here, requires that I decline the offer. Allow me to serve you and the rest of our settlement by remaining here and caring for it while you are gone. If something were to go awry, and you and Josephus did not return, at least I would be here to finish your work."

"That is very noble and selfless of you, Malchus, and I should have expected nothing less. You always think of others before yourself," replied Joseph. "Very well, you shall remain."

Boudicca then spoke up. "Master Joseph, I am but a young girl. I have been trained in the sword but have yet to see battle, and I am untested. Do you think I can be of service?"

Joseph replied, "Yes, my dear, it is my assessment that your innocence and courage will be a valuable asset to have in this confrontation. You are virtuous and brave, and you have been proven to have faith. Remember that you could not have boarded the Ship of Solomon without it. We would be honored if you would make the journey with us." The others all added their support.

"Very well, then," said Boudicca, "count me in."

"So be it," said the prophet. "Now, about the process. We will summon the image of the Teacher, speak with him, and request that he transport all of us back to our home. The trip will be unlike anything you have experienced before and will leave you feeling disoriented for a short while. Fear not, it is temporary and will pass quickly. When we arrive, we will guide you to the Keeping Room, where we will speak with the Teacher. Those of you without swords involved in the process, please hold on to tightly to the stone, the cup, and the Sword of Judgment. They need to come back with us, also." Then, speaking to the Guardians, he said, "Let us now initiate the process."

Jeff stepped into position with the others, feeling relief at the thought of returning home. When everyone was in place, the Guardians held their swords out in front of them over the roaring fire. They positioned their swords so that the tips were almost touching.

Jeff took a deep breath and concentrated on one thought; contact with the Teacher. Immediately, the image of the Teacher burst into view. Almost life-sized, the image of the ancient man floated above their outstretched swords above the flames.

"I see that you have decided to seek my help," said the image. "Is it time for your return?"

"It is," said the Meglio. "We have obtained what we need and now must determine the place of confrontation. The twelve standing around the fire will all need to be returned. Can you make that happen?"

"I can," replied the Teacher. "Have you prepared them for the experience?"

"Of course," replied the prophet.

"Then let us begin," said the image. "I am initiating the process now. Your point of return will be the fire pit by the river."

The swords began to glow, and the fire rose higher in response to the departure of the Teacher's image. There was a bright flash of pure, white light, and all twelve brave and virtuous warriors departed from Glastonbury.

Malchus stood alone by the fire, determined to do his duty, but speculating on what wonders he might be missing.

CHAPTER TWENTY-ONE

RETURN TO THE KEEPING ROOM

As the women gathered around Susan's fallen and writhing body, the Teacher reappeared.

"I have initiated the return of your family," the image announced. "They will be arriving shortly at the fire pit by the river. Please send a party out to meet them and bring them here immediately. They will know how to help Susan."

"I will stay with her," Carolyn offered. "The rest of you, go meet them. Stay together and be careful. It may be dangerous out there. The landscape is different than you remember, and it's probably getting dark. Go!"

Alex, Colleen, Katie, Livvy, and Ellie, rushed out of the Keeping Room, up the stairs, and out of the already open door into the remains of the old barn.

"Stay together, but move quickly," instructed Alex. "We want to get them back here as soon as possible."

"Yes!" exclaimed Katie. "My mom's life might depend on it!"

They made their way past all the burned-out hulks of Leviathan armored vehicles and fallen trees while struggling to stay close to each other. As they got near the river, there was a blinding flash of light, and they all hit the ground.

"Was that an explosion?" asked Ellie.

"I don't think so," said Livvy. "There was no concussion. Maybe it was them returning. Hurry, let's go!"

They resumed their trek, and when they arrived at the fire pit, they saw twelve people standing there.

"Dad!" Ellie shouted as she ran to the prophet and jumped into his arms. Alex and Livvy ran to their grandfather, hugging and kissing him.

"Well, this is *quite* a welcome!" exclaimed the Meglio. "We must do this more often. What are you all doing here?"

"Grandpa, hurry!" exclaimed Katie. "We *have* to get back to the Keeping Room! Mom invoked Protocol 17, and now she is hurt. You *have* to help her!"

"Robert, stay with our guests and make sure they get to the Keeping Room as soon as they are ready to make the walk," said the Meglio to his father-in-law. "The rest of you, head to the Keeping Room, now!"

The Gray Champion checked on the guests. Josephus seemed to have experienced very little impact from the trip through time, presumably because the Sword of David had protected him. Also, Joseph of Arimathea seemed in great shape. Perhaps the cup had also shielded him from the effects. Boudicca was in the worst shape. She had crawled over to the river and was now heaving mightily.

When the Gray Champion got to her, he said softly, "Take your time, child, it's only nausea. It will pass. It happens to almost all of us the first few times. All will be well."

Then he dipped his hand into the river and used the water to cool her face and the back of her neck. As he did, he realized how much this young woman reminded him of Catherine. So strong and so full of life. It made him more determined than ever to save his daughter and to keep this child safe from Azazel.

When the heaving subsided, he asked, "Are you well enough to walk?"

Remaining silent, and looking embarrassed by her show of weakness, Boudicca just nodded.

"Okay then," said the Gray Champion, "follow me to the Keeping Room." He reached down and took her hand, offering her support, and together they began the walk.

"What happened here, Robert?" asked Joseph as he surveyed the horrendous scene of destruction.

"This was where the first battle of the war for freedom against the Leviathans started," Robert replied.

"What kind of weapon could cause such destruction?" asked Joseph incredulously.

"This was caused by my daughter," replied the Gray Champion as he stopped to touch one of the overturned and melted vehicles, emphasizing his point. "She alone defeated the Leviathan forces, utilizing the dark energy of the universe."

"A woman caused all this destruction?" asked Boudicca. "She must be very powerful. Will I get a chance to meet her?"

"If we are successful in our mission," Robert replied gently, "I will introduce you myself. You remind me very much of her."

"Can she use such a weapon against Azazel?" asked

Joseph.

"Apparently not," replied Robert. "That's one of the reasons we need to destroy Azazel ourselves."

"I see," said Joseph. "We are going to only get one chance at this, I assume."

"Yes," replied Robert, "if we're lucky."

He pushed off the overturned vehicle and took a step away. Then something caught his eye. It was an orb of glimmering metal lying almost under the vehicle. Squatting beside it, he recognized that this was the same vehicle he and the Meglio had seen before their trip to Glastonbury.

Reaching down, he pushed a bit of dirt away and picked up the orb. He noted that it was cold and heavy as he put it in his pocket. Standing, he wondered what the quantum computer would discover about the strange Leviathan alloy. Time for that when this was over, he thought as he joined the others.

As they approached the heavy door, the Gray Champion smiled gently as he saw Colleen peeking out. Then her head disappeared, as she raced down the steps. He picked up his pace, racing down the stairs after her.

"Mom!" he heard her shout as she raced into the Keeping Room to her mother's side. "They're back! Grandpa and the others are back! They will know what to do to help you. Hang on."

As the Gray Champion entered the Tech room, he saw the Meglio kneeling beside his struggling daughter, whispering in her ear.

"I am here for you, sweetie," he murmured. "You are so brave and so strong! We will bring you back to us, just have faith."

"Grandpa," said Billy, "can we use the swords to help Mom like we did Great-Grandpa?"

"I believe so," replied the Meglio. "We all have the same blood running through our veins and gender makes no difference. There is a DNA connection that the swords will recognize. But first, we must know exactly what took place here."

The image of the Teacher spoke. "She was required to address the world in the same way that the Gray Champion did. The same process was used, and apparently with the same result."

"You authorized this? You allowed this?" shouted the Meglio, obviously struggling to control his anger. "My wife is in the hands of a demon Watcher and you thought it was a good idea to put my only daughter at risk, also?"

"I actually encouraged it," admitted the image with no remorse in his tone. "Based on my understanding of Protocol 17 and given the dire situation of the forces of freedom, I took the required actions programmed into the quantum computer for the circumstances. It clearly states that in the absence of the Meglio and the prophet, Susan would assume the acting role of prophet and handle any and all family business, up to and including offensive action. Her speech was not an offensive action, but it was still necessary."

"I would have hoped that there would have been some discretion used before exposing my daughter to such danger," growled the Meglio. "Have you been able to analyze her quantum state? Are there any other entities infesting her essence?"

"That's hard to say, Meglio," replied the image. "Her quantum signature is sound, but there is something else there. I cannot get a fix on it. It is powerful, yet seemingly benign."

"Well, one way or another, we will find out what it is!" declared the Meglio. "Heroes, prepare for the healing process. Stand around Susan with your swords drawn."

"Would you accept a bit of advice, Meglio?" asked the Gray Champion, gently placing a hand on his son-in-law's shoulder.

"Of course," replied the Meglio.

"Since there is a possibility that there is another quantum entity inhabiting her essence along with her own, I recommend that we kill anything that comes out of her before it has a chance to do any damage."

"How do you propose we do that, Robert?" asked the Meglio. "We have nothing that can harm a quantum being."

"Use the Sword of Judgment," replied the Teacher. "I don't have time to tell you why just yet, but it is your only choice. It has great and unusual powers. Trust me."

"Prophet, take the Sword of Judgment from Josephus and stand with the boys," commanded the Meglio. "When they revive Susan, if anything rises out of her, cut its head off, understood?"

"With pleasure," replied the prophet.

The Meglio addressed the heroes. "Proceed."

They slowly brought their swords into contact with Susan's writhing body, and Robert watched as they began to glow. It was a soft, golden glow which radiated warmth. As the glow increased in intensity, Susan began to struggle and strain. She thrashed about so much that Colleen, Carolyn, and Alex struggled to restrain her. At last, she let out a horrific scream and lay still. The swords stopped glowing and returned to their original state.

"What happened, Grandpa?" asked Joe. "Did we lose her?"

"Is she okay?" asked Katie.

Before the Meglio could answer, Susan began to vibrate on the table, and a form began to slowly rise from her body. The Gray Champion felt his stomach clench at the sight.

"Prophet, prepare to strike!" shouted the Meglio.

As the form rose further out of Susan's body, they could see that it was very faint and wraithlike in appearance.

Still, the Gray Champion thought, it could be dangerous and needed be eliminated. "Strike, Rob; strike now!" he hissed.

The prophet drew back the Sword of Judgment preparing to strike. When the head was fully visible above Susan's chest, the prophet started his slashing swing.

"STOP!" cried the Gray Champion. "That's Catherine!"

The prophet heard the command but could not stop the sword from completing its arc. He swung right through the form of his mother. The form disbursed like smoke at the wave of a hand.

Looking at the Meglio and his great-grandfather, he cried, "What have I done? Did I just destroy Mom?!"

CHAPTER TWENTY-TWO

GRANDMA SPEAKS

Billy watched in horror as the prophet stood, visibly trembling. Had he really just destroyed his own mother? The thought was too terrible to bear! As Billy was trying to decide whether to try and comfort his uncle, the misty form reconstituted itself and hovered over the body of Susan. It began to speak in a barely audible voice.

"Listen to my daughter, for I have imparted knowledge to her." Then the smoke-like image vanished.

"Teacher, record and analyze this; *all* of it!" shouted the Meglio as Susan began to speak.

"My daughter, I give to you now the words of Enoch and Seth, which are the keys to understanding and defeating the Watcher Azazel. They are words of power and hope. Tell the family to fight the battle, for the victory is sure.

"These are the words from the tablets of Enoch:

"And he said unto me: 'Observe, Enoch, these heavenly tablets, read what is written thereon, and mark every individual fact.'

"And I observed the heavenly tablets, and read everything

which was written thereon and understood everything, and read the book of all the deeds of mankind, and of all the children of flesh that shall be upon the earth to the remotest generations.

"And I saw written on them that generation upon generation shall transgress, till a generation of righteousness arises, and transgression is destroyed, and sin passes away from the earth, and all manner of good comes upon it.

"I know a mystery and have read the heavenly tablets, and have seen the holy books, and have found written therein and inscribed regarding them: That all goodness and joy and glory are prepared for them.

"I have given wisdom to thee and to thy children, that they may give it to their children for generations, namely this wisdom that passeth their thought.

"And those who understand it shall not sleep, but shall listen with the ear that they may learn this wisdom, and it shall please those that eat thereof better than good food.

"Then, I know another mystery, that knowledge will be given to the righteous and the wise to become a cause of joy and uprightness and much wisdom. And to them shall the treasures be given, and they shall believe in them and rejoice over them, and then shall all the righteous who have learnt therefrom all the paths of uprightness be recompensed.

"And when sin and unrighteousness and blasphemy and violence in all kinds of deeds increase and apostasy and transgression and uncleanness increase upon the earth, in those days, violence shall be cut off from its roots, and the roots of unrighteousness together with deceit, and they shall be destroyed from under heaven.

"And all the idols of the heathen shall be abandoned, and the temples burned with fire, and they shall remove them from the whole earth, and the evil ones shall be cast into the judgment of fire, and shall perish in wrath and in grievous judgment *forever.*

"And the righteous shall arise from their sleep, and wisdom shall arise and be given unto them. And after that, the roots of unrighteousness shall be cut off, and the sinners shall be destroyed by the sword, and those who plan violence and those who commit blasphemy shall perish by the sword.

"And at its close shall be elected the elect righteous of the eternal plant of righteousness, to receive sevenfold instruction concerning all His creation. And after that, a sword shall be given to the righteous and sinners shall be delivered into their hands.

"Woe to those who build unrighteousness and oppression and lay deceit as a foundation; for they shall be suddenly overthrown, and they shall have no peace. For from all their foundations shall they be overthrown, and by the sword shall they fall. Woe to you, ye rich, for ye have trusted in your riches, and from your riches shall ye depart.

"And whose souls follow after idols; for they shall have no rest. Woe to them who work unrighteousness and help oppression, and slay their neighbors until the day of the great judgment. In those days, the nations shall be stirred up, and the families of the nations shall arise on the day of destruction to know liberty once again.

"And your righteous ones in those days shall be a reproach to the sinners and the godless. Wherefore fear not, ye that have suffered; for healing shall be your portion, and a bright light shall enlighten you!

"Now, I read from the Book of Seth, words that were given to him by Adam.

"Adam wept before the Lord God, and begged and entreated Him to give him something from the garden, as a token

to him, wherein to be comforted. And God looked upon Adam's thought, and sent the angel Michael as far as the sea, to take from thence golden rods and bring them to Adam. This did God in His wisdom, in order that these golden rods, being with Adam in the cave, should shine forth with light in the night around him, and put an end to his fear of the darkness. And the angel brought the golden rods to God, by the Tree of Life, in the garden.

"Then God said to the angel, 'Dip them in the spring of water that flows from the Tree of Life; then take them and sprinkle their water over Adam and Eve, that they be a little comforted in their sorrow, and give them to Adam and Eve.' And the angel did as God had commanded him, and brought them to Adam and Eve on the top of the mountain upon which the evil one had placed them when he sought to make an end of them. And when Adam saw the golden rods, he rejoiced and wept, because he knew that the gold was one of the tokens of the kingdom whence he came.

"Then God said unto Adam, 'Thou didst ask of Me something from the garden, to be comforted therewith, and I have given thee this token as a consolation to thee; that thou trust in Me and in My covenant with thee.

" 'But, O Adam, put this token by thee in the cave; the gold that it may enlighten thee by night, to comfort thee in thy sorrow.'

"Then God commanded the angel, Michael, to give it to Adam. And he did so.

"And God commanded him to bear up Adam and Eve, and bring them from the top of the high mountain, and to take them to the Cave of Treasures. There, they laid the gold on the south side of the cave, for the mouth of the cave was on the north side. The angel then comforted Adam and Eve, and departed.

"The gold was seventy rods; these remained by Adam in the Cave of Treasures; and God declared that the cave be

undetectable and inviolable forever, therefore was it also called the 'Cave of Concealment'. But others say it was called the 'Cave of Treasures', by reason of the bodies of righteous men and precious gifts that were in it.

"These things did God give to Adam, on the third day after he had come out of the garden, in token of the three days the Lord should remain in the heart of the earth. And these things, as they continued with Adam in the cave, enlightened him by night; and by day they gave him relief from his sorrow.

"And when the prince of the lower order of angels, Azazel, saw what great gift had been given unto Adam, he was jealous of him from that day, and he did not wish to worship him. And he said unto his hosts, 'Ye shall not worship him, and ye shall not praise him with the angels. It is meet that he should worship me, because I am fire and spirit; and not that I should worship a thing of dust, which hath been fashioned of fine dust.'

"Azazel and his Watchers would not render obedience to God, and of his own free will, he asserted his independence and separated himself from God. So they were swept away out of heaven and fell, and the fall of himself and of all his company from heaven took place on the sixth day after Adam and Eve departed the garden, at the second hour of the day. And the apparel of their glorious state was stripped off them. And behold, from that time until the present day, he and all his hosts have been stripped of their apparel, and they go naked and have horrible faces.

"These Fallen Watchers built for themselves a place of gathering. It is called Grigori Tipi. There, they carved their knowledge on twelve pillars, revealing the secrets of the universe to mankind for their destruction to be revealed at the end of time. There are twelve pillars in a circle surrounding the two central pillars at this place. These Watchers are giants. They cover themselves with coats of feathers to conceal their fallen nature.

They possess visages like vipers and are as serpents in their hearts. Many of their number descended among mortal kind on the plain of Sanliurfa and did take mortal wives, who produced giant offspring called Nephilim.

"They eat no food, nor become thirsty, nor find obstacles. And these spirits shall rise up against the children of the people and against the women, because they have proceeded forth from them.

"These are the Grigori, who, with their prince Azazel, rejected the Lord of Light, and after them are those who are held in great darkness and took to themselves wives, and befouled the earth with their deeds. Who in all times of their age made lawlessness and mixing, and giants were born and marvelous big men and great enmity. The whole earth has been corrupted by Azazel's teachings and of his own actions; and therefore write upon him all sin. Azazel taught the people the art of making swords and knives, and shields, and breastplates; and he showed to their chosen ones bracelets, decorations, shadowing of the eye with antimony, ornamentation, the beautifying of the eyelids, all kinds of precious stones, and all coloring tinctures and alchemy.

"By his own teachings he shall be destroyed! Oh man, be warned, when darkness mixes with light a neither-or is born. But know that these Watchers will be punished both before and on the Day of Judgment."

Susan stopped speaking and opened her eyes and said, "Mom?" Then, looking around, she spotted her father, the Meglio.

"Daddy, I saw Mom," she said. "I saw her in a cave. She came to me and touched me. I've never felt such love, joy, and warmth. Is she here? Is she safe?"

"Shh, just rest, sweetie," said the Meglio running his hand over her brow. "Rest, and we shall discuss this later when you feel better. I am so proud of you. You have your mother's strength and the heart of a lion."

"I'll stay with her, Dad," Carolyn said to her father-in-law. "You all go and deal with the information that she just gave us. Just figure this all out so we can get Mom back, please."

With Susan recovering, introductions and an orientation were in order.

"It's certainly a blessing to have so much of my family here safe and together at this dangerous time," the Meglio began. "My beautiful and brave granddaughters, daughter-in-law, my daughter, son, and grandsons. But we have a few more relatives that I need to introduce."

He turned and gestured toward Joseph and the others in turn. "I would like to introduce to you one of the revered patriarchs of the family, Joseph of Arimathea, his son Josephus, and the royal ward of Joseph, Boudicca, Princess of the Iceni tribe. They will be accompanying us and fighting by our side when we confront Azazel. Their help has been essential to our success to this point, and without them, we would not have been able to obtain the three sacred items so critical to our victory."

Livvy was beside herself with excitement. "Did you say Boudicca? You mean the very same Boudicca from British history? The one who led an uprising against the occupying forces of the Roman Empire?"

At this point, her sister Alex put her hand over Livvy's mouth to stop her from revealing more of Boudicca's future and said, "I think what my sister is trying to say is that she is very happy to meet you. We are all thrilled to meet you."

Tearing Alex's hand from her mouth Livvy said, "Why did you do that, Alex, that was so *rude*! I was just trying to find out if she is the same person who—"

Once again, Alex, this time joined by Ellie, covered Livvy's mouth and started to drag her into the next room as she struggled against them.

"Excuse us," Alex said. "We just need to talk to my sister for a minute."

Jeff grinned and took a couple of sideways steps toward the doorway. His grin broadened as he heard the girls struggling to keep Livvy quiet to no avail.

"Have you two lost your mind?" Livvy sputtered. "What was that all about?"

"Livvy," said Alex, "you can't go spouting off about the future of these people. They are from the *past*. Maybe it's not good for them to know their future. You could say something that might change history, and that would be bad. Didn't you learn anything from *Doctor Who* and all those time travel stories you've read?"

"Oh dear! I didn't think about that," replied Livvy, sounding chagrinned. "I was just so excited to meet her. She's one of my favorite heroes from history. She led an army against the Romans and almost won. It's an incredible story!"

"Well then, let's keep it that way and not say anything more about it," advised Ellie. "We don't want you to lose your heroine."

"All right," said Livvy, "but don't *ever* do that again. Keep your grimy hands to yourselves, understood?"

Alex and Ellie put their arms around Livvy and said, "You got it," as they walked back into the Tech Room.

When they returned, Jeff caught Alex's eye and gave her a thumbs up. She grinned and nodded, then they joined the others as they mingled and discussed the new arrivals and how thrilled they were to meet them all. Colleen and Katie were discussing Josephus.

"I read about him in some the research I did on the

Holy Grail legends," said Colleen. "He was the keeper of the Holy Grail after Joseph of Arimathea died. Some of the legends even say that Josephus was the first and greatest knight, and that all the others were given their knighthood from him. Even Galahad, whom they say was his great-grandson. Apparently, he was really a great warrior but also the first Bishop of England. The first warrior priest of England."

"I had read some of that but never read the stuff about Josephus," said Katie. "How cool is it that we are related to him? Kind of connects us to the Knights of the Round Table!"

"Okay, everyone," said the Meglio, "I'm sorry to interrupt this family reunion, but we have urgent business at hand. We must discuss the information given to us by your grandmother through your aunt, Susan. Please take seats around the table."

The round table was huge, but not big enough for all of them to sit around. "Elders around the table and the youngest please stand behind those seated," instructed the Meglio.

Joseph of Arimathea, the Gray Champion, the Meglio and the prophet and Josephus took seats. Next was Billy, then Jeff, then Joe and Robbie and Nick. Katie and Colleen joined them, along with Alex. The rest, Ty, Livvy, Ellie and Boudicca stood behind the others. "Looks like we still have to sit at the kiddie table," whispered Ty to Livvy and Ellie, causing them to giggle.

When everyone was settled, The Meglio summoned the Teacher. "Teacher, please join us." The image of the teacher appeared in the middle of the round table.

"You heard and recorded all that was given to us by Catherine through Susan," said the Meglio. "Please tell us what your analysis of the information revealed."

CHAPTER TWENTY-THREE

THE SITE OF THE FINAL CONFRONTATION

"Based on the information given through Susan, and from the segments of the ancient tablets Catherine imparted to her, I know where she is being held," announced the Teacher. "She is imprisoned in the cave referred to as the Cave of Treasures located on Mount Charaxio in the Eastern Taurus Mountains, overlooking the traditional site of the Garden of Eden. My analysis has turned up confirming references in the Nag Hammadi library in Alexandria, Egypt. There, the book known as the 'Gospel of the Egyptians' reads:

"This is the book which the great Seth wrote and placed on a high mountain, where the sun has not risen, nor is it possible. And since the days of the prophets, and the apostles, and the preachers, the name has not risen upon their hearts, nor is it possible an ear has not heard it. The great Seth wrote this book with letters in one hundred and thirty years. He placed it in the mountain that is called Charaxio, in order that in the end of the times, and the eras, it may come forth and reveal this incorruptible holy place.

"These are truly enigmatic words, for they speak of a book concealed 'in' a mountain, the location of which, and even the name thereof, has not been uttered since the time of Seth. But here, we have the name revealed in this text. But, you may ask, where is Charaxio, the true hiding place of the secrets of Adam?

"Charaxio is said to be located where the sun has not risen, nor is it possible. I recognize this statement as referring to the Land of Darkness. This land was outside of the place that God chose for Eden, and it is where the Watchers aligned with Azazel, descended to Earth, and began to take mortal wives. It is called the Land of Darkness because of this transgression and because it is virtually impenetrable due to the vast ranges of the Taurus Mountains surrounding it.

"I can confirm that Mount Charaxio overlooks Eden and the Land of Darkness, for I have read the Book of Seth myself, and I have seen the pillars that Azazel carved to reveal and memorialize the secrets of the Watchers. They are located at the place of confrontation. We heard Susan refer to this place as Grigori Tipi. It is known in your time as Gobekli Tepe, situated on the plain of Sanliurfa, in southeastern Turkey, fifty miles east of the Euphrates River."

"That's wonderful news, Teacher!" exclaimed the Meglio. "But I have an additional question. You said that you, yourself, have read the Book of Seth and that you have seen the pillars carved by Seth at the place of confrontation? How is this? And why have you not given us this information before?"

"In order to answer your question, I must now reveal to you my true name. It will make all things clear," stated the image. "I am Enoch, son of Jared, father of Methuselah, the seventh generation from Adam. I am the author of the Book of Enoch. I am referred to as the Scribe of Judgment and lived on the Earth for three hundred and sixty-five years before I was taken by God to be with him in heaven. My name means 'dedicated or initiated teacher'. That is my purpose. That is why I was sent to you. To teach you the things you need to know to be able to initiate the judgment of Azazel."

"You are Enoch?" asked the prophet. "The real and biblical Enoch?"

"I am," replied the image of Enoch.

"Then, you could have told us all of this from the very beginning," replied the prophet, anger in his tone. "Why didn't you reveal all of this, so that we didn't have to suffer with the thought of my mother being held by Azazel for so long? We could have saved ourselves the trip to Britain and have rescued her by now."

"You did not have what was needed," replied the image of Enoch. "Because of your trip to Britain, you are now fully armed for the confrontation. The best teachers lead their students and allow them to educate themselves and reach their own understanding. True knowledge must be earned, and it must come from within. Everything you have gone through to this point has been part of a necessary process. You are finally ready."

"Are you a quantum being?" asked the Gray Champion. "Is that how you have access to the quantum computer?"

"No, I am a spiritual being," replied the image of Enoch. "When I was translated to heaven, that was the form I was translated into. But all spiritual beings have access to all of God's creation, including the quantum aspects. I am here by the will of God."

The Gray Champion still looked puzzled. "Earlier, when we were trying to heal my granddaughter, Susan, you said that we needed to use the Sword of Judgment to destroy any evil entity which might rise from her body. Why didn't you know it was Catherine? You also said that you would tell us later why this sword would be effective to that end. Please reveal that information to us now."

"Yes," replied the image of Enoch. "It is time for that information. First, I am spirit, but I am not all-knowing. Only the Maker of Heaven and Earth is omniscient. The reason that the Sword of Judgment was required is that it is the only sword on Earth made from the golden rods that God gave to Adam for his enlightenment and comfort.

"As you recall from what was revealed to you from the Book of Seth, these rods were dipped into the water that flowed from the Tree of Life at the center of the Garden of Eden. They were infused with the life force, what is known to you as 'quintessence' from that tree. When used on humans, the gold of this sword can impart comfort, understanding, life, and healing. When used against demons, it brings death. That is why I told you to use it to protect yourselves."

"Is that why it did not destroy the quantum essence of my mother when I swung the sword to destroy what was emerging from Susan?" asked the prophet.

"That is correct," replied Enoch.

"So how did the rods of gold that God gave to Adam get made into the Sword of Judgment, and how did it get into the hands of Solomon?" asked Ellie.

"Ellie, as I am sure you remember from the scriptures," replied Enoch, "Solomon had a dream in which the Lord said that he could have anything his heart desired. Solomon's answer was, 'So give your servant an understanding heart to judge your people to discern between good and evil. For who is able to judge this great people of yours?'

"God said to him, 'Because you have asked this thing and have not asked for yourself long life, nor have asked riches for yourself, nor have you asked for the life of your enemies, but have asked for yourself discernment to understand justice, behold, I have done according to your words. Behold, I have given you a wise and discerning heart, so that there has been no one like you before you, nor shall one like you arise after you. I have also given you what you have not asked for, both riches and honor, so that there will not be any among the kings like you all your days.'

"One of the 'riches' that God gave to Solomon to fulfill his request for wisdom and God's reward for not asking for wealth or long life, was Adam's gold from the Cave of Treasures.

"At the instruction of Michael the Archangel, Solomon then fashioned the Sword of Judgment from some of the gold. In this way, he ensured that he would always judge God's people with wisdom and discernment. When he judged, he was always in possession of the sword, which ensured a correct verdict. Do you now understand?"

"I do," replied Ellie.

"There is more," Enoch continued. "The Cup of the Lord was also fashioned from this same gold. Joseph of Arimathea, I know you are familiar with the history of the cup as the keeper of it, but it had not been revealed to you before that the gold given to Solomon by the angel of God, which he used to fashion the cup, was the very same gold that God gave to Adam. It was infused with quintessence from the Tree of Life. So, the cup you keep has the same power over evil that the sword has, possibly more."

"That's why when you were telling us about it, you referred to it as the Cup of Quintessence!" exclaimed Jeff. "Now I understand. It would seem that we have two very powerful Watcher weapons in our possession. That's very good news."

"Yes, that is true," replied the image of Enoch, "They are weapons of life, and it is fitting that they be used to defeat Azazel, since he showed man how to make weapons of war and death. But they must be used by people of the highest virtue and wisdom. Joseph must wield the cup, but make sure that you choose wisely who will wield the sword."

"Before we make that choice," said the Meglio, "we need to know more about the place of confrontation. You said this place is called Gobekli Tepe. Please tell us all we need to know about this place."

"Of course," said the image of Enoch. "As stated earlier, it is the place of falling. It is the exact spot where the rebel angels aligned with Azazel fell to earth, and where they began to take human wives. Using their vast knowledge and strength, they erected twelve huge, megalithic, T-shaped pillars on which they revealed the forbidden knowledge they wished to impart to mankind.

"These pillars were to be a representation of the twelve ruling Watchers and the information each of them was responsible for imparting to mankind.

"This site was used by the Watchers for many years and then was buried forever by sand when God flooded the earth. It has only recently been rediscovered and uncovered by modern archeologists. That is the main reason you needed to return to this present time. I could have sent you there while you were in 37 AD, but all you would have found was a vast mound of sand, as it had not yet been uncovered by man. This is the first time in recorded history that it has been accessible."

"How long has it been buried?" asked Nick.

"As your people account for time now," replied Enoch, " 'the Falling' took place in 10,850 BC. So, it was covered over in 9,850 BC and has remained that way since then."

"Wow!" exclaimed Robbie. "It has to be the oldest structure on earth then."

"That is true, and it is also the most powerful nexus of energy on the planet. It was ripped open by the falling of the Watchers," added Enoch. "Evil is very strong in that Land of Darkness. As you know, the only thing more powerful than darkness is light. The smallest amount of light is always enough to dispel the deepest darkness.

That is what you will be there to do. Bring the light of virtue and defeat darkness, a profound darkness that has been in this world for nearly twelve thousand years. You have seen that light before in your Swords of Valor. That light, combined with the quintessence of the Sword of Judgment and the cup, will be the keys to victory."

"Can we dispense with all the background information and begin the process of destroying that demon?" asked Susan as she and Carolyn entered the room. "My mother's essence is in danger, and you sit here talking about nexuses and quintessence. The time to act has arrived. I say we get to it."

"Are you feeling better?" asked the Meglio.

"Physically, yes," Susan replied, "but emotionally, not so much. My encounter with Mom's essence just made me realize how much I miss her and how hard it would be to lose her again. For some reason, listening to this discussion from the other room has annoyed the heck out of me. Stop the dithering and get to the point where we save Mom!"

Joe and Nick stood from their chairs and invited Susan and Carolyn to sit around the table. They accepted and sat.

"What do you mean when you say 'we'?" the Gray Champion asked Susan.

"Just what I mean," she replied, "I'm going with you."

"Susan, I understand your desire to help," said the Meglio, "but you're needed here. When we leave for the confrontation, you must remain here to monitor the situation at home and protect those that remain behind."

"We'll see," said Susan, who then turned to the image of Enoch. "Get on with the plan."

"You heard my daughter," the Meglio instructed Enoch. "Let's get to it."

"Very well," began the image, "I will transport twelve of you to Gobekli Tepe. Once there, you will need to work fast. The darkness of the place will be palpable and very draining on you and the weapons. I assure you that Azazel will be aware of your presence. Assume positions inside the circle in front of each of the twelve pillars facing the center pillars of Seth.

"Joseph should position himself at the pillar of Azazel, the largest one, standing upon the Stone of Jacob. He will be carrying the cup. Whoever is carrying the Sword of Judgment needs to be standing at the pillar to his right. Use the Swords of Valor to summon Azazel just as you did to summon the Swords of Terror. The singing of the swords will be heard not only by Azazel, but by the archangels themselves.

"The stone will open the portal to the spiritual realm. When that happens, be prepared to act quickly. Azazel was incredibly powerful as a purely spiritual being, and in his spiritual/quantum hybrid form, he may be even more dangerous. Only time will tell. That is all I can tell you at this point. What happens during the confrontation is in your hands. Make sure to follow the leading of the swords and to rely on virtue as your guide. Trust in the power of the cup and fulfill your destiny. There is much at stake."

"Why can't you tell us what to expect after Azazel arrives?" asked Ty. "Can't you tell us how to actually kill him?"

"I cannot reveal what has not happened yet," replied Enoch. "As for how to kill him, that has not been given to me, therefore I cannot reveal it to you. But I can tell you that you have all you need."

"That is all very well and good," said Susan, "but you still have not told us how defeating Azazel will rescue my mother! When we defeat him, if we defeat him, are we just supposed to climb Mount Charaxio and find her? Will she be free to come to us? How do we know she will not still be trapped in the Cave of Treasures forever?"

"Again," replied Enoch, "all will be revealed in time. Trust the process."

"Sure, trust the process," said Susan, rising to her feet. "I have very little patience for trust right now. We need assurances and facts. My whole family is at risk, and you want me to be okay with sending them out there to face an incredibly powerful demon Watcher on his own turf on trust alone?"

"Would it be better if I used the word faith?" asked Enoch. "You are a woman of faith. You know the biblical definition of faith; 'Now faith is the assurance of things hoped for, the conviction of things not seen.' Simply put, the biblical definition of faith is 'trusting in something you cannot explicitly prove'."

"I have faith and understand what it is," replied Susan, looking Enoch in the eye. "I have faith in God.

You are not Him. That is all I will say about that." She turned away and took her seat.

"Then you have spoken wisely," said Enoch. "That is *my* final word on the subject."

"When can we make the trip to Gobekli Tepe?" asked the Gray Champion. "I agree with my granddaughter, time is wasting. Regardless of whether Azazel is aware of our arrival, we should proceed quickly. We want the element of surprise, however short a window we may have, to be on our side."

"Robert, don't you think we need more preparation?" asked the Meglio.

"No, I do not," replied his father-in-law firmly. "This is not a battle that will be won by preparation. The battles of the past may have been won from the outside in, meaning that preparation, physical weapons and superiority have carried the day. But this battle, this final battle will determine who wins this war. This battle must be fought from the inside out. This is a battle of the heart, of the will, and of the spirit.

"I told you before when we talked outside that many times I have acted rashly and emotionally, and that is why you make a better Meglio than me. But this is not one of those times. Believe me when I tell you that action must be our default position today. Quick, decisive action. Our brains need to be put on the back burner, and we must let our hearts lead us now. Now is the time to act. Immediately."

"I can send you there as soon as you are ready," said Enoch. "I agree with the Gray Champion. There is no better time than now."

CHAPTER TWENTY-FOUR

CATHERINE'S FAITH

Catherine sat in the Cave of Treasures feeling defeated. She knew that she had made a quantum connection with Susan, but she still was not certain that it would matter. She had seen the condition of her father, the Gray Champion, after his speech, and was worried that Susan would be in the same catatonic state after her speech to the world. Would she be able to recover?

She had not actually seen her father recover from his ordeal. When she was taken by Azazel, he was still lying on the round table, unmoving. If Susan was in the same condition, how could she possibly communicate to them all the knowledge she had transferred to her? Would they even be able to understand it even if she could tell them?

So many questions. After her brief time of being free to explore all the secrets of the universe, not knowing was an excruciatingly painful experience. Of course, there was always her faith; a faith that had not been diminished by her captivity.

Strange, she thought, how the greater her uncertainty was, the greater the supply of faith she seemed to have, needed to have. Was it some sort of spiritual survival mechanism?

She resolved to focus on her faith and not the questions that swirled around in her quantum mind.

"Faith," said Azazel derisively as he suddenly descended into the cave. "Faith is merely a self-delusion, my dear, using words and sentiments to create an emotional sleight of hand founded on irrational notions. Faith is trying to force reality to submit to wishes. It is simply trying to create truth from a lie, by seeking to surpass unpleasant reality with the allure of fantasies. Faith is the haven of the uneducated, the uninformed, and the deceived. Intelligent, logical beings have no need for such fairy tales.

"Yes, my dear, I know your thoughts. You think that faith will make all things go well for you and your family. If it was not so laughable, I would pity you."

A bit startled by the sudden appearance of the Watcher and the revelation that he could read her thoughts, Catherine took a deep breath to compose herself, then replied, "How nice that you make such grand pronouncements about something you know nothing of. I find that pitiful."

"Still impertinent, I see," said Azazel. "Maybe your mind is still struggling to accept your fate? But then again, maybe not. For as I see it, faith is the abandonment of rational thought and the renouncing of logic. It's the surrender of the primary difference between humans and lower animals. It's the desperate desire to trust and to give up doubt and logic to simple belief. It is fueled by the desire to abandon those things and place all your hope and confidence in someone or something hidden and mysterious. Of all the theoretical virtues, faith is the most overly hyped, the most overly glorified, the ultimate deception. I view that as sinister and profoundly evil, so who is the pitiful one here? Maybe a little pain will quench that faith of yours?"

"Faith is a gift of God, which can neither be given nor taken away by promise of rewards or threat of torture," replied Catherine. "Your ignorance is showing once again, Azazel. But then, you were never given the gift of faith, were you? Angelic beings don't need faith, do they? They are immortal, powerful, and self-reliant. So sad, another gift of God denied to you. Maybe you are jealous?"

"Prideful, yes," admitted Azazel, "jealous, no. For if you knew what I know, you would be the jealous one."

"And what would that be, O Prideful One?" sneered Catherine, "Please, enlighten me once again."

"I know of your betrayal!" he roared back at her. "You and your kind are fools! Do you think I was unaware of what was hidden in this cave or that you would explore and find it? That is exactly what I intended. My plan was for you to find it, and despair that you couldn't tell your family.

"But I must congratulate you. You did find a very creative way to transmit the information to your family, bravo. But I must also thank you, my dear, for you have unwittingly fulfilled my desires. Because of the information you imparted to your daughter, they will now walk into my trap willingly and with great vigor.

"Oh, what a scene it will be! The swords will sing, we will appear as if summoned, and they will wave their swords at me, thinking I will cower and beg for mercy. Is that not pitiful? I am the merciful one! I will have mercy on the Earth by ridding it of the unworthy, slimy infection that is mankind. I will give to the Earth the gift of a worthy species to inhabit and care for it. The Earth will become proud once again, a true reflection of its master."

"Really?" replied Catherine. "Now who is the one trying to breathe life into a lie with the beauty of wishes? You have not been able to accomplish that dream in a multitude of millennia with all of your pride and power. Now you have convinced yourself that it will come to pass just because you wish it to be so. Maybe you do have faith Azazel, as misplaced as it may be."

"The time is right. All of the chess pieces are in place, and I am about to declare checkmate," Azazel announced. "The pawns have all been taken, the rooks and bishops are under my control, and the knights will soon be destroyed. After all, I have already captured the queen, and she cannot defend the king. I control the board. Game over."

"It is never over until the last move is made," observed Catherine.

"It *is* over, and I will make you watch it happen," sneered Azazel. "Then, I will deal with you in the way that you deserve to be dealt with. Oh, how I will enjoy wringing the insolence and impertinence out of you."

Then he swiftly descended upon her and once again grabbed her by the hair. He held her face so close to his that she could feel the heat of his fetid breath and taste his wickedness upon her tongue.

"You will be my Eve, and you will serve only me. Together, we will create a new world and a new species. That is something for which you need no faith, for it is fact."

"Shut up and take me to watch your defeat," demanded Catherine as she laughed in his face. "I need something to look forward to."

"It is not time yet," Azazel growled. "But soon. Very soon."

CHAPTER TWENTY-FIVE

PREPARING FOR GOBEKLI TEPE

Susan watched as the heroes collected their swords and those who were going discussed their assignments. She felt such a mixture of emotions; sadness that she couldn't go with them, anxiety at what they were about to face, and the burden of the responsibility she would bear should they not return. God, please be with them, she prayed silently.

Before leaving, the Meglio gathered Susan, Carolyn, and his granddaughters together and said, "If we do not return, the responsibilities of the family fall to you. You must continue to guard the Swords of Valor and lead the other Guardian families. This day, I have witnessed courage, bravery, virtue, and valor in each one of you, and my heart is full. I now go into this battle knowing that the family legacy is safe and that regardless of the outcome, all is well. Now, all of you except Susan, kneel."

The women knelt before the Meglio as he drew the Sword of Humility and said, "Today I officially appoint you all soldiers of the Guardians of the Swords of Valor. From this day forward, you will serve the family with valor and virtue. Be strong, be brave, and stay virtuous, and no evil will ever harm you. Now, rise and know that I love you all."

They stood and hugged the Meglio, their grandfather.

"You will return to us, Grandpa," said Alex. "You are the greatest man I know, and I know you can defeat Azazel. Please, be careful."

Her grandfather hugged her back. "I love you, too, Alex. Always remember that, and when things get tough, I am depending on you to strengthen the others, understood?"

"Understood," said Alex, releasing him and wiping the tears from her eyes.

Then, turning to Susan, he said, "I know you wanted to join us on this mission, but I also know it is best for you to stay here. I need you here with the others. You are the matriarch of this family now, and if we don't make it back, there is no one that I trust more to lead the families through this crisis than you. Please understand that it has nothing to do with your bravery or courage. In fact, that is why you must stay. You are the one that must lead them all if we fail."

"I understand," replied Susan, "but it hurts to know that you will be facing this without me by your side. I have always been there for you and Mom and the family, and it feels like I am abandoning you at the time of your greatest need. Are you sure?"

"I am," replied her father. "Having lost your mother, the last thing in the world I want to lose is you. Stay here and know that you have my love and appreciation. This will be the much harder duty, I assure you."

"I love you, Daddy," said Susan as she hugged him, hoping it would not be for the last time.

Then, she went to her brother, Robert, the prophet,

and instructed him firmly. "Take care of him, you hear? I will hold you personally responsible if he gets hurt. Do you understand?"

The prophet hugged his older sister and replied, "Got it, Sis. I will do everything I can, but you know how he is."

"I know, stubborn and single-minded. Regardless, protect him and the others. Promise me."

"I promise," replied the prophet.

"That goes for me, too!" said his wife, Carolyn. "Don't leave me here alone to deal with these kids!"

The prophet laughed. "Got it, honey. I know how hard that would be… for them!" They all laughed as Carolyn hugged him tightly.

The Gray Champion watched from across the room. With great satisfaction, he observed his great-granddaughters being commissioned into the ranks of the Guardians. Enjoying the feeling, he rocked back on his heels a little and placed his hands in his pockets. His right hand touched the metal orb he'd placed there.

Without drawing attention to himself, he went to the control panel of the quantum computer. He pulled the round ingot of the strange alloy from his pocket.

Quietly, he asked, "Enoch, can you analyze this material?"

"Of course," came the equally quiet response. "I have already scanned its molecular structure. Information on this alloy is only found in a high-security Leviathan database that I have managed to gain access to, and is not recorded anywhere else in the world. It is potentially the world's strongest and lightest metal.

It appears that it is made by temperature-treating an alloy of iron, aluminum, magnesium, and carbon, which would induce the alloy B2 to form evenly throughout the steel.

"Then, with the additions of the metals below in very specific proportions:

    30% Magnesium
    10% Aluminum
    10% Gallium
    10% Iron
    10% Carbon
    20% Osmium
    10% Beryllium

"Each material adds a different, unique property to the unusual alloy. Gallium is a mainstay semiconductor in a wide variety of electronics and has the bizarre property of beating like a living heart when it reacts with certain other metals. Beryllium is naturally invisible to x-rays, and osmium is the world's densest metal.

"The resulting material, in which the B2 hexagonal lattice structure reinforces the supple austenite matrix, has impressive tensile strength.

"Upon accessing several Leviathan databases, I have discovered that this Leviathan alloy, codenamed MAGIC OB, has a higher strength, lighter weight, increased control of light spectrum, and greater chemical reactivity than any approximate counterparts.

"This new metal has a strength-to-weight ratio that matches even our best titanium alloys, surpassing even the alloy used in the door of the Keeping Room, but at one tenth the cost of manufacture. Light like aluminum, but as strong as titanium alloy, this material has the highest strength-to-weight ratio known to mankind.

"I think you can see that this alloy is a metal that can change the world. Perhaps I might suggest its use by the

Guardians to construct new Swords of Valor for the new female Guardians.

"If you were to empower this material with dark energy during the forging process, these new swords would have some of the very same abilities as the ten original Swords of Valor, as well as some new, unique, and powerful ones.

"If you place the alloy within the compartment on the console, we can begin the replication process. It will take some time, but sufficient quantities could be produced by the time of your return to begin the forging of the new swords at your convenience."

Upon hearing the response, he considered for a moment all that he'd just learned, then he placed the metal orb in the compartment that had opened in the control panel. This promised to be interesting.

"Everyone, assemble in the main room," instructed the Meglio. The Gray Champion rejoined the group. "We will not be departing from the fire pit by the river this time. With the new capabilities of the quantum computer, we can leave from here. It will also conserve the swords' energies and virtues. We're going to need every bit of it tonight."

Everyone left the Tech Room and moved to the main Keeping Room area. When the twelve were gathered in a circle, the Meglio spoke.

"Enoch, we are ready for the leaving process. Please begin. Everyone, focus your thoughts on Gobekli Tepe, and remember, when we arrive, head straight for your positions. Focus on your assignments."

"Leaving process initiated," said the image of Enoch. "Godspeed, and may the Lord be with you."

The room was filled with a deep humming sound, which increased by the second. The group of twelve were enveloped in a glowing quantum cloud, and then, in a flash of pure, white light, departed for their confrontation with Azazel.

Susan felt as if her heart had been ripped from her body. She looked at Carolyn, Katie, Colleen, Alex, Livvy and Ellie. Their expressions mirrored her own emotions. Their family members were going off to confront unimaginable evil, and they were left behind to worry, wonder, and watch. She shook herself mentally. Now was not the time to indulge in worry and doubt! Now was the time for diligence and attentiveness.

"Let's not just stand here doing nothing," she said with authority. "You are guardian soldiers now, so assemble in the Tech Room, and let's figure out how to monitor their progress. And while we're at it, let's pray for their success. Enoch, will you lead us in prayer? You remember how to pray don't you?"

"I practically invented it," the image of Enoch quipped. "Let us begin."

⚬⚬⚬

Back in the Cave of Treasures, Azazel released Catherine from his grip.

"I sense turmoil in the quantum realm," he stated. "I believe it is time for us to depart this cozy cave. Stand up!" he commanded her.

"I would rather sit, thank you," she replied obstinately.

"Very well," Azazel sneered. "Then I will drag you there, willing or not."

He once again dug his talons into her hair and dragged her up with him through the ceiling of the cave to meet the Guardians at Gobekli Tepe.

As he rose, he could not help thinking about the place that had been chosen as the place of confrontation. It was his first home on earth. It was his place of falling. Intended by God to be a place of exile, to him, it was anything but. It was there that he truly became a leader, a teacher, and a sovereign. The Earth had become a place that he could mold into his own image.

Now that it had been uncovered by the humans after thousands of years under the cover of the sands of the desert, he would finally accomplish that millennia old promise to himself.

Chapter Twenty-Six

The Final Confrontation

Billy took a deep breath. He was used to time travelling with the swords, but he knew some of the others were not. He looked over at Boudicca. She didn't seem as shaken as she had the first time.

"Everyone okay?" asked the Meglio a few seconds after the team arrived. "Any travel sickness?"

"A little," admitted Boudicca, "but not as bad as last time. I am fine."

"Good," replied the Meglio, looking around, surveying their location, and then pointing, "There, to the left, is our target. The stones of Gobekli Tepe. Quickly, let's get into position!"

Billy looked where his grandfather had pointed. The circle of standing pillars was a good one hundred yards from where Enoch had placed them. He joined the others as they hustled to the forbidding, moonlit circle of stone.

Catching up to the Meglio, he asked, "Why didn't Enoch send us back to 10,000 BC? When we went to assess Stonehenge, we had to go back to 37 BC because that was when it still was at the height of its power. Why wasn't it the same with this place?"

"I'm not sure," replied the Meglio. "It's possible that it's because this place may still be in use by Azazel and is still at the height of its power. It was never really destroyed, just covered over and perfectly preserved. I'm sure that Azazel still considers it his home. That makes this place even more dangerous, and possibly more powerful, now than before."

They arrived at the site and gathered together for a moment. In the full moonlight, Billy could clearly make out the carved inscriptions on each stone "T" pillar.

"There," said the Gray Champion. "That one is the largest pillar, the one Enoch identified as Azazel's. Joseph, that's your position. The rest of you take your positions accordingly. Meglio, to the pillar on his right and prophet, to the pillar on his left. Josephus, bring the Stone of Jacob and the Sword of Judgment."

Josephus complied quickly. "Go and position the stone at the foot of the pillar for your father to stand on," commanded the Gray Champion, "and give the Sword of Judgment to the Meglio."

Josephus handed the Sword of Judgment to the Meglio with a bow, and then carried the stone to the foot of Azazel's pillar. Joseph of Arimathea followed close behind, carrying the cup, held protectively in his hands beneath his cloak. The others, now having the orientation, quickly moved toward their assigned positions in front of their appointed pillars.

As he turned around, Billy was surprised to see the Meglio hadn't immediately gone to his position. Instead, he'd followed the prophet and stood respectfully before him. With a slight bow of his head, he handed the Sword of Don Quixote to his son.

"You take this," the Meglio said. "Remember, it is now a Sword of Valor. Use it well."

"But it's yours," said the prophet.

"I have the Sword of Judgment, and I can't have you facing Azazel weaponless," replied his father.

"But prophets don't carry swords. We lead by example and through inspiration," Rob objected.

"You are not leading tonight, Rob," said the Meglio putting his hand on his son's shoulder, "you are following and fighting. Remember that. Whatever happens, know that I love you, and I am proud of you."

"Enough talking, you two," said the Gray Champion. "Take your positions. Heroes, when you get into position, do *not* move. Do not abandon your posts. You carry the Swords of Valor, and it is important to wield them this day in complete faith and trust. Stay where you are until this is over. Do not abandon your positions for any reason. This confrontation is at the core of it, a test of faith. Standing your ground and trusting is critical. Do not waver. Your eyes and ears may deceive you, so just trust, have faith, and obey."

Billy straightened his posture and stood tall before his assigned pillar. He glanced at his cousins, who had taken their positions as well, brothers standing side by side. Boudicca and Josephus also stood side by side in front of their assigned pillars. Finally, the Gray Champion took his position at the pillar to the right of the Meglio.

"Now," he commanded, "raise your swords!"

Out of sight, high above the scene, Azazel watched as the Guardians and the visitors from the past took their positions, desecrating and befouling his home by their presence.

"Look how they foul everything they touch," said

Azazel to his captive. "Soon, they will be no more. Their infestation of this world will be just a memory, and together, you and I will rectify God's first and only mistake. Maybe then, He will see that I was always right."

"And maybe," said Catherine, "you will burn in hell for all eternity."

He gave her a quick sideways glance, and then resumed watching the scene below. "Dealing in wishes once again, I see," he said. "Enjoy your final wish, my queen, for soon you will see them all die; your family along with your wishes. Quiet now, they are summoning me; or so they think!"

Far below, the swords began their song. Just as they had during the first Final Process, the swords pulled themselves free from the grip of their owners, hovered before them, then spun and whirled wildly. They emitted various tones, which together composed the Song of Calling. It went on for about a minute, increasing steadily.

"Time for us to attend the festivities, my dear," said Azazel as he began his descent to the stone circle. "Stay silent, or I shall not provide them with a merciful death."

Jeff, being familiar with the calling process, watched expectantly while Josephus and Boudicca looked stunned by the sight. As they gaped at the spinning swords, Azazel swooped down, making a comet-like streak through the nighttime sky, looking like a falling star, finally stopping his approach a few dozen feet above the center pillars.

In his grasp, Jeff saw their grandmother struggling to free herself.

"He has Grandma with him," he said to Billy. "That's good, at least we won't have to search for her when this is over."

"I know," Billy replied, "but without our swords in our hands, the game has changed. I hope Grandpa has a plan B."

"Oh, my," said Azazel mockingly, "look what your powerful swords have done! They have made me fall once again. Please, have mercy on me," he continued, his tone becoming increasingly derisive.

Then, his tone and expression morphed into anger.

"Do you think me so weak as to be subject to your playthings?" he roared. "I am Azazel, Prince of the Watchers, and lord of this world! It was I who gave mankind swords, and I shall now take them away!"

Then, with a violent sweep of his hand, the spinning Swords of Valor were cast away into the night, leaving the Guardians with only the swords of Josephus, Boudicca, and the Sword of Judgment.

Suddenly, the night sky was riven by lightning and the sound of thunder as two magnificent archangels appeared in heavenly splendor high above the stone circle.

"Ah, I see I was not the only one summoned by the swords," said Azazel, calling up to the archangels hovering above. "Michael and Gabriel, my old friends, have you come to watch me achieve my final victory? Very well then, watch closely, for you must tell it all to God as faithful witnesses. Tell Him I have finally rid the world of the vermin that He created. Tell Him that I will create a new race of giants to worship Him properly and be worthy to be called His children!"

The archangels said nothing in reply. They only hovered silently above while the lightning and thunder continued to crackle and boom.

"Servants and messengers are all you are and all you

will ever be," continued Azazel, taunting the archangels. "Watch and see what a true king and warrior does, and maybe you will join me when I am done. I could use a servant or two."

Then, he turned his attention back to the Guardians. "What will you do now that your toy swords have fled? Where is your virtue and valor now?"

"We still have the Sword of Judgment," said the Meglio. "That is all we need. Be assured that it is time for your judgment, and it *will* take place here tonight."

"And as for our virtue and valor," the Gray Champion added, "those qualities now, as they always have, reside within us. The swords were just the physical manifestation of them. Nothing you can do can take them away from us."

"Really?" replied Azazel. "We shall see, for fear also resides in you, and fear can easily overwhelm virtue and valor. It will be amusing to see the war raging inside as you struggle to fight back the fear which I shall soon ignite in you."

"It is you who will soon fear," said Joseph of Arimathea, taking the cup from under his cloak and holding it high for Azazel to see. "This is the cup of the one who overcame fear and death, the Cup of Life. Come, and drink from the Cup of Wrath. Come and drink if you are brave enough!"

Azazel looked at the cup and was silent for a moment. Then, he raged, "It is you who will drink from the cup of MY wrath, Joseph!"

Still dragging the quantum body of Catherine, he flew to where Joseph was standing and ordered, "Kneel before me, Joseph of Arimathea! Kneel to your king or die."

"I will not kneel to you or any other," replied Joseph,

"I kneel only before the Lord of All. It is you, Azazel, who must kneel before me!"

Azazel bared his serpent fangs and snarled, "I did not kneel before Adam when I was commanded to do so by God Himself; I will not kneel to you!"

His powerful arm shot out, and he seized Joseph by the neck. As he struggled to lift Joseph high into the air, he found that he could not. Joseph's feet were firmly set upon the Stone of Jacob, and he was immovable.

"Let him go!" shouted Catherine as she struggled to free herself from Azazel's grasp. "You have me, leave them alone."

Paying no attention to his struggling captive, Azazel growled and gave up trying to move Joseph. He turned his attention to the prophet, then said to Catherine.

"Shall it begin with your beloved son, my dear? Yes, I think that is appropriate. It is always the son who should suffer for the sins of the mother and father."

The prophet, standing there weaponless, said, "Let her go, and I will give my life willingly."

Azazel laughed, "As if you had any say in the matter!"

Azazel's free hand shot out and grabbed the prophet by the throat and lifted him off the ground. "Now it begins," he announced as he began to crush the prophet's windpipe, his talons drawing blood.

Jeff watched in horror. They had been warned not to move from their positions once the action began, as it would disrupt the process, but he was torn between obedience and action. He remembered his great-grandfather's warning about how the things that were going to see and hear might deceive them. He decided to obey, but also to pray and believe fervently for the return of the swords. Desperately looking around the stone circle at the others, he saw similar conflict etched on their faces. He heard Ty shouting.

"Robbie! We have to help Dad!"

"No!" shouted Robbie, "Don't make the same mistake you've made before. Stay put. Don't abandon your post. Trust and obey, do you hear me? Don't move!"

"Robbie is right!" shouted Jeff. "Obedience and faith are more important right now than action. We can't defeat Azazel physically, so be obedient. Trust and believe that the swords will return. Summon them. Concentrate. Now! Do it all of you!"

Helplessly, Jeff looked back at the prophet and could only watch as the prophet struggled, writhed, and twisted in the hand of Azazel.

Then, suddenly, the Sword of Judgment flashed in the moonlight and severed the arm of Azazel. The arm and the prophet fell to the ground.

As a black tar-like substance began to ooze from the place where his arm had hung, Azazel whirled around and looked at the one who had maimed him.

"No one harms my family without paying a very high price," growled the Meglio, brandishing the Sword of Judgment. "Not even a demon Watcher. Prepare for your final judgment!"

Enraged, Azazel released his grip on Catherine and dove on the Meglio, sinking his bared fangs deep into the arm holding the Sword of Judgment. With the talons of his only remaining hand, he began to dig into the Meglio's chest, trying to rip his heart from his body.

The Gray Champion, knowing the heroes were obeying the command to stand fast, raced to help his fallen son-in-law, leaping into the fray.

"Deal with me, you coward!" he shouted, while, with a mighty effort, he pulled the Watcher off the Meglio.

Azazel was immensely powerful, and it seemed his rage at being wounded fueled him with even more power. He whirled to face the Gray Champion while the Meglio, lying on the ground behind him, was fading fast with the Sword of Judgment still in his hand.

Catherine, now free from the grasp of Azazel, looked at the Sword of Judgment still in her husband's hand. While Azazel was completely focused on his struggle with her father, she raced to where he was lying, snatched up the sword, raised it high, and drove it powerfully through the leathery wings covering the back of the Watcher, deep into his heart as he struggled with her father.

Azazel jerked around to see who had impaled him. "Catherine, my queen, it seems that I have not yet rid you of faith," he growled. "It must be an immense faith to believe that anything of this world can kill me. Now, unfortunately, I must destroy that faith once and for all, and you with it. You have proven yourself unworthy to be my consort. It seems I must now conscript your daughter into my service. Let that be your last thought as you die at my feet!"

As Azazel rose menacingly to his full height before her, Jeff saw her look behind the evil Watcher at the body of her husband, torn and unmoving lying on the ground, with her father trying to revive him. Jeff could almost feel her hope and faith beginning to dissolve inside her just as Azazel had predicted.

Suddenly, from the distance came the sound of singing, and the Swords of Valor whirled into sight. They came diving down and drove themselves into the ground in front of each of the heroes who had remained steadfastly at their assigned pillars. Immediately, the swords began to vibrate and glow.

Upon the return of the Swords of Valor and in response to their song, the Sword of Judgment, still piercing the heart of Azazel, burst into flame. It was a terrible, fierce, and consuming fire which quickly enveloped Azazel. He began to scream as his body began to change.

His wings incinerated first, then his outer skin charred and sloughed away, and finally his bones crumbled into black, charcoal-like chunks. His disembodied screaming continued audibly as his inner quantum form began to be consumed. His spiritual entity became visible in the flames, which seemed to be congealing and melting.

As the flames began to die and the Sword of Judgment fell to the ground, all that remained was silence and a puddle of black, tar-like ooze, which wriggled and writhed like a wounded viper.

Although Jeff felt rooted to his spot, frozen with the shock of what he'd just witnessed, Joseph, it seemed, was not. He left his position on the Stone of Jacob and picked up the Sword of Judgment. He drove the tip of it into the writhing, black, snake-like mass, skewering it. Then, he held it high for all to see.

"Behold Azazel, the mighty Watcher, the scapegoat of God, and the enemy of man," said Joseph. "His judgment is almost complete!"

Then Joseph placed the still writhing remains of Azazel into the Cup of Life. The remains stopped struggling and began to sizzle and bubble furiously.

The archangels still hovering high above the stone circle of Gobekli Tepe descended, stood at the two central pillars, and addressed the Guardians.

"Your task is complete, faithful servants of God!" said Michael in a booming, authoritative voice. "We will take the cup and pour the remains into Dudael, the place of imprisonment for Azazel, cohort of Samyaza, who is already there waiting for him."

Gabriel added, "For the Lord has commanded, 'Bind Azazel hand and foot, and cast him into the darkness: and make an opening in the desert, which is in Dudael, and cast him therein. Place upon him rough and jagged rocks, cover him with darkness, and let him abide there forever. Cover his face that he may not see light. And on the day of the great last judgment, he shall be cast into the fire."

Joseph approached the archangels and handed them the cup.

"When our task is complete," said Michael to Joseph of Arimathea, "we will return the cup to you."

With that, the archangels departed.

Jeff watched them go, and finally felt an overwhelming sense of relief... until he heard a familiar voice that shouldn't have been in this place.

CHAPTER TWENTY-SEVEN

THE COST OF VICTORY

"Daddy!" shouted Susan as she ran to her fallen father lying on the ground. He was surrounded now by her mother, the Gray Champion, and the rest.

"Daddy, are you okay?" asked Susan. "Enoch sent me here for you. We saw what happened on the monitors in the Keeping Room, and I had to come. Please tell me you are okay!"

The Meglio was still conscious but mortally wounded. The sight of his only daughter brought a faint smile to his face.

"We won, sweetie," he said. "We have done our duty. We have fought the good fight and finally rid the world of Azazel."

"I know, Daddy, we all saw it. We are so proud of you," said Susan. "Enoch is ready to bring us all home as soon as you give the command. Do it now, so we can take you back there, and heal you with the swords."

Catherine touched her daughter on the shoulder. "Susan, his wounds are deep. They go right to his quantum essence. The swords cannot heal that part of him. Say your goodbyes here and now."

"NO! I will not!" sobbed Susan. "I refuse to give up, we can help him. We can heal him." Then, standing to her feet, she commanded, "Bring the swords. *All* of them! *NOW!* Joseph, bring the cup! We must use all of them to heal him!"

"The cup is gone," said Joseph. "The archangels took it with them."

"Fine," said Susan, "then the swords will do. Stand around him and touch him with the swords, now!" she commanded her nephews and her sons.

They complied quickly and began the healing protocol. Nothing happened. The swords remained cold.

"I told you, Susan, the swords cannot help him now. They are temporarily drained of their power. It will take hours for them to regain their virtues," said Catherine. "Say your goodbyes please, quickly."

Susan stared into her mother's quantum visage, still unwilling to accept the truth. She turned to her brother, the prophet, who was standing next to their mother and started to pound his chest.

"You were supposed to protect him! You were supposed to bring him back safely! You promised! You *promised!*" Then she began to weep and buried her head in his chest.

"I know," said the prophet struggling to talk. "I am sorry, I failed you. I failed us all."

As the two siblings, their mother, the Gray Champion, and all the rest gathered around the Meglio, Susan and Rob knelt by his side, each taking a hand.

"Daddy, we love you so much!" cried Susan as her tears fell heavily upon the broken body of her father, the Meglio. "You have always been my one and only hero. You were the first man I ever loved and have always been my knight in shining armor."

"I know, honey," said the Meglio weakly. "I know you love me. You have always showed me that in everything you did. Just let me go, it is my time. Just remember and be strong for the rest of the family."

"Dad," said Rob, "I'm sorry I failed you. I love you."

"There is no failure, Rob," whispered the Meglio. "I know you know that. I have heard you tell that to thousands of other people. There is only learning and growth. There can be no failure when the proper end has been attained, whatever that end is, and however painful it may be. This is the proper end. You have won your victory. You have proven your virtue. You are now complete."

His eyes closed for a few seconds, then he continued. "God has given us all beauty for ashes, the oil of joy instead of mourning, and a garment of praise instead of a spirit of despair. Rejoice, for all is well."

The Meglio turned to gaze at his wife as the last moments of his life ebbed from him. "Catherine, my love, you have always been my life, my strength, and my only love. I don't think I could bear eternity if I could not spend it with you. Will I see you again?"

She smiled as she gazed back at him. "You will, my love, very soon. Then we will have eternity to share together."

"Will there be dancing, my love?" asked her husband weakly as the life drained from him, "How I have missed dancing with you!"

"Of course, my love. What would eternity be without dancing?" replied Catherine, smiling.

The Meglio returned her smile. The light of love shown from his eyes briefly, and then departed as he took his last breath.

The night was giving way to sunrise as the Guardians stood around the body of their Meglio. Susan stood with Rob's comforting arm around her shoulders, gazing upon their father's bloody and broken body.

Suddenly, the Swords of Valor rose once again and began to sing. This time, it was a song of melancholy, but one still full of love and victory. She watched in awe as the Meglio's wounded quantum essence rose from his dead body, limped to his wife, and took her hand.

Susan knew that there was much to deal with back home. Joseph of Arimathea, Josephus, and Boudicca needed to be returned to their proper time and place. The world would need all the help they could provide to regain its freedom and liberty. There was much unfinished business to attend to.

She looked up into her brother's face, seeking the strength and comfort she knew would be there. As if sensing her emotional turmoil, he looked down and gently pulled her closer to him. In that moment, she knew there would be time to deal with all of that later. The missions, the pain, the anguish, and the struggle could temporarily be forgotten as they each dealt with the loss of their beloved father and grandfather.

For now, she stood silently huddled with her family in the rosy, golden glow of sunrise, listening to the melancholy song of the swords. She smiled a sad, tender smile as she watched the wounded quantum essence of the Meglio, after so many lonely years, once again dance with his wife.

EPILOGUE

The priest read a final passage of scripture:

"Isaiah 27:1- *In that day, the Lord with his sore and great and strong sword shall punish leviathan the piercing serpent, even leviathan that crooked serpent; and he shall slay the dragon that is in the sea.*"

Then, he closed his bible. "A humble giant has fallen," he said, as he started to wrap up his praise for the man lying in the coffin there before him. "I read that final scripture as evidence that this man fulfilled the will of God right up to the time of his death. May the memory of his obedience, heroism, and humility live on after him, blessing all of us who knew him and benefitted from his bravery and service to humanity."

He concluded his graveside comments, blessed the coffin and the mourners, and signaled to the workers to lower the coffin into the cold, damp earth. Before the workers began, the eleven cousins, all of them now Guardians, surrounded the coffin and raised their swords. As they stood silently honoring their grandfather the Meglio, their swords began to glow softly, signaling the presence of virtue.

Susan and Rob stood under the threatening sky, watching their sons and daughters, nephews and nieces honoring their father. Rob remembered the events of only a few days before in the aftermath of their victory over Azazel.

After having watched their father and mother's quantum essences dance to the song of the swords at the stone circle of Gobekli Tepe, they were joined by the image of Enoch.

"All is now as it should be," announced Enoch. "The judgment of God upon Azazel has been carried out, and mankind has been given another opportunity to create a world where virtue, valor, faith, freedom, and liberty reign.

"You have all done the will of God, but there is much that remains to be done. Continue to live in virtue and valor, and all will be well."

"What will become of Grandpa and Grandma?" asked Jeff.

"They have an eternity to explore the secrets of God's universe," replied Enoch.

"Will Grandpa's quantum essence be healed?" asked Joe.

"It has already begun," Enoch assured him. "His connection is so strong with your grandmother that just her touch has begun the healing process. It is that way with great love, healing is always the first effect."

"Will we ever see them again?" asked Ty. "Can they come to us? Can we speak with them?"

"As quantum beings, they have the freedom to interact with both the physical and spiritual worlds," replied Enoch, "and they are still in possession of their free will. So, if they choose it, they have the ability to interact with any of you with whom they have a quantum connection. Trust that when they deem it helpful and beneficial, they will be available to you."

"What do we do about Joseph, Josephus, and Boudicca?" asked Billy. "They know so much that could impact the course of history. If we send them back to their time knowing and remembering all they just experienced, it could change the

timeline."

"I have the ability to send them back without remembering anything of their experiences here," revealed Enoch, "but they will have been fundamentally changed to some extent. The quantum memory of their recent experiences will remain with them, imprinted on their quantum essences.

"The impact of the virtue and valor that have been imparted during their time with you will influence their behavior for the rest of their lives. They have much they must accomplish, and they will need the strength that the inherent memory of this experience will provide."

Then he addressed Joseph of Arimathea. "Joseph, you are charged with returning the Sword of Judgment and the Stone of Jacob to their former resting place. The sword with the strange belt, the Sword of David, must also be returned to the Ship of Solomon, for it must ultimately be wielded by your great-great-grandson, Galahad. He is the chosen one spoken of in the scroll of Hiram of Tyre.

"I will return you to your time, retaining the knowledge of your experiences here, but when your tasks are complete, you will remember no more. The cup will be waiting for you upon your arrival in Glastonbury, as the archangels promised."

"Thank you, Enoch," said Joseph. "I will be faithful to my work and to the quest. I will return all that was borrowed."

Then addressing Boudicca, Enoch revealed, "Young lady, you have many adventures ahead of you. Know that there will be sorrow and strife. You have a very important role to play in the history of your people. Be strong! Be brave and understand that you have all the strength and virtue you need to fulfill your destiny, no matter how powerful the enemy. Know this also; there are some defeats that have greater value than victory. Such is your fate."

"Will I be afraid?" asked Boudicca.

"You will be afraid, but you will not fail to act, for you have much virtue inside of you now. Fear not, for you will be remembered for all time."

Finally, addressing Josephus, Enoch said, "Josephus, you also will be a leader of men. As you are of the Prophet generation, you will be the first bishop of the land.

"In that role, you will be responsible for the souls of many, but through you will arise the greatest knights of all time, the Knights of the Round Table. As such, that makes you the First Knight, the one to initiate all the rest that will come after you.

"The valor and virtue imparted to you through your experiences here will always lead you and guide you and be imparted to all you initiate. Virtue is the key! Do not stray from its path."

"Thank you, Enoch," replied Josephus. "I am humbled and vow to impart the blessings of virtue on all I serve."

"Now," said Enoch, "say your goodbyes and I will return you to your time."

After the return of Joseph, Josephus, and Boudicca, Enoch addressed the remaining Guardians.

"It is time for you to return to the Keeping Room. I will send you there, but will not be returning with you."

"Where will you go?" asked Nick.

"I have a very pleasant task to fulfill," replied Enoch. "I will be the guide for your grandfather and grandmother as together we explore the secrets of God's universe. As I was once guided by the faithful Watchers, so I shall now guide your grandparents. What a wonderful adventure that will be!"

"Who will be guiding us?" asked Robbie. "Who will we be interacting with when we speak with the quantum computer?"

"You may choose whomever you wish, but you no longer have need of a guide," replied Enoch. "You have all the virtue you need within yourselves. Rely on that virtue and your faith,

and you will always choose wisely. That is the gift you have given yourselves because of your heroism today. You have proven yourselves faithful and obedient in the face of pure evil and temptation, have been refined by the fire of battle and been purified. Be bold and sure, for the world needs your leadership now. Go and fulfill your destiny with virtue and valor!"

"We still need a Meglio," stated the prophet. "Susan and I are prophets, it is not our place to fill the position of Meglio."

"You already have a Meglio," stated Enoch. "Remember, everything happens for a reason." Then, addressing the Gray Champion, Enoch asked, "Are you ready to resume your duties to your family as Meglio?"

"It would be my honor to lead my family once again," replied Robert Ogilvie Petrie. "My grandchildren and great-grandchildren need me, and I will not abandon them in their time of need. I will live the rest of my life in service to them and the world."

Enoch returned them and the body of their grandfather to the Keeping Room shortly thereafter. Upon their return, there were tears of sorrow for their fallen grandfather, but joy in the return of the ones who had survived.

The first order of business was to check on the status of the battle for freedom. After confirming with the quantum computer that the forces of freedom had beaten back the Leviathans on all fronts because of Susan's inspirational address, they began the preparations for the Meglio's funeral.

As Robert's thoughts returned to the present, he felt the strong arms of their grandfather, the Gray Champion, pull him close. He looked over and saw that his other arm had pulled Susan close, as well.

"I am so proud of both of you," he said. "I wish your grandmother could be here to share in this. She would be so proud, also."

"Who knows?" said Susan, "Maybe Mom and Dad will meet up with her and tell her all about this? After everything we have experienced, we now know that anything is possible."

"That's true," agreed Rob. "In fact, that gives me a great idea. Grandpa, when we get back to the Keeping Room, I will show you how to program Grandma Petrie's personality into the quantum computer. I think the image of Grandma Petrie would make our interaction with it so much more fun!"

"That would be a blessing, Rob," said his grandfather. "I have missed her so much. Can we program her with the ability to make liver and onions? I can't eat any more of your father's Italian food."

"Sure Grandpa, anything for our new Meglio!" said Susan. "Hey, if the quantum computer could take that Leviathan metal alloy you gave it, replicate it, and produce brand new Swords of Valor for the female Guardians, then I am sure it can make you some food that you actually like!" She grinned and hugged him tightly.

The team of Guardians of the Swords of Valor walked away from the graveside into a bright, new world, where a glimmer of freedom and liberty, fueled by virtue and valor, was beginning to shine.

Melillo Family Tree

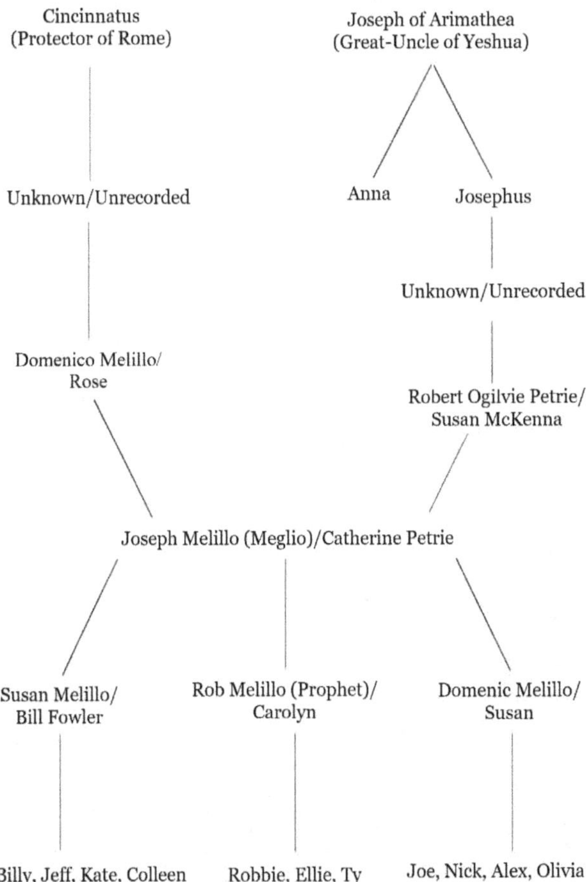

ACKNOWLEDGEMENTS
AND
AUTHOR'S NOTE

Dear reader, we have reached the final chapter in the Swords of Valor trilogy. Thank you for taking the journey with me.

This has truly been a labor of love. I have rarely enjoyed anything so much in my life as writing this story. It has been a way for me to honor my family, pay tribute to some of the greatest heroes and thinkers of history, and most of all, to honor God and His word.

There have been many biblical and pseudo-biblical references in these stories. This is intentional. The Bible and everything in it are given to us for our edification and comfort. There is much treasure to be gleaned from its pages if we will open our hearts to its truth.

After having finished this trilogy, I realized that what I was creating after all was an "alternative history" story about my family. I love alt-history stories, "what if" stories, and looking at life from a different point of view.

I have stated before that the majority of the story is taken from fact, history, and science with a minor portion being fiction or speculation. In *Sword Above All,* I also added a healthy portion of mythology, legend, and speculative history.

For example, it has never been proven that Jeremiah

the Prophet brought Tea Tephi to Ireland with the scribe Baruch. Many people in Britain believe that, but the proof is thin. Also, although the Golden Sword is referenced in the Book of Maccabees as stated in this story, it was in a dream, and it has never been asserted that the sword was real nor that the prophet brought it with him to Ireland.

However, it is stated that he did bring the pillow stone of Jacob with him, and that it is known today as the Coronation Stone, The Stone of Scone, The Stone of Destiny, or Lia Fail. The Stone of Destiny is an ancient symbol of Scotland's monarchy, used for centuries in the coronation of its kings, and later, the monarchs of England and those of the United Kingdom. The stone was last used in 1953 for the coronation of Elizabeth II of the United Kingdom of Great Britain and Northern Ireland.

The story of the Ship of Solomon is from the *Vulgate Queste del Saint Graal and Estoire del Saint Graal*, written in the 13th century. I love everything related to King Arthur and the Knights of the Round Table and the Grail Quest, and I was thrilled to be able to include the legends of Solomon's Ship and the sword with the strange belt.

I also used the *Vulgate Cycle* version of this legend, as it is connected directly with the Ship of Solomon and Galahad. I cannot tell you how happy it made me to be able to connect the dots in this story so that by the end of the trilogy, I and my family were related to not only Joseph of Arimathea, but Galahad, the Knights of the Round Table, and much of British royalty!

Here is something really strange: after completing the story and including the parts about the Hill of Tara and the Mound of the Hostages, I was given one of those send away DNA tests by my daughter. I sent it in and, to my surprise, one of the comments said that I was related to Niall Nolligach, an Iron Age king.

Well, do you know what that means? According to the internet, the Mound of the Hostages/Duma na nGiall is named after one of the most-famous high kings of Ireland, Niall Nolligach, who, like all Iron Age kings, took members of other royal families "hostage" to deter aggression, hence his nickname, Niall of the Nine Hostages." I don't know about you, but that gave me chills.

I touched on more legends when I dealt with Jesus accompanying Joseph of Arimathea to the British Isles. There is much written about this and many people will defend this belief, but it is not disclosed anywhere in scripture. Could it have happened? Sure. Did it happen? Who knows?

According to the research I did, Joseph of Arimathea really did have children named Anna and Josephus. According to some legends, Anna married one of the local kings, and her line became one of the key ancestral lines of British royalty. It also said that after Joseph of Arimathea died, Josephus was the one who carried on protecting the Grail.

Everything written here about Enoch, the fallen angels, the Watchers, and Azazel, was taken from either the *Book of Enoch* or the Bible. The information given to Susan by Catherine from the tablets she found in the Cave of Treasures, and the info about the gold of Adam, came directly from the *Book of Enoch* and the apocryphal works, the *Book of Seth* and the *Second Book of Adam and Eve*.

Speculative science also took center stage in this book. Quantum computers, quantum essences, dark energy, dark matter, quintessence, quantum holographic images being transmitted to every device on the planet, along with time travel all had their place. I truly believe that we will see greater understanding of these concepts as science digs deeper. Will all of these concepts become reality or be able to be accessed for the use of mankind? Who knows? I hope so.

In this story, I say that Robert Ogilvie Petrie, the Gray Champion is of the Royal Stewart Clan. That is not true. He was of the MacGregor Clan. So, as it turns out, we are not, as a family, related to any of the current British royalty, but we are related to the famous "Scottish Robin Hood" figure, Rob Roy MacGregor.

What we know of the clan's origins is a mixture of ancient tradition and verifiable fact. The clan's motto, "*S Rioghal Mo Dhream*", meaning "Royal is our race", reflects the family's claimed connection to Celtic royalty. They are also said to have fought alongside William Wallace in the first Scottish war for independence.

Boudicca. I loved this character. According to Wikipedia, she *"was a queen of the British Celtic Iceni tribe, who led an uprising against the occupying forces of the Roman Empire in AD 60 or 61. She died shortly after its failure and was said to have poisoned herself. She is considered a British folk hero."*

That does not tell even a small portion of her story, and I encourage you to read about her. Her strength, power, determination, and leadership qualities were amazing. I took liberties with the time frames involved. Since some of the dates that I found were very close to crossing over into the 37 BC timeframe of the story, I fudged a little, because I love her story and wanted her as a female hero of virtue and valor in the story.

The information about Gobekli Tepe is accurate. It is believed to be the oldest man-made worship structure in the world and has been carbon dated to be at least eleven thousand years old. I encourage you to research it and discover all the amazing aspects of this archeological treasure.

Now, here is something I want to make clear. The

speech that Susan as the Spirit of Liberty, and for that matter the address The Gray Champion gave to the world in the second book, were created by melding together bits and pieces of some of the most inspirational speeches ever given relating to liberty, bravery, endurance, and the value of freedom. I have referenced some of the authors or orators in the body of it, but not all, as it would have been very disruptive to the flow. As you read through it, I hope you felt some of the sheer power that some of these words and quotes still have to influence the hearts of men and women.

The speeches talk a lot about virtue, valor, bravery, and courage. That is on purpose. It is an absolute truth that freedom and liberty require virtue, valor, bravery, and courage to sustain them. One of the subtle messages of this series is that virtue is costly. It is costly to us, and if we're not willing to give of ourselves for the families, communities, and nations in which God has placed us, what will be the cost of the absence of our virtue?

The Meglio/Grandfather in this trilogy is the "nexus of virtue", the prime mover and motivator of the virtue of the younger heroes. It's a role he didn't ask for, a role he might have never wanted, and a role he could have walked away from at any time if he'd ever chosen to be selfish, but he doesn't. Joseph the Meglio gives everything he has for his family, his country, and still, it demands more (even to the point of returning from the dead). His virtue demands his very life twice. Although the price he paid for virtue was costly, he was the one man who could pay it, thereby standing against a great tide of evil.

In practicing costly virtue, we imitate Christ, who was no stranger to giving all he had in service to others; to giving all he had to not just hold back evil but defeat it. And when we find ourselves broken because of the cost of our virtue, that is also an imitation of Christ, who wept and sweated blood in a garden.

I hope these books inspire you to ask yourself, am I willing to stand at the bridge and give in tangible ways to my neighbors, friends, and enemies? To give whether they deserve it or not, and whether or not it benefits me? To set aside my ambitions and dreams, to sometimes defer my own hope for the sake of the hope of others?

Jesus kept no hope back for himself when he sweated blood in the garden of Gethsemane and gave himself over to be the hope of the world. We would do well to try to do the same.

Finally, I would like to thank my family for allowing me to tell much of our story, to use their names and character traits… flaws, humor, and all…to create a fun and interesting hybrid tale of reality and fantasy.

I was so thrilled to finally get to introduce you to the female heroes of the family in this final book of the Trilogy. They truly are a powerful, creative, brave, and intelligent group of heroes and are certainly excellent examples of virtue and valor. I could easily see my sister Susan stepping up and taking control as she did in this story if our family were ever threatened in this way. She is far more powerful and influential than she knows.

I always daydreamed that someday my father would take me aside and reveal to me all the stunning family secrets he had been keeping silent about all my life. Then I would find out that I was really from Krypton, or that there was a Bat Cave under the house, or that he was really King Arthur reborn, or that he had a wonderful, powerful mystical sword that he needed to give me, along with a quest to go with it. None of that happened, so I had to write the story for myself.

I loved doing it. I hope you enjoyed it, too.

DJM

ABOUT THE AUTHOR

Domenic Melillo is a husband, father, son, and brother living in Wake Forest, North Carolina. He graduated from Villanova University, where he received his Bachelor of Science in Accounting. He also received his MBA in Banking and Finance from Hofstra University. He has worked in the mortgage industry for thirty-six years.

His passion for writing and poetry was inspired by his father, Joseph Melillo, who read to his children many of his favorite poems from the all-time greats. All of Domenic's writings take inspiration from real life events.

Through his writing, he strives to highlight and contrast the light and dark sides of life, or as he calls it, "the duality of our existence". He is drawn to the themes of family, faith, heritage, loss, and redemption. He is an avid student of history, and in many ways strives to embody many of the characteristics of one of his heroes, Don Quixote, in that he longs to see things as they should be, not as they are.

Domenic has been described as a soul living out of his time, and yearns for the days of chivalry, virtue, valor, and honor, writing in the hope of inspiring families and society to return to these foundational qualities.